# Wheels
# Within Wheels

## F. Paul Wilson

(i)
infrapress

MANUFACTURED IN THE UNITED STATES OF AMERICA

ISBN 0-9766544-3-1

Published by Infrapress,
a division of Writers.com Books
Akron, Ohio

www.infrapress.com
publisher@infrapress.com

www.writers.com/publishing/infrapress
publisher@writers.com

LIBRARY OF CONGRESS CONTROL NUMBER: 2005930735

The novel *Wheels Within Wheels* was orginally published in the United States of
America in 1978 by Doubleday and Company Inc. It was first published in Great
Britain in 1980 by Sidgwick and Jackson Limited. A novelette version appeared as
"Wheels With Wheels" in *Analog Science Fiction/Science Fact,* Vol. LXXXVIII, No. 1:
September 1971.

A version of "Higher Centers" was published in *Analog Science Fiction/Science Fact,* Vol.
LXXXVII, No. 2: April 1971.

A version of "The Man With the Anteater" was published in *Analog Science Fiction/
Science Fact,* Vol. LXXXVII, No. 5: July 1971.

*Book covers and interior designed by Paula Guran*

*For John W. Campbell, Jr.,*
*of course*

# Preface to *Wheels Within Wheels*

*Wheels Within Wheels* is listed as my second novel. And it almost is. (A novel, that is.)

It's rooted in the high point of my writing career to that time: When the original "Wheels Within Wheels" novelette snagged the cover of the September 1971 *Analog* with a fabulous (not a word I use very often) cover by John Schoenherr that perfectly captured the menacing elements of the story. Talk about a thrill. To a newbie SF writer in those days it was equivalent to a garage band making the cover of *Rolling Stone*. I didn't have it made, but I felt I had *made* it.

After *Healer*, Doubleday wanted another novel. I decided to follow the same process that had sparked that book: Take one of my *Analog* stories and use it as a springboard. "Wheels Within Wheels" begged for expansion, and so it got the nod.

Doubleday offered a fifty-percent increase in my advance (up to a whopping $3000), and Jim Frenkel took paperback rights for his SF line a Dell.

I was cruising.

*WWW* the novel is less episodic than *Healer*, and certainly hangs together better, but it still strikes me as not quite as cohesive as a novel should be.

Perhaps I'm being too tough on it. The important thing now is that after twenty-eight years—I wrote it in 1977—it still works on many levels. But not all.

Its main failings are those suffered by any science fiction written in the seventies, in the Dark Ages before …

…the microchip revolution: Computers you can hold in your palm? Get out.

...the communications revolution: Word Wide Web—are we talking giant spiders? Email—what's that? Wireless telephones the size of a cigarette pack—crazy.

...the nascent genetics revolution: Whatever I say here won't come even close to the imminent reality, so why set myself up for a fall?

Please keep all these in mind while you're reading.

That aside, I think the plot is still strong and engaging, and the mysteries fairly presented.

As for style, well, I keep running into spots where I step in and out of point of view, a carelessness that I now find infuriating. And exclamation points—sheesh. I use more in *WWW* than in all my novels since 1990. Same for adverbs.

The good news (for me at least) is that all this tells me I've learned a lot about writing through the intervening years.

I've made some changes here—mostly cleaning up—but I don't see the point in doing a top-to-bottom rewrite. A lot of people love these novels as is, and major changes would be unfair to folks who want a uniform set of the originals.

But wait—there's more...

*WWW* became a milestone in my career when the Libertarian Futurist Society selected it for the first Prometheus Award. I had never heard of LFS and was delighted to learn I was a winner, but bowled over when they told me the award consisted of a certificate (no surprise there) and 7.5 ounces of gold in bullion coin. (Yes!) Gold at that time was running around $200 per ounce, so the award's value equaled half the novel's advance from Doubleday.

I was now an award-winning author. Cool. I still have the coins... somewhere.

Now to the short stories...

Here are the first ever reprintings of "The Man with the Anteater" and "Higher Centers." I could have included them in my first story collection, *Soft and Others*, but decided against it for a simple reason.

I'm not crazy about them.

Yes, they follow my continuing theme of the individual versus the system, but they're preachy, didactic, pedantic...I could go on, but you'll see for yourself. As I said in the preface to *Healer*, back in those days we were learning our craft in public. These stories were written in 1970 (equivalent to the late Jurassic Period for some of you) and occupy the lower-left end of my learning curve.

I still like what I said, just not how I said it.

"Higher Centers" (*Analog*, April 1971) is a parable of Big Brother versus local/market control. (Guess which side I come down on.) It has a clever maguffin, but it's as subtle as a dropped anvil.

"The Man with the Anteater" (*Analog*, July 1971) is even less subtle and, in many ways…ridiculous. It starts off with a few paragraphs directed straight at the reader—something I'd consider *verboten* only a few years later. In the finale I pull a Melville: I stop the narrative to give a short lecture on antbears. Oy. But the story belongs here because its protagonist is Josephine Finch's grandfather and Peter Paxton has a cameo.

So here now you have—along with *Healer* and *An Enemy of the State*—the entire core of my LaNague Federation fiction. (Yes, *Dydeetown World* and *The Tery* exist in that future history, but they're not part of the main line.)

I've never liked being pigeonholed, but in this business a reputation for anything (other than lousy writing) is good. *Wheels Within Wheels* and the Prometheus Award started people referring to me as " that libertarian sci-fi writer."

Read on and see why.

F. Paul Wilson
The Jersey Shore
September 2005

# CONTENTS

In the light of what we know today, it is difficult to imagine how the Restructurist movement engendered any popular support at all. But it did. Whole sectors at one time declared themselves "Restructurist" and agitated for what they called reform legislation.

But "reform" was a gross misnomer: the Restructurist hierarchy was composed of first-order reactionaries, economic royalists who were avowed enemies of the free market. Their political philosophy had been thrown out by the LaNague revolution and the Federation charter kept it out. But they hung on, cloaking their ambitions in feigned social concern, mouthing humanitarian slogans as they maneuvered to exert control over interstellar trade.

from STARS FOR SALE:
AN ECONOMIC HISTORY OF OCCUPIED SPACE
by Emmerz Fent

# PROLOGUE

The room was a special one, situated in the far corner of a building on the outskirts of the Federation complex. The Continuing Fund for the Restructuring of the Federation had leased it more than twenty standard years before and had footed the bill for all the extensive and expensive renovations.

The windows had been removed and the openings filled in and sealed. The wall spaces had been filled with a heavy mixture of synthestone and lined with a micromesh grid which, when activated, would distort not only the vibrations in the walls themselves but any electronic transmissions down to but not including the subspace level as well. The grid encapsulized the room and door, ensuring that an external amplifier attempting to monitor voices within the room would pick up only an indecipherable garble of sounds and no more. A psi-shield had been added as a final touch. Nothing within, short of a subspace transmitter, could beam a message out, and even the most compact s-s set in existence couldn't hide here.

Especially here. The walls, floor, and ceiling were completely bare and the lamps were self-powered floor models. All the furniture was made of the transparent crystal polymer that had been so popular two decades before. No hiding place in the room for any sort of monitoring device and any attempt to insert one into the Wall would disrupt the micromesh and set off a malfunction signal. It was the "safe room" reserved for special meetings of the upper echelon of the Restructurist movement. Elson deBloise had called for such a meeting today.

Douglas Habel entered first. He was the grand old man of the movement, now in semi-retirement. He avoided the head seat with some effort—that belonged to Elson now—and situated himself along the far side of the conference table.

Philo Barth came in soon after. Paunchy, ribald, a seemingly supercilious individual, he was firmly entrenched as a Federation representative from his sector.

" 'Lo, Doug," he said, and fell heavily into a chair. He and Habel discussed in low, casual tones the upcoming hiatus during which all the representatives would return to their respective homeworlds.

Doyl Catera entered next, a scowl on his face. He was young, an up-and-coming bright star in the Restructurist firmament, but his moods were mercurial...and he despised the "safe room." Nodding to the other two, he threw himself into a chair and waited in moody silence.

Before long, Elson deBloise made his entrance, carefully timed for last. He had a heavy build, dark brown hair graying just the right amount at the temples, and a presence that reeked of self-assurance.

DeBloise slid the door shut behind him and pressed a button at its center which would mesh it with the grid woven around the rest of the room. Without hesitation, he then took the seat at the head of the table and extracted a small noteplate from his pocket.

"Well," he said affably, "we all know why we're here, I guess."

"Not why we're here, no," Catera said with biting precision.

DeBloise maintained a friendly tone. "Doug, Philo, and I are well aware of your objections to the security precautions in this room, Doyl, but we feel they're necessary evils."

"Especially at this point of the game, Doyl," Habel said. "We're on Fed Central and this planet is run by the pro-charter forces. And while I must admit that during my long career they have, as a group, respected our security, there are others outside the political community who have no such scruples. I have reliable information that someone has been keeping close watch on our movements lately, especially yours, Els. I don't know who's behind the surveillance as yet, but at this stage of our plan, I must emphasize that we cannot be too careful. Is that clear, Doyl?"

"All right." Catera's tone was resigned. "I'll go along with the security charade for now. Let's get on with our business and get it over with."

"I'm all for that," Barth muttered. "The subject is money, I believe."

"Isn't it always?" deBloise replied.

He had remained carefully aloof from the preceding exchange, maintaining a pose of lofty equanimity. He despised Catera for his reckless maverick tendencies and, although he rarely admitted it even to himself, for his potential threat to deBloise's position as standard bearer of the movement. But nearly three decades in active political life had taught him to hide his personal feelings well.

"The sector treasurers are raising a bit of a fuss about the amount,"

Barth said. "They can't imagine what kind of project could possibly require such a sum."

"You all stuck to the agreed-upon pitch, I hope," deBloise said with an eye toward Catera.

Catera held his gaze. "Of course. We told them it was for a penetrating investigation into the way the LaNague Charter is failing many of the Federation planets. It was stretching the truth to the limits of endurance, but I suppose we can ultimately defend our sales pitch if the plan goes awry."

"Have no fear of that," deBloise assured him. "But the money—are the treasuries going to come through with what we need?"

Barth nodded. "They'll come through, but reluctantly. If it hadn't been for Doug's little speech, they'd still be holding out."

Habel beamed. He had recorded a short, stirring message for the representatives to carry with them to the sector committees. In it he had exhorted all committed Restructurists to rise to the challenge of the day; to free the monies that would allow the Restructurist leadership to gather the necessary information to open the eyes of the Federation Assembly and turn it around.

"It was a good speech, even if I say so myself."

"It was," deBloise agreed, "and it seems to have worked, which is of primary importance. Now we can finally set the plan into motion."

"I still have my reservations, Elson," Catera said, and the other occupants in the room held their breath. Catera's sector was one of the richest and they were counting on it for a large share of the money. If he held back...

"How could you possibly object to the plan, Doyl?" Habel said with all the fatherliness he could muster.

"It's a moral question, actually. Do we have the right to play political games with a technological innovation of this magnitude? It has the capacity to revolutionize interstellar travel and could eventually make all planets neighbors."

"We're not playing games, Doyl," deBloise replied with passion. "What we intend to do will move us closer to the goals of the movement. An opportunity like this presents itself once in a lifetime—once in a millennium! If properly handled, it can bring all our efforts to fruition. And if we don't seize it now and use it to our advantage, then we don't deserve to call ourselves Restructurists!"

"But I've been to Dil. I've—"

DeBloise held up a hand. "We've agreed to mention no names at any time. We all know who you're talking about and we all know where he lives."

"Then you all know that he's an unstable personality! His device could be lost to us forever!"

"Don't worry about that," Barth said. "When were in power he'll have to give it up. No individual quirks will stand in our way—we'll see to that."

Catera frowned and shook his head. "I still don't like it."

"You'd better like it!" deBloise hissed. He was on his feet and speaking through clenched teeth. Whether there was genuine concern on Catera's part or just the start of a power play, deBloise could not be sure. But he intended to get a commitment here and now. "The movement is a little over a hundred years old now and we've made considerable gains in that time. It started as a handful of discontented representatives and now entire sectors think of themselves as Restructurist. But we've become stagnant and we all know it. Oh, we make grand gestures and sweeping generalizations in public, but our point of view seems to have peaked. Some of our analysts even see the start of a downswing on the marginally committed planets."

He paused to let this sink in.

"Our speeches no longer cause even a ripple in the Assembly and we introduce amendments to the charter that are knocked down time after time. Our constituents are going to start wondering if we really know what we're doing and it may not be too long before we find others sitting in our seats in the Assembly unless we do something now!"

A prolonged silence followed as Catera gazed at his shoes through the transparent tabletop. Finally: "I'll see to it that the funds I control are deposited in the account tomorrow."

"Thank you, Doyl," deBloise replied in a conciliatory tone as he seated himself again. "How much can we count on?"

Catera shrugged. "Don't know exactly. It's in mixed currencies, of course. I think the total will come to about half a million Federation credits after conversion."

"Excellent! Philo?"

And they went on totaling the contributions, unaware that the entire meeting was being recorded.

*The course of public events is often shaped by seemingly unlikely individuals occupying seemingly marginal positions. As for the present state of Occupied Space, a good part of the credit or blame—depending on your philosophical viewpoint—probably belongs to the members of a single family, the name of which is no doubt unfamiliar to you unless you're involved in interstellar trade. The family name? Finch.*

from STARS FOR SALE:
AN ECONOMIC HISTORY OF OCCUPIED SPACE
by Emmerz Fent

# I
## OLD PETE

"Ah, how I'd love to wring that man's neck!" Old Pete said to the air.

He lay stretched out on the sand listening to the recording as Ragna's G2 primary beat down on him from a distance of approximately 156 million kilometers. He was eighty-one years old but neither looked nor felt it. His legs were scrawny, true—"chicken legs," he called them—and the skin was loose at his neck and wrinkled around his eyes, with the frontal areas of his scalp sporting nowhere near the amount of hair they had of old; but when he walked he moved briskly and lightly with swinging arms and a straight spine.

He loved the sun. Loved to sit in it, bake in it, broil in it. His graying hair had been bleached white by that sun and his skin was a tough, dark brown that accentuated the brown of his eyes. Minute collections of pale, flaky skin dotted his extended forehead. Actinic keratosis, a doctor had told him…or something like that. From too much sun, especially through Ragna's relatively thin ozone layer. Can lead to skin cancer, the doctor had said. Be smart. Use this lotion. It'll dissolve the keratoses. And start using this sun-screen lotion daily. Either that or stay in the shade.

Old Pete did neither. If the keratotic areas took a malignant turn, well, they had a lotion for that, too. Until then he'd enjoy his sun to the fullest.

And it *was* his sun. At least the part of it that shone down upon this particular island. The Kel sea stretched away in all directions to an unbroken horizon where it merged with the lighter blue of the sky. The island, an oblong patch of sand and rock about a kilometer long and half that distance across, supported a single house, some scattered scruffy trees, and little else. But it belonged to Peter Paxton and to him alone. He had purchased it shortly after leaving IBA and rarely left it. A luxury flitter was moored on the roof of the house for those occasions when he did.

So he lay supine on the beach, seeing red as the sun transilluminated his eyelids, and listened to a recording of other men's voices. His right hand held a printed transcript but he preferred to hear the original. The nuances of inflection and tone not reproducible on paper were as important to him as the content of the words themselves.

Nor did he need the transcript to tell him who was speaking at any particular moment. He'd never met the men on the recording but was as familiar with their voices as he was with his own. Old Pete had been keeping tabs on the Restructurist hierarchy at sporadic intervals for a number of years now, but his surveillance had increased in intensity with the news not too long ago that something special and oh-so-secret was afoot in the inner circle. He was determined to find out what it was.

As the recording came to a close, he sat up with a grunt.

"Poor Doyl Catera—almost got himself in trouble there for a moment. His sense of ethics made a serious attempt to break through to the surface. Almost made it, too. Then deBloise brought up elections and the threat of being replaced in the Assembly—the things that really matter to a politico—and ethics went plunging into the pit again. Ah, well," he sighed. "To be expected, I suppose."

The visitor to the island sat impassively on the other side of the player. Old Pete looked at him.

"What do you make of all this, Andy?" he asked.

Andrew Tella shrugged. He was short, dark, and still carried himself in a manner that hinted at his former years of rigid training in the Federation Defense Force. He didn't want to express an opinion. He was an operative. His job was to gather information and he did his job well. His client, Old Pete, had just mentioned ethics and Tella did not like to discuss ethics. Not that the subject itself made him uncomfortable, it was just that his code of ethics was somewhat different from most other people's. He had no compunction about prying into matters others wanted to keep secret. Events occurred, facts existed. They belonged to those who could discover them and ferret them out. That was the part that kept him in this business: the process of discovery. And even that became a humdrum affair at times…finding out what a client's wife or business associates or competitors were planning or doing. Then someone like this Peter Paxton came along and it was a whole new game. A man with no political connections who wanted to know the secret goings on of some of the biggest names in Federation politics. Here was a challenge, and a profitable one to boot.

Receiving no verbal reply, Old Pete went on. "You did a good job. Actually got a recording device into their security conference room. How'd you manage that?"

"It wasn't all that difficult," Tella replied with a self-satisfied grin. "They have all these elaborate security precautions—the distorter grid, the guard, that trite transparent furniture. But they don't scan the people coming into the room. I simply planted a recorder in the heel of Catera's left shoe the night before the meeting and retrieved it two days later. You just heard the results."

Old Pete laughed and looked toward the horizon. "I'd give anything to stick this under deBloise's nose and play it for him. But unfortunately that's out of the question. I've got to let them go blithely on their way thinking it's all still a big secret." He paused. "You know, that's the second time we've heard them mention Dil. I think it's about time you took a little trip to that planet to see if you can find out what's so important to them there."

"That might not be the most practical approach," Tella replied. "I could waste a lot of time on Dil before I learned a thing. The Federation Office of Patents and Copyrights would be a better starting point. We are, after all, looking for what was called a 'technological innovation,' and only a raving madman would fail to register something like that before marketing it. And I happen to have a few contacts in that office."

"I suppose that's true," Pete agreed with a nod. "Tell me: you ever do any industrial espionage?"

Tella hesitated, then: "A few times, when I was starting out. That's where I got my contacts at the Office of P&C. Never was very good at it, though."

Old Pete raised an eyebrow at this and Tella caught it.

"I don't consider myself a thief," he said defensively. "I dig up information that other people would rather keep hidden but I do not steal the products of another man's mind. That's why I joined up with Larry. He feels the same way."

Old Pete lifted his hands an amused look on his face. "Did I question your ethics?"

"Your expression did."

"You're too touchy. I knew all about you and Larry Easly before I hired you. Research, you know. I was looking for undercover operatives who took their work and their reputations seriously and you two fit the bill. Now get to Fed Central or Dil or wherever you feel you've got to go and find out what you can about this device deBloise and his rats are meddling with."

Somewhat mollified, Andy Tella nodded and reached over to the player set between them. He held a small box over the top of the set, pressed a button, and a tiny silvery sphere popped out to be magnetically scooped into the box, which then closed with a snap. He rose to his feet.

"You've got resources, Mr. Paxton," he said, letting his eyes roam over the house and island, "but you're going to need more than you've got if you figure on putting a kink or two into their plans."

"What makes you think I want to interfere at all? How do you know this isn't all just idle curiosity to fill an aging man's final hours?"

Tella grinned. "Who're you trying to con? You mentioned research before. That's my field. You think I'd snoop around Fed Central for you before checking out who you are, where you've been, and how you got there? In your whole life, as far as I can tell, you've never done a single thing without an ultimate purpose in mind. And this isn't just politics for you—you've got a personal stake here, but that's your business. I'm merely warning you: you're dealing with some pretty powerful characters here. You're going to need help, Mr. Paxton."

Old Pete resumed his supine position on the sand and closed his eyes. "I'm all too well aware of that. But for the time being, let's see if we can find out exactly what they're up to." Without opening his eyes, he waved a hand in Tella's direction. "Get in touch when you have something."

The receding sound of Tella's footsteps vibrated through the hot sand to the back of Old Pete's skull as he lay there and considered his options. Things were beginning to come to a head. He would have to start setting the stage for a countermove now or risk being caught off guard when the time for action arrived.

And that meant he would have to go back to IBA.

A flood of memories swirled around him. Interstellar Business Advisors... he and Joe Finch had founded the company on a shoestring more than half a century before. Fifty-four years ago to be exact. Hard to believe that much time had passed. Then again, when he considered all they had accomplished in that period, it seemed a wonder they'd had enough time at all.

It had begun back on Earth when a very young Peter Paxton received word from Joseph Finch, editor and publisher of Finch House Books, that his manuscript on the theory and practice of business on an interstellar scale had been accepted. Mr. Finch wanted to meet with him personally.

The meeting still remained fine-etched in his mind: Joe Finch slouching behind his cluttered desk, fixing him now and again with those penetrating eyes, and telling him how his book was going to revolutionize interstellar trade. And imagine! Written by a man who had never even weekended on the moon! They spent the afternoon in the office. Joe Finch's range of interests and knowledge was impressive. He was an omnivore with an insatiable appetite for information. He spoke at length on the fine points of the latest attempts to mine the neutron stars, then switched to an impromptu dissertation on the reasons for the most recent additions to Earth's list of extinct flora and fauna. He gave a technical explanation of his own experimental techniques in holographic photography and then expounded on his perdurably unorthodox view of Earth's current fiscal and political situation. And through it all ran an invisible thread of logic that somehow strung everything into a cohesive whole.

They talked for hours in the office and then went to Finch's house, where he lived alone except for his giant pet antbear. The rest of the night was spent in the living room, talking and drinking Joe Finch's horde of natural scotch whiskey until they both passed out in their chairs.

Never in his life among the teeming homogenized masses of Earth had Pete met such a forceful personality. That night was the beginning of a close friendship. So close that when Joe fled Earth after incurring the wrath of the planet's chief administrator, Peter went with him. The antbear came along, too.

They ran to Ragna, rented an office, and decided to put Pete's book into practice rather than publish it. Obtaining a business loan on Ragna was no easy matter in those days, but they swung it and announced the opening of Interstellar Business Advisors—a big name on a little door.

Soon they began advising. A few small-time independent traders with timorous plans for growth or consolidation were the first clients. Pete plugged the type of product, the demographics, the population projections, political vagaries, et cetera, of the sectors in question into his theoretical programs and ran them through a computer. The results were then run through Joe

Finch, who processed them with his indefinable combination of intuition and marketing experience, and a strategy was formed.

Success was slow in coming. The efficacy of an IBA program was never immediately apparent. The final proof was, as ever, in the marketplace, and that took time. But Joe and Pete chose their clients carefully, weeding out the fantasists and quick-credit artists from the serious entrepreneurs, and after six or seven standard years word got around the trade lanes that those two fellows in that little office on Ragna really knew what they were doing.

The fitful trickle of inquiries soon swelled to a steady stream and IBA began renting more space and hiring ancillary personnel. Each of the partners had found himself a mate by then. Joe became the father of Joseph Finch, Jr., and life was good.

The company continued to expand, and after two standard decades it held advisory accounts with a large number of the mainstay firms in interstellar trade, many of which would not make a move into a new market without first checking with Joe and Pete. But the accounts the partners liked most were the small, marginal ones that involved innovative products and processes, the speculation jobs that taxed their ingenuity to the limit. The big, prestigious accounts kept them solvent, the speculatory ones kept them interested. They charged a flat fee for service to the former and arranged a percentage of the adjusted gross over a variable period of time for the latter.

Time passed.

They grew rich. And as news of the Earthside exploits that drove Joe from the mother planet filtered through to the outworlds, he became a celebrity of sorts on Ragna. A psychological malady known as "the horrors" was sweeping across the planets and a few IBA staff members were struck down. Pete's childless marriage broke up. A man calling himself The Healer appeared out of Tolive saying he could cure the horrors, and apparently he could. IBA contracted the construction of its own office building and began renting space to other businesses.

They had bizarre experiences, like the time Joe and Pete were almost swindled out of a fortune by an accelerated clone of Occupied Space's most famous financier. The clone had to be destroyed, of course—the Clone Laws on almost all planets dictated that—which was a shame because they had both found him charming.

They had near tragedy when Joe, Jr., was almost killed by a radiation leak at a construction site shortly after he joined the firm. He was only eighteen at the time and managed to pull through.

And they had joy with the arrival of Josephine Finch, augmenting Junior and his wife after five years of marriage—a little late by outworld standards, but worth the wait to all concerned.

Then tragedy struck full force. Joe's flitter had a power failure while he, his wife, and daughter-in-law were two kilometers in the air.

Things were thrown into disarray for a while. Joe had been talking of retiring in the next few months when his seventy-fifth year coincided with IBA's thirty-fifth, but no one had taken that too seriously. Everyone fully expected to see him in his office every morning long after he had officially retired. Now he was gone and IBA would never be the same.

Everyone, including Pete, looked to Joe's son to fill the void, but Junior balked. For reasons apparent only to himself, he left Ragna with no particular destination in mind and was never seen or heard from again until his body was found a year later in an alley in a backwater town on Jebinose with a Vanek ceremonial knife in his heart.

Junior had placed control of his stock with Pete and his death left Pete in complete control of IBA. But Old Pete—it was at about that time that the "Old" became an integral part of his name—wanted no part of it. He appointed a board of directors with himself as chairman and made it a point not to attend any of the meetings. This went on for a number of years. The directors adapted to the company and kept it going at an adequate pace, although not with the spirit and verve of the original, and became entrenched in the process. Old Pete never noticed. He had taken up a new hobby—politico-watching, he called it—which occupied most of his time. His purposes were his own, his methods were the best money could buy. The hobby seemed to satisfy the sense of political mischief he had inherited from Joe.

The status quo might have remained undisturbed indefinitely had not an attractive and rather hostile nineteen-year-old girl walked into his office one day and demanded control of her father's stock in IBA. Josephine Finch had come of age.

Old Pete gave her the stock without hesitation. As Junior's only descendant, she had a right to it. She went on to request temporary proxy power of *his* stock and, for his own reasons, he gave it to her. And that's when Josephine Finch began to turn IBA upside down. The outcome was a flurry of resignations from the board of directors and the forced retirement of Old Pete himself.

Retirement afforded him more time to devote to his politico-watching and now he had stumbled onto something that threatened all of interstellar trade. He didn't know just what was being planned, but if the Restructurists were talking in units of a half-million Fed credits, it was big…very big. And if it was good for the Restructurists, it was bad for him—bad for IBA, bad for the companies he had counseled over the years, bad for all the freedoms that had made his life so worth while.

Tella was right. This was too big for him. He was going to need help and the only place he could go to was IBA. He didn't relish the thought. There remained quite a residue of ill feeling between Jo and him, all of it on her side. He had been surprised and hurt by the forced retirement, especially after letting her use his stock against the board of directors, but he had not fought it. He had been seriously considering dropping his nominally active role in the company for some time but had never got around to doing anything about it. The forced retirement made up his mind for him and he left quietly for the Kel Sea island he had purchased shortly after Junior's death.

No, he bore no ill feelings—the girl reminded him too much of Junior for that—but he wished he could say the same for Jo. He couldn't understand her. There had been an undercurrent of hostility in all her relations with him, and for no apparent reason.

Old Pete sighed and rose to his knees, then to his feet. He hated to leave the island. Even more, he hated the thought of facing that fiery little girl again. Because seeing her always brought back memories of Joe, Jr.

And remembering Junior always made Old Pete a little sad.

## II

## JUNIOR

The two men gazed at the bustle of the spaceport below them.
"But where are you going?" the older one asked. He appeared genuinely concerned.

Joe Finch, Jr., shrugged. "Really haven't decided yet. Probably into the outer sectors."

"But the company—"

"It's only for a year, Pete, and I'm sure IBA won't miss me. If anyone can take care of things, it's you. I haven't contributed much since Dad's death anyway."

"But you just can't drop everything and take off like this," Paxton protested. "What about Josephine?"

Junior put his hand on Paxton's shoulder. They were close—Junior had called him "Uncle Pete" as a kid—and Paxton now and then tended to take on a fatherly attitude, especially since the death of Joe, Sr.

"Look. Jo's ten now. I've tried to be a mother and a father to her for the three years since the accident. She's perhaps overly attached to me at this point, but she'll survive a year without me. I'm thirty-three and I've got to get away for a while or I won't be much of anything to anybody. Especially to me."

"I know what's going on inside that head of yours," Paxton said gravely, "so don't take this wrong…but can't you climb a mountain or something?"

Junior laughed. "I've no desire to be a mountain hanger. I…I just don't feel part of IBA, that's all. It's not my company. It's yours and Dad's. I had nothing to do with its founding or growth. It's just being handed to me."

"But the company has a lot of growing to do," Paxton said. "You could be a big part of that. In fact, IBA's future will ultimately depend on you, you know. If you run out on it now, there's no telling what—"

"IBA's present momentum," Junior interjected, "will easily carry it another decade with little help from anyone. I've got no qualms about taking out a year to go somewhere."

"And do what?"

"I dunno...something." He extended his hand. "Good-by, Pete. I'll contact you when I get where I'm going."

Peter Paxton watched the slouching figure amble off in the direction of one of the shuttle ramps, a man in the shadow of his father, the only son of Joe Finch trying to prove to himself that he was worthy of the title. It was distressing to see him wander off like this, but Paxton had to admire him for having the guts to do it. After all, it was only for a year. Maybe he could find himself in that time, or do something to put him at ease with himself. He wouldn't be much use around the company in his present state anyway.

So both men parted convinced that it was for the best and only for a year; neither realized that one would be dead before that year was up.

JUNIOR DIDN'T KNOW exactly why he picked Jebinose. Maybe he had heard about its minor racial problem once and the memory had lingered in his subconscious, waiting for the opportune moment to push him in the planet's direction. Maybe he was drawn to situations in flux. Jebinose was in minor flux.

The planet's background was a minor blot on the early history of man's interstellar colonization. In the old days of the splinter colonies, exploration teams were sent out in all directions to find Earth-class planets. At that time the Earth government was offering a free ride to a suitable planet to any dissident group that desired an opportunity to realize its own idea of a perfect society. The policy served many purposes: it disseminated Terrans in a rough globe of space with Earth holding a vague central position; it allowed humanity to start dehomogenizing itself by cutting divergent parts off from the whole and letting them develop on their own; it took enormous pressure off the Earth bureaucracy—the real reason for the plan's inception—by forming an exit route for the malcontents and freethinkers on the planet.

A lot of planets were needed and this put considerable pressure on the exploration teams. Sometimes they became careless. A major criterion for colonizable classification was the absence of an "intelligent" native species. No one was quite sure of just exactly what was meant by "intelligent," but tool-making was the accepted rule of thumb for dividing the thinkers from the non-thinkers. There were countless long, ponderous discussions on the wisdom of using a single criterion to determine a race's position on the intellectual scale but those discussions took place on Earth. The actual decisions were left up to the explorer crews; and as far as they were concerned, tool-making was it.

The Jebinose blunder, however, had nothing to do with interpretation of the rules. The planet was given an "M" classification (Earth-type, suitable for settling) after the most cursory of examinations. The colonists were indeed surprised when they discovered that they were sharing the planet with a tribe of primitive humanoids.

No one knows too much about the early colonial history of Jebinose. The splinter group that landed there was composed of third-rate syndicalists and was conspicuous only by reason of its particular ineptitude at the task of colonization. But for the Vanek, not a single member would have survived the first winter.

The Vanek are an alien enigma. They are quiet, humble, peaceful, fatalistic. Few in number, they are intensely devoted to a rather vague religion which bids them to welcome all newcomers to the fold. Their civilization had reached an agrarian plateau and they were quite willing to let it remain there.

Humanoid with blue-gray skin and long, spindly arms, they found it easy to befriend the colonists. It was not long before the Vanek had completely swallowed them up.

The cross-breeding phenomenon between human and Vanek has yet to be explained. There are many theories but no single one has received general acceptance. No matter…it worked. The Jebinose colony, as in the case of many other splinter colonies, was forgotten until the new Federation tried to order the chaos of the omnidirectional human migration. By the time it was rediscovered, human and Vanek genes had been pooled into a homogeneous mixture.

Much heated debate ensued. Some argued that since the original colony had been completely absorbed, resettlement would, in effect, be interference with an alien culture. Others argued that the Vanek were now part human and thus had a right to Terran technology…and besides, Jebinose was favorably situated in regard to an emerging trade route that had great potential.

Jebinose was resettled. The emerging trade route, however, failed to live up to its potential. The planet had an initial spurt of growth in its population as spaceports were constructed and cities grew up around them. Then the population stabilized into a slower, steadier growth pattern and some of the hardier citizens moved to the hinterlands where the Vanek lived and technology was at a low level. Jebinose was typical of many middle level planets: modern cities and relatively primitive outlands; not a backwater planet, but hardly in the thick of interplanetary affairs.

The Vanek tribes were scattered over the planet, mostly in the agricultural areas. It was through one of these that Junior wandered. He was tall and wiry with a good amount of muscle on a light frame. The unruly sandy hair that covered the tops of his ears and curled at his neck was his mother's; the long straight nose, blue eyes and sure movements were his father's. His face was fair, open, likable, ready to accept the universe on its own terms until he found good reason to change it. Although there was no physical abnormality, his shoulders were perpetually hunched; he'd been told all his life to straighten his back but he never did.

His wandering eventually brought him to the town of Danzer. It was a tiny place, the town center consisting of eight wooden buildings, a general store/restaurant among them. A few rugged-looking ground cars rolled up and down the dirt street that ran through the middle of town. On each side of the street ran a raised wooden boardwalk. Junior found a shady spot on the south side, unslung his backpack, and sat down.

He had been walking for days and was bone weary. A cool breeze helped evaporate the sweat beading his face as he put his head back against a post and closed his eyes. And to think he had considered himself in good physical condition. That was rough terrain out there. Those gentle rolling hills that looked so beautiful from a distance were sheer torture on the upside, especially with an extra tenth of a G to work against. He could have rented a flitter or a ground car; could have bought one outright. But he hadn't wanted to do it that way. Now he wondered if that had been such a wise idea.

He reopened his eyes as the last drop of sweat dried and noticed a middle-aged man staring at him from across the street. The man continued to stare for a short while longer, then he stepped off the boardwalk and crossed over to Junior for a closer look.

"You're new around here, aren't you?" he said in provincial tones and stuck out his right hand. "I'm Marvin Heber and I like to know everyone in Danzer."

Junior shook that proffered hand—it was lightly callused; not a field worker's hand. "My name's Junior Finch and, yes, I'm new around here. Very new."

Heber sat down beside him and tipped back the brim of the cap he was wearing. His face was a weathered ruddy brown up to the hatband line about two centimeters above his eyebrows. At that point the skin abruptly turned white. He was gaunt and about average height. Some of his teeth were missing—a sight Junior was not at all used to—and it appeared he had neglected to apply a depilatory cream that morning. Hardly an arresting figure, this Marvin Heber, but something in the quick, searching eyes told Junior that this man was quite a bit more than he seemed.

"Just moving in, huh?"

"No. Moving through, actually. I've been wandering around the region just to see what I can see."

"See anything interesting?"

The man was nosy and did not make the slightest attempt to hide it. Junior decided to be as oblique as possible.

"Lot of virgin land left around here," he replied.

Heber nodded and eyed the newcomer. "If you want to settle, I'm sure we can help you find a place."

"Who's *we?*"

"Me, really. I was using the plural in the editorial sense."

Now Junior was certain this man was more than he seemed. He fumbled for something to say next and was getting nowhere when the approach of an odd-looking figure changed the course of the conversation. An elderly, spindle-armed beggar in a dusty robe came up to him and asked for alms. His skin was bluish gray and his black hair was pulled back from a high forehead and wound into a single braid that was slung in front of his left shoulder.

Junior fished in a pocket, came up with a few small coins, and dropped them into the earthen bowl extended in his direction.

"Wheels within wheels, *bendreth*," the beggar said in high, nasal tones, and then continued his journey down the street.

"That was a Vanek, right?" Junior asked as he watched the figure recede. "I hear they're common in this region but that's the first one I've seen close up since I arrived."

"As a group they keep pretty much to themselves and only come into town to buy supplies now and then. There's always a beggar or two about, however."

Junior made no reply, hoping his silence would draw Heber out.

"They spend most of their time on their reservation—"

"They're confined to a reservation?"

"Confined is hardly the word, my young friend. Before the Federation would allow resettlement of this planet, the Vanek leaders were approached and asked if they objected. Their reply: 'Wheels within wheels, *bendreth*.' When asked to choose whatever areas they would like reserved—without limit, mind you—for their exclusive use, they replied, 'Wheels within wheels, *bendreth*.' So their nomadic patterns were observed and mapped out and everywhere they wandered was reserved for their exclusive use." He grunted. "Waste of good land if you ask me."

"Why do you say that?"

"They don't wander anymore. And there aren't all that many of them. Never was. Their total population peaked at about a hundred thousand planet-wide fifty standard years ago. They've leveled off at about ninety thousand now. Looks like they'll stay there, too."

"Why'd they stop wandering?"

"Don't have to any more. All they've got to do is sit around meditating and carving their little statues."

"Eh?"

"That's right. Little statues. But you won't see any around here. Some company in the city buys them up as fast as the Vanek can turn them out and sells them as curios all over Occupied Space. 'Handmade by alien half-breeds' I believe the ads run."

"You know," Junior said, straightening up, "I think I've seen one or two in gift shops." He had a vague memory of oddly grained wood carved into intricate and bizarre landscapes and tableaux. He also remembered the price tags.

"Then you realize why the Vanek have no financial worries."

"Why do they beg, then?"

Heber shrugged. "It's somehow mixed up with their religion, which no one really understands. Mostly it's the old Vanek who do the begging; I guess they get religious in their dotage just like a lot of humans. You heard him say, 'Wheels within wheels' after you gave him some coins, didn't you?"

"Yeah," Junior replied with a nod. "Then he said, '*bendreth*,' or something like that."

"*Bendreth* is the Vanek equivalent of 'sir' or 'madam.' They say that to just about everybody. 'Wheels within wheels,' however, has something to do with their religion. According to tradition, a wise old Vanek philosopher with an unpronounceable name came up with the theory that the universe was a conglomeration of wheels: wheels within wheels within wheels within wheels."

"Wasn't too far wrong, was he?"

"No, I guess not. Anyway, he managed to tie everything—and I mean everything—into the workings of these wheels. Got to the point where the only answer or comment he could make about anything was 'Wheels within wheels.' It's a pretty fatalistic philosophy. They believe that everything works out in the end so they rarely take any decisive action. They figure the wheels will turn full circle and even things up without their help."

He paused for a breath, puffing out his cheeks as he exhaled it. "Did you notice the cracks in the begging bowl, by the way?"

Junior nodded. "Looked like it had been broken and then glued back together again."

"That's part of the religion, too. You see, that old philosopher went to a banquet once—this was in the ancient days when the Vanek were a rather lusty and barbaric race—and the chief of this particular tribe sought to question him on his philosophy. Of course, the only answer he could get was 'Wheels within wheels, *bendreth*.' This annoyed him but he contained his anger until they all sat down at the eating table. During the meal it is said that the old philosopher uttered his favorite phrase over 250 times. Finally, the chief could take no more and broke a heavy earthen salad bowl over the old man's head, killing him. So now all Vanek beggars carry an earthen salad bowl that they have broken and then repaired as a sign that the philosopher did not die in vain."

Junior shook his head in wonder. "Sound like strange folk. How do the local Terrans get along with them?"

Heber shot him a sidelong glance, then answered. "I guess 'get along' is about the only way you could put it," he admitted. "There's no animosity between the two groups but there's certainly no friendship either. The Vanek are not easy people to warm up to. They float in and out of town and have no effect on the rest of us. Some of the city folks have been making noises about Terrans discriminating against the Vanek and I suppose there are plenty of instances where it happens, but it's a passive thing. When you come down to it, most Terrans around here just don't have any respect for the Vanek because the Vanek don't care about respect and consequently do nothing to engender it.

"And it's not racial antagonism as many outsiders might think." Again, the sidelong glance at Junior. "The fact that the Vanek are partially alien has nothing to do with it. That's a minor difference. It's other differences that cause problems."

"Like what?" Junior asked on cue.

"For one thing, there's no first person singular pronoun in the Vanek language. Some of the early anthropologists at one time thought this was a sign of group consciousness, but that was disproved. It's just that they don't think of themselves as individuals. They're all one on the Great Wheel. It makes it hard for Terrans to relate to them as individuals and thus it's hard to respect them as individuals.

"And there's more. The people around here are hard workers. They sweat their guts out trying to get a living out of the ground, and here are these skinny Vanek sitting around all day whittling wood and making a fortune. The local Terrans don't consider that an honest day's work."

"So it comes right back to lack of respect again," Junior said.

"Right! But try to convince the legislators in the capital about that! They're getting together some sort of a bill to combat the so-called discrimination against the Vanek and it looks like it'll pass, too. But no law's going to make a Terran respect a Vanek and that's where the problem lies."

He kicked a stone out into the middle of the street. It was a gesture of disgust. "Damn fools in the capital probably don't even know what a Vanek looks like! Just trying to make political names for themselves."

"Well," Junior began, "equality—"

"Lip-service equality!" came the angry reply. "A forced equality that might well cause resentment on the part of the Terran locals. I don't want to see that. No, Mr....Finch, wasn't it?" Junior nodded. "No, Mr. Finch. If equality's going to come to Danzer and other places like it, it's gotta come from the locals, not from the capital!"

Junior made no comment. The man had a good point—an obvious one to Junior—but Junior couldn't decide whether it was sincerely meant or just an excuse to oppose some legislation that happened to interfere with his racial prejudices. He noted that Heber made no alternative proposals.

Heber glanced at the sun. "Well, time for me to get back to work," he said.

"And just what is it you do, if I may ask?"

"I'm the government in town, you might say—mayor, sheriff, judge, notary, and so on." He smiled. "Nice to have met you, Mr. Finch. Hope you enjoy your stay around here."

"Nice to have met you, Mr. Heber," Junior replied.

And he meant it…with only a few reservations. Heber was an outwardly pleasant and garrulous type but Junior wondered why he had taken so much time to explain the Terran-Vanek situation to him. Politics, maybe. If enough outsiders could be turned against the pending antidiscrimination bill, maybe it wouldn't pass. Whatever his reasons, Heber had been highly informative.

Junior forced himself to his feet and walked across the street to the general store. A land-rover passed close behind him as he crossed. Ground transportation was the rule here, probably because flitters were too expensive to buy, run, and service. Heber was right about the hard work involved in living off the land on Jebinose, and the rewards were minimal. The farmlands, for all intents and purposes, were economically depressed. That would help explain a part of the poor Terran-Vanek relations: the local Terrans were in control as far as numbers and technology were concerned, and they owned all the businesses; but the Vanek held a superior economic position solely through the sale of their carvings. The situation was tailor-made to generate resentment.

Junior found himself indifferent to the conflict. It was unfortunate, no doubt, that there had to be friction between the two races, but if these Vanek were as fatalistic as Heber said, then why bother with them?

He approached the general store building. The foodstuffs and supplies piled out front in their shiny, colorful plastic or alloy containers struck an odd contrast to the weather-beaten wood of the store. All the buildings in Danzer were handmade of local wood. Prefab probably cost too much.

A hand-lettered sign proclaiming that Bill Jeffers was the proprietor hung over the doorway and Junior's nostrils were assailed by a barrage of odors as he passed under it. Everything from frying food to fertilizer vied for the attention of his olfactory nerve.

His pupils were still adjusting to the diminished light of the store interior when Junior bumped into someone just inside the door. Straining his eyes and blinking, he saw that it was a young Vanek.

"Sorry," he muttered to the robed figure. "Can't see too well in here just yet." He continued on his way to the main counter in the rear, unaware of the intense gaze he was receiving from the Vanek.

"Yes, sir!" said the burly bear of a man behind the counter. His two huge hands were resting palms down on the countertop and his teeth showed white as he smiled through an unruly black beard. "What can I do for you?"

"I'd like something to eat. What's on the menu?"

The big man winked. "You must be new around here. You don't get *a* meal here, you get *the* meal: local beef, local potatoes, and local greens."

"All right then," Junior said with a shrug. "Serve me up an order of the meal."

"Fine. I'm Bill Jeffers, by the way," he said, wiping his right hand on the plaid of his shirt and then jabbing it in Junior's direction.

Junior shook hands and introduced himself.

"Staying around here long, Mr. Finch?"

Junior shook his head. "I doubt it. Just wandering around the area."

These rurals, he thought. Nosy. Always the unabashed questions about who you were and how long you were staying. Junior was used to people obtaining this sort of information in a more indirect way.

Jeffers nodded at Junior, then looked past him. "What'll it be?"

"The meal, *bendreth*," said a high-pitched, sibilant voice behind him.

He turned and found himself facing the Vanek he had accidentally jostled on his way in.

"Hello," he said with a nod.

"Good day, *bendreth*," replied the Vanek.

He had a slight frame, smooth grayish skin with a hint of blue in it, and piercing black eyes. There was an indigo birthmark to the left of midline on his forehead.

"How are you today?" Junior asked in a lame effort to make conversation.

Despite his years with IBA and its myriad contacts throughout Occupied Space, he had never been face to face with an alien. Although most of the Vanek were thought to carry traces of human genetic material, they were, in every other sense, true aliens. And here was one now, standing next to him, ordering lunch. He wanted desperately to strike up a conversation, but finding a common ground for discussion was no easy matter.

"We are mostly well," came the reply.

Junior noted the plural pronoun and remembered what Heber had told him. It was gauche to bring it up, but it might help to open a conversation.

"I've heard that the Vanek always use the word 'we' in the place of 'I,'" he said, cringing and feeling like an obnoxious tourist. "Why's that?"

"It is the way we are," came the impassive reply. "Our teachers tell us that we are all one on the Great Wheel. Maybe that is so. We do not know. All we know is that we have always spoken thus and no doubt we always shall. There is no Vanek word for the single man."

"That's too bad," Junior said with obvious sincerity, and then instantly regretted it.

"And why do you say that, *bendreth?*" The Vanek was showing some interest now and Junior realized that he would have to come up with a tactful yet honest answer.

"Well, I was always raised to believe that a race progresses through the actions of individuals. The progress of the Vanek, in my estimation, has been terribly slow. I mean, from what I can gather, you've gone nowhere in the past few centuries. Maybe that's the result of having the word 'I' absent from your functional vocabulary. I hope I haven't offended you by what I've just said."

The Vanek eyed him narrowly. "You needn't apologize for speaking what you think. You may—" His words were cut short by the arrival of the meals: steaming mounds of food on wooden slabs. Each paid for his portion in Jebinose script and Junior expected the Vanek to follow him to one of the small tables situated in the corner to their left. Instead, the alien turned and walked toward the door.

"Where're you going?"

"Outside. To eat."

"It's too hot out there. We'll sit at one of these tables."

The Vanek hesitated and glanced around. The store was empty and Jeffers had disappeared into the back. Wordlessly, he followed Junior to a table.

Both were hungry and, once seated, began to eat. After rapidly swallowing two mouthfuls, Junior spoke around a third. "Now, what were you about to say?"

The Vanek looked across the table at him and chewed thoughtfully. "You may be right. Once we might have said that we have progressed as far as we desire. But that doesn't hold true any more. We Vanek have shown ourselves quite willing to accept and utilize the benefits of a civilization technologically far superior to our own. So perhaps it has not been by desire that our culture has been stagnated. Still, there is more to culture than technology. There is—"

"Hey!" came a shout from the rear of the store. "What's he doing over there?"

Junior looked past the Vanek and saw Jeffers standing behind the counter, glaring in his direction.

Without looking around, the Vanek picked up his slab and walked out the door. Junior watched in stunned silence.

"What was that all about?" he asked. "I was talking to him!"

"We don't allow any Vaneks to eat in here," Jeffers told him in a more subdued tone.

"Why the hell not?"

"Because we don't, that's why!"

Junior could feel himself getting angry. He put a lid on it but it wasn't easy. "That's a damn humiliating thing to do to somebody, you know."

"Maybe so. But we still don't allow any Vaneks to eat in this store."

"And just who are the 'we' you're referring to?"

"Me!" said Jeffers as he came around from behind the counter and approached Junior's table. He moved with surprising grace for a man of his size. "It's my place and I've got a right to call the shots in my own place!"

"Nobody's saying you don't, only you could show a little respect for his dignity. Just a little."

"He's a half-breed!"

"Then how about half the respect you'd accord a Terran? How's that sound?"

Jeffers's eyes narrowed. "Are you one of those meddlers from the capital?"

"No," Junior said, dropping his fork into his mashed potatoes and lifting his slab. "I only arrived on the planet a few weeks ago."

"Then you're not even from Jebinose!" Jeffers laughed. "You're a foreigner!"

"Aren't we all," Junior said over his shoulder as he walked out the door.

\* \* \*

THE VANEK WAS SEATED on the boardwalk outside the store, calmly finishing his meal. Junior sat down beside him and put his own slab aside. He was choked with what he recognized as self-righteous anger and couldn't eat. It was a strange sensation, rage. He had never experienced it before. He'd had his angry moments in the past, of course, but he'd never run across anything like this in the three odd decades of his tranquil and relatively sheltered life. This was pure, self-righteous, frustrated rage. And he knew it could be dangerous. He breathed deeply and tried to cool himself back to rationality.

"Is it always that way?" he asked finally.

The Vanek nodded. "Yes, but it is his store."

"I know it's his store," Junior said, "and I certainly appreciate his right to run it as he wishes—more than you know—but what he did to you is wrong."

"It is the prevailing attitude."

"It's a humiliating attitude, a total lack of respect for whatever personal dignity you might possess."

There was that word again: respect. Heber had said that the local Terrans had none of it for the Vanek. And maybe they had no reason to respect these introspective, timid creatures, but…

Thought patterns developed after years at IBA whirled, then clicked into place, and Junior suddenly realized that of all the Terrans in Danzer, Bill Jeffers owed the Vanek the most consideration.

"But we're going to change that attitude, at least in one mind."

The Vanek threw him a questioning glance—the similarity in facial expressions between the two races struck Junior at that moment. Either they had always responded alike or the Vanek had learned to mimic the Terrans. Interesting…but he let the thought go. He had other things on his mind.

"You're going to take me to your tribe or camp or whatever it is," Junior said, "and we're going to figure out a way to put some pressure on Mr. Jeffers."

The pressure of which he was speaking was the economic kind, of course. Economic pressure was a household word as far as the Finch family was concerned.

The Vanek sighed. "Whatever your plan is, it won't work. The elders will never agree to do anything that might influence the course of the Great Wheel. They'll reject whatever you suggest without even hearing you out."

"I have a feeling they'll agree. Besides, I have no intention of asking them to do anything; I'm going to ask them not to do something."

The Vanek gave him another puzzled look, then shrugged. "Follow me, then. I'll take you to the elders. But you have been warned: it's futile."

Junior didn't think so. He had found something unexpected in the attitude of the young Vanek—whose name, he learned as they walked, was pronounced something like Rmrl. He'd read it in the flick of his gaze, the twist of his mouth, and realized that for all his detached air, for all his outward indifference, this particular Vanek was keenly aware of the discrimination he faced daily in the Terran town. Junior had seen through the carefully woven façade and knew that something could be done, must be done, and that he could do it.

III
JO

Dark brown skin and eyes against a casual white jump and short white hair: Old Pete was a gaunt study in contrasts, moving with such ease and familiarity through the upper-level corridors of IBA that the receptionist in the hall hesitated to accost him. But when he passed her desk on his way to the inner executive offices, she felt compelled to speak.

May I help you, sir?"

"Yes." He turned toward her and smiled. "Is The Lady in at the moment?"

She answered his question with another. "Do you have an appointment?" Her desktop was lit with the electronic equivalent of a daybook and an ornate marker was poised to check off his name.

"No, I'm afraid not. You see—"

"I'm very sorry." The finality in her tone was underscored by the abrupt dimming of her desktop. "Miss Finch can see no one without an appointment." The daybook read-out was her ultimate weapon aid she was skilled at using it to control the flow of traffic in and out d the executive suites.

The old man rested a gnarled hand on the desktop and leaned toward her. "Listen, dearie," he said in a low but forceful tone, "you just tell her Old Pete is here. We'll worry about appointments later."

The receptionist hesitated. The name "Old Pete" sounded vaguely familiar. She tapped her marker once, twice, then shrugged and touched a stud on the desktop.

A feminine voice said, "Yes, Marge," from out of the air.

"Someone named Old Pete demands to see you, Miss Finch."

"Is this some sort of joke?"

"I really couldn't say."

"Send him in."

She rose to show him the way but the old man waved her back to her

✳ 31 ✳

seat and strode toward an ornate door made of solid Maratek firewood that rippled with shifting waves of color. The name *Josephine Finch* was carved in the wood at eye level, its color shifts out of sync with the rest of the door.

*Old Pete?* thought the woman within. What was he doing at IBA? He was supposed to be in the Kel Sea, out of her sight and out of her mind. She dropped a spool of memos onto the cluttered desk before her. After taking an all-too-rare long weekend, work had accumulated to the point where she'd have to go non-stop for two days to make up for the extra day off. Project reports, financial reports, feasibility studies, new proposals—a half-meter stack had awaited her return. The interstellar business community, at least that portion of it connected with IBA, had apparently waited until she'd left the office three days ago before unloading all its backed-up paperwork.

At times like this she idly wished she had an accelerated clone to share the work load. But as it stood now with the Clone Laws, she'd go to jail and the clone would be destroyed if anyone ever caught on.

A clone would be especially nice right now, just to deal with Old Pete. But he was here and there was no avoiding a meeting with him. It wasn't going to be pleasant, but she'd have to do it herself.

The door opened without a knock and there he stood. He'd changed. His skin was darker and his hair was whiter than she'd ever seen it. Over all, his appearance was more wizened, but the changes went deeper than that. Jo had always thought of Old Pete as the perfect example of a high-pressure executive—his movements had always been abrupt, rapid, decisive, his speech terse and interruptive. He appeared much more at ease now. There was a new flow to his movements and speech.

He had changed, but the feelings he engendered in her had not. The old distrust and hostility rekindled within her at the sight of him.

For a heartbeat or two after coming through the door, the old man stood with his eyes fixed on her, his mouth half open, frozen in the instant before speech. Abruptly, he appeared to reassert control over himself and arranged his features into familiar lines.

"Hello, Jo," he said softly, closing the door behind him. "You're looking well."

And she was. A few pounds in the right places had matured her figure since the last time the two of them had faced each other. She was wearing a clingsuit—blue, to match her eyes—and she wore it well; in the past she had been too thin by most outworld standards, but the extra weight on her light frame brought her close to optimum. Her dark hair, its normal sandy color permanently altered years before to a shade closely matching her late grandfather's, was parted in the middle, curving downward into a gentle frame for her oval face, and then cut off sharply below the ears. Between the straight line of her nose and a softly rounded chin, her lips would have appeared fuller had they not now been compressed by irritation.

"You're not looking so bad yourself," she replied stiffly. "Island life seems to be agreeing with you. How've you been?" She really didn't care.

"Can't complain."

The amenities went on for a few more minutes with Jo doing her best to be as pleasant as possible. Old Pete's return irritated her. IBA was running smoothly now, and all because of her. What did he want here anyway? She resented anyone from the old days intruding on IBA. It was her company now—the Finch flair had been restored and IBA was reasserting its claim to pre-eminence in its field.

Old Pete. Of all the people from the past, he was the last she wished to see at her door. And he must know that. She'd made no secret of it when he was forcefully retired; and even now, years later, she could feel the hostility radiating from her despite her calm and cordial demeanor.

Old Pete was glancing around the room. A figure standing in a far corner caught his eye and he whirled. "Joe! Good—" Then he realized he was looking at a hologram. "That's one of the most lifelike holos I've ever seen," he said with obvious relief as he moved around to view it from different angles. "For a moment I actually thought—"

"The founder's portrait has to go somewhere," Jo said.

"Co-founder, you mean."

Jo hesitated, then backed down. He was right and it would serve no purpose to get petty with him.

"The late co-founder," she finally replied, then made an attempt to bring the conversation toward the bottom line. "What brings you back?"

Frowning, he eased himself into a chair across from Jo's desk and stared at her. "I don't know how to put this, exactly. In a way, I'm here to ask IBA to help me, the Federation, and IBA." His mouth twisted into a wry smile. "Sounds kind of convoluted, doesn't it?"

"Sounds like you're hedging," Jo replied without returning the smile.

Old Pete's laugh was genuine. "Just like your grandfather! Okay, I am hedging, but only because I've got to somehow convey to you a convincing version of a vague concept formed from speculation based on incomplete and/or secondhand information."

"What is it, then?" she snapped, then reminded herself to show restraint and have patience. He was, after all, an old man.

"I've uncovered a plot against the Federation charter."

Jo let the statement hang in the air, waiting for more. But her visitor out waited her.

Finally, "What's that got to do with IBA?" she asked grudgingly.

"Everything. The charter severely limits the activities of the Federation; it restricts it from meddling in planetary affairs and from interfering in interplanetary trade. For the past couple of centuries it has bound the planets tightly together while managing to stymie the bureaucrats at every turn. But there's a delicate balance there, easily upset. If the charter should be changed or, worse yet, thrown out somehow, the politicos at Fed Central who are so inclined will have free rein to indulge their whims."

Jo shrugged. "So what? That doesn't affect IBA. We have absolutely no connection with anyone in the Federation. We don't even have a connection in the Ragna Cooperative. So how can any political machinations be of any consequence to us?"

"If the charter goes, so does the free market," he told her.

A drawn-out, very dubious, "Ohhhh?" was her only reply.

Old Pete grunted. "Jo, what do you know about the Restructurist movement?"

"It's a political group that wants to make some changes in the Federation," she replied. "DeBloise is their current leader, I believe. Beyond that, I don't know much about them. Nor do I care much about them or any other political group."

"You'd better start learning. To say they want to 'make some changes in the Federation' is to put it lightly…turn it inside out is more like it! The Fed was designed to keep the lid on interplanetary affairs: mediate some disputes, promote a little harmony while simultaneously maintaining a low level of constructive discord, and quashing the violent plans of some of the more acquisitive planetary regimes. But that's not enough for the Restructurists. True to their name, they want to restructure the entire organization…turn it into some sort of social and economic equalizer that'll regulate trade in free space and even get involved in the internal affairs of some of the planets."

Jo remained unconcerned. "They'll never get anywhere. From what I understand, the Fed charter is defensively worded in such a way as to make it impossible for anyone to get around it."

"You forget: there's an emergency clause that allows for a temporary increase in the scope of Federation activity should it or its planets be threatened. Peter LaNague, who designed the charter, disowned it after that clause was attached over his protests."

"I'm aware of all that," Jo said with forced patience. The conversation seemed to have veered off its original course…or had it? In spite of the pile of work spread out before her, she felt compelled to follow Old Pete's train of thought through to its finish. "And it seems every time I catch a vidcast, there's a news item about another attempt to invoke the security clause in the Fed charter. And every time it's voted down. Even if they do succeed in invoking it, so what? It's only temporary."

"That's where you're wrong, Jo. If you look at the history of old Earth, you'll find that very seldom, if ever, is any increase in governmental power temporary. The emergency clause is probably the key to Restructurist control: once they invoke it they'll have their foot in the door and the Federation will never be the same again. I don't want to see that happen, Jo. Your grandfather and I were able to make IBA a going concern because of the Fed's hands-off policy toward any voluntary transactions. It's my personal belief that we Terrans have come as far as we have in the last couple of centuries because of that policy. I don't want to see it changed. I don't want to see the Federation regress toward empire—it arose from the ashes of another empire—but I see it looming in the future if the Restructurists have their way."

"But they won't," Jo stated.

"I wouldn't be too sure of that. Many of those Restructurists may seem like starry-eyed idealists, but a good number are crafty plotters with power as their goal. And Elson deBloise is the worst of the hunch. He's an ambitious man—a mere planetary delegate ten years ago, he's now a sector representative—and this plot, whatever it is, centers around him and his circle. I've made a connection between deBloise and an as yet unnamed man on Dil. The man is some sort of physicist, probably, and if deBloise thinks he can be of use, then both he and the Federation had better be on guard!"

Jo was struck by the old man's vehemence. "Why not go directly to the Federation if you think something dirty is up?"

"Because I don't have a shred of tangible evidence. I would look like a nut and deBloise would have plenty of time to cover his tracks. Frankly, I'd rather not even involve the Fed. It's not set up to deal with deBloise's type. I'd much prefer to handle everything behind the scenes and avoid any open involvement with the politicos. To do that I need IBA's contacts."

"It's always been a company policy to stay out of politics," Jo said after a moment of silence. "It's one of our by-laws, as a matter of fact."

Old Pete's face creased into a smile. "I know. I wrote it."

"Then why the sudden change of heart?"

"No change of heart, really. I still don't think business should have any connection with government. It's dangerous and it's usually sneaky. When a businessman and a politician get together, certain things are bound to occur." He ticked the points off on the fingers of his left hand. "The businessman is usually one who's found that he hasn't quite got what it takes to make it in the free market, so he will try to persuade the government to use its coercive power to help him gain an advantage over his competitors: a special sanction, an import quota, a right of way, et cetera. The politician will find that if he complies he will grow richer in power and/or material wealth. The colluding business will aim for a monopoly over a particular market while the politician will aim in turn for further extension of political influence into the marketplace by controlling that monopoly. They both wind up winners. The losers: everybody else.

"So I still say, government should have no influence in the economy and business should have no influence in government. And that's the way it's been under the LaNague Charter. You, don't see any lobbyists at Fed Central because the Federation has denied itself any and all economic power. Nobody's getting any special favors and I want to keep it that way. And the only way for me to do that is to meet a few politicos head-on."

Jo drummed her fingers on the desk and studied the old man. His concern was genuine. And despite the conspiratorial overtones of his suspicions, Jo had an uneasy feeling that he could be right. The Restructurists had been rather quiet of late. Maybe something was brewing after all.

But a secret plot to trigger the emergency clause of the Federation charter? Unlikely. But then again …Old Pete had never been known to be prone to hysteria, nor to paranoia. He was getting on in years, true, but not that far on. He and her grandfather had possessed two of the shrewdest minds in the interstellar market in their day and she sensed that Pete's was still sharp. If he thought there was something in the wind that threatened IBA, then it might be wise to give him the benefit of the doubt.

Jo withheld complete acceptance. She'd help, even if it meant continued close contact with Pete, but she'd keep an eye on him. If he was wrong and his suspicions had no basis in fact, then little was lost except some time and personal aggravation. If he happened to be right, however…well, IBA was her home and her family. Anything that threatened it, threatened her.

"I've always found ç," she said after a long pause, "though rarely verifiable. But if it's in IBA's interest, I'll do what I can."

Old Pete's body relaxed visibly as he heard this. "Good! You can help me dig. I've already got someone checking out this fellow on Dil. We'll have to keep a watch on all the Restructurist eminentoes to see if anything else is about to break."

Jo nodded. "I can see to that. I'll also send someone of my own to Dil to see what can be uncovered there." She rose to her feet, anxious to end the meeting. "In the meantime…

Old Pete sat where he was and held up his hand. "Not so fast."

"What's the matter?"

"If we're going to be working together on this thing," he said, "let's get one thing settled: Why do you hate me?"

Jo's voice rose half an octave. "I don't hate you."

"Yes, you do. And I'd like an explanation. You owe me that much, at least."

She wondered at times if she owed him anything; then at other times she felt she owed him everything. But always, when she thought of him, old hatreds rose to the surface. She hesitated.

"I'm waiting," Old Pete said patiently.

Jo shook herself and made ready the reply that was as unpleasant for her to say as it was going to be for Old Pete to hear.

"If it hadn't been for you," she said slowly and distinctly, "my father would be alive today."

Old Pete's face registered the expression she had expected: shock. And something more…he was hurt, too.

After a long pause, he spoke in a low voice. "How could you think such a thing?"

"Because it's true! You probably talked him into that sabbatical of his. And if you didn't talk him into it, you could have talked him out of it. But however it was, you got control of his stock and sent him off to be killed!"

Old Pete suddenly looked all of his eighty-one years. A lot of things were suddenly very clear to him.

"You must believe that Junior insisted on leaving …I did my best to dissuade him, but you can't talk a Finch out of anything once he's got his mind set on it. He thrust the stock on me for safekeeping until his return—he only planned to be away a year."

"But he never returned and it all turned out very nicely for you, didn't it?"

"You're not thinking very clearly, little girl," Old Pete said as anger began to absorb the hurt. "Think! What did I do with that stock? Did I set myself up as all-powerful ruler of the IBA complex? Did I remake the company in my own image? Did I milk it dry? No! No to all of them! I set up a board of directors to run things for me because I'd lost interest in the whole affair. Joe dead, and then Junior dead…all within four years…" His voice softened again. "I just didn't feel like going on with any of it any more."

In the long silence that followed, Jo was almost tempted to believe him. His hurt at what she had said seemed so real. But she couldn't accept it. Not yet. There was something locked away in Old Pete, something he would never let her see. She had no idea what it was or what it concerned, but it was there. She sensed it. And she couldn't let the old hatreds go. She had to have someone to blame for losing a second parent by the time she was eleven years old, for the years spent with an indifferent uncle and a preoccupied aunt.

"Well," she faltered, "someone made him leave. Someone got him out of the picture."

"Yes, and that someone was Junior himself."

Jo's voice broke. "Then he was a fool!"

"You can't understand why he left, can you?" Old Pete said softly, as if seeing Jo for the first time. "And I think I know the reason. Since you were in your teens you've known what you wanted and you had to work to get it. You had to confront me, then the board of directors, and then you had to prove yourself to the interstellar traders."

He rose and began to pace the room.

"It was different, however, for Junior...perhaps we shouldn't have called him that but it got to be a necessity when he and his father were working together. You'd say 'Joe' and they'd both say 'What?' But anyway, it was different for him. He grew up in your grandfather's shadow; he was Joe Finch's son and everything was cut out for him. He had a prefab future in IBA and most sons would have slipped right into the mold.

"But not Junior. IBA was a golden apple waiting to be plucked and he walked away. Oh, he hung on and gave it a try for a couple of years after his father's death, but it just wasn't for him. At least not yet. He didn't feel he'd earned it. It was no accomplishment for him to take over IBA. He balked." Old Pete snorted. "That Finch blood, I guess."

"And you couldn't change his mind?"

He shook his head. "No. Tried up to the last day. He said good-by not knowing where he was going; I said good-by figuring to see him again in a year or so. You know the rest."

"What there is to know, yes." Jo slumped in her chair. "I'm sorry, but I don't care to talk about this any more."

Old Pete ignored her. "You know, I just realized what's missing in this office: a picture of Junior. Jo, you really shouldn't reserve all your ancestral reverence for your grandfather."

"Please," Jo said, "not now. I'll have someone show you to the guest suite."

"Quite all right," came the smiling reply. "I know exactly where it is—I helped design this building, don't forget." He turned at the door. "A nice little holo of your father would go very well on the desk there. Think about it. Junior was really quite a fellow in his own way. And you're closer to him than you'll ever know."

Jo remained in her chair after he had gone. It was a long time before she was able to get back to her work.

# IV
## JUNIOR

The Vanek village was an odd place, almost humorous in its incongruities. Sitting in front of their smooth-domed mud huts, the Vanek women, almost identical to the men in appearance, prepared the coming meal or mended clothes; the men whittled their statuettes and tableaux as they had no doubt done for centuries; the children romped as all children have romped for eons. A timeless scene at first glance. Then one noticed that the pump over the well in the center of the village was of Terran design and powered by solar batteries. A closer look and one noticed that fine strands of insulated wire ran from hut to hut. And filtering through the primitive background noise of the village in its natural surroundings was the hum of a modern generator. The Vanek had looked upon electric lighting and had seen that it was good...at least in this particular village.

Rmrl left Junior standing by an odd-looking contraption while he went to confer with the elders. It was a series of intricately carved gearlike wheels suspended on axles set at crazy angles. Junior touched one of the smaller wheels and it began to rotate; he gave it a push to move it faster and suddenly all the wheels were turning. The rates and angles were all different, but all were turning.

He returned his attention to Rmrl, who was approaching a large hut that stood apart from the others. The mud on the walls had been etched with countless, intricate gyrating designs.

The young Vanek was met at the door by a wizened figure. As their conversation grew animated, other figures appeared in the doorway. Fingers pointed, hands gestured back and forth, a confusion of high-pitched voices drifted toward Junior as he watched with interest. Finally, Rmrl turned away. The door closed behind him.

"They do not wish to listen," he said with an expressionless face as he returned to Junior's side. "I'm sorry, *bendreth*."

"There's hardly any need to apologize to me," Junior grunted. "I'm not the one on the dirty end of the stick."

"Pardon, *bendreth*?"

"Nothing. Just an expression."

He watched the rotating wheels and pondered the situation. His first inclination was to drop the whole matter and continue his hike through the region. If they were content with the situation, then let it be. He had always despised people who thought they knew what was best for others, and feared that he might be falling prey to that very same attitude in regard to the Vanek.

If they don't want my help, then why should I even bother? They could be right…bringing things to a head may not be the best answer. And if they don't want to move, why should I push them?

Then he caught the expression on Rmrl's face—the tiniest glimmer of unhoped-for hope had been doused. Hidden, but it was there.

Junior found himself striding toward the Elder Hut.

"*Bendreth!*" Rmrl cried. "Come back! It will do no good! They will refuse to listen!"

Ignoring him, Junior pushed through the door and entered the hut.

It was dark inside, the only illumination coming from a single dusty incandescent bulb, primitive in design and low in wattage, hanging lonely and naked from the ceiling. There was a dank, musty odor, but what he could see was reasonably clean.

Seven scrawny, robed figures started up from the floor at Junior's precipitous entrance. He noted their frightened expressions and quickly held out his empty palms.

"I mean you no harm. I only wish to speak to you."

Rmrl came up behind him and stood in the doorway, watching.

"We know what you wish to say," replied one of the elders, the most wizened of the lot. "You wish us to take action to influence the Great Wheel. We will not. It is forbidden and it is unnecessary. The Great Wheel has a wisdom of its own, indecipherable in mortal terms, and brings all things 'round in good time. We will do nothing to alter its course, *bendreth*."

"But I'm not going to ask you to do anything," Junior said quickly. "I want you to try and not do something."

The seven muttered among themselves at this. If this is what you have to go through to get anything moving in this place, Junior thought, small wonder they still live in mud huts!

The same elder turned to him again. He was apparently the chief or something. "We have decided that under those circumstances it would not be unorthodox to listen to you, *bendreth.*"

Junior shot a quick glance at Rmrl and then seated himself on the hard-packed earth of the floor. The elders did likewise. It was as he had expected: the elders, and probably most other Vanek, were dogmatists. Not doing something, according to the letter of their creed, was quite different from doing something.

"What we are dealing with here," Junior began, "is really a very simple problem. On one hand we have Bill Jeffers, a man who is quite willing to sell you food, clothing, and fuel for your generator, but is loath to let you eat in the store where you buy all these things. Now is neither the time nor the place to make a moral judgment on the rightness or wrongness of this policy. He owns his store and what he wants to do with it is his business. It's just a fact we have to deal with.

"Just as it is a fact that you Vanek do not like this policy."

The elders glanced warily at each other as Junior said this, but he hurried on with his speech.

"It is another fact that you Vanek make up a good part of Jeffers' business. You earn your money, and where and how you spend it is your business. You have something Jeffers wants—money. And in return for spending your money in his store you would like to be treated with the same respect he accords his Terran customers."

The chief elder opened his mouth to speak but Junior cut him off: "Don't deny it. You hide it well, but it gnaws at you."

The old Vanek hesitated, then gave him an almost imperceptible nod. This pushy Terran had suddenly risen in the elders' collective estimation.

"Okay. Now, the next step is to bring this point home to Jeffers. To accomplish this, all you've got to do is stay away from his store until he gets the message that unless he bends a little, his gross income from now on will be a lot less than what he's used to. And don't worry about him getting the message; he's a businessman and you'll be speaking his language."

The elders stared at Junior in open-mouthed wonder. They had little knowledge of the economic forces at work around them. The general store was a tremendous convenience to them. No longer did they have to till the fields in the hot sun, no longer did the fullness of their bellies depend on the success of the harvest. Let the Great Wheel bring whatever weather it may, as long as the Terran curio dealers bought the statuettes and carvings, the Vanek would never go hungry.

So, since the day of its construction, the general store had been looked upon as a boon from the Great Wheel. But now this Terran was revealing that their relationship with the proprietor of the store was one of interdependence. It was all so obvious! Why hadn't they seen it before?

"You are very wise, *bendreth*," the chief elder said.

"Hardly. It's all common sense. What's your decision on the matter?"

Muttering and mumbling, the elders grouped into a knot on the far side of the hut. A few seemed to be opposed to the idea—it would influence the Great Wheel. Others contended that they had managed without Jeffers and his store in the past and certainly it would not be unorthodox to get along without him now. The latter argument prevailed.

The chief elder turned to Junior. "We have agreed to your plan, *bendreth*. The word shall be passed to our brother Vanek in this region that we no longer buy from Jeffers." He hesitated. "We still find it hard to believe that such action on our part will have any effect."

"Don't worry," Junior reassured him. "He takes you all for granted now; but he'll change his tune once the receipts start to dwindle. You'll all suddenly become very important to Bill Jeffers. Wait and see."

The elder nodded absently, still not quite believing. The meek had been told they had power, yet they were unsure of its use, unsure that it really existed.

Junior left the hut in high spirits. It was all so simple when you used your head. In a few days Jeffers would start to wonder why he hadn't seen any Vanek around his store lately. He would get his answer and the choice would be his. Junior had little doubt as to what that choice would be.

He felt good. He was doing something worthwhile and doing it on his own. No one was paving the way for him. He was breaking his own ground.

The sun was down behind the trees as he unrolled his sleeping bag in the middle of a small clearing somewhere between the Vanek village and Danzer. He'd sleep well tonight, better than he had in many years.

Dawn broke chilly and damp. Reaching into his sack, Junior brought out a container of breakfast rations and activated the heating strip. Two minutes later he was downing a hot meal.

The sun was up and chasing the ground fog as he moved toward Danzer at a brisk pace. His plan was to go to town and hang around Jeffers' store to watch how things developed as the day wore on. And should the shopkeeper begin to wonder where all the Vanek were keeping themselves, Junior would be sure to offer his opinion.

Yes, he was thinking, today ought to prove very interesting.

Jeffers was on a short ladder, stocking one of the shelves, when Junior walked in.

"G'morning, Finch," he said with a glance over his shoulder. Junior was surprised that he remembered his name. "Cooled off from yesterday?"

"Entirely."

"Good. Looking for breakfast?"

"Had some already out in the field. But I'll take some coffee if you've got it."

Jeffers smiled as he poured two cups at the counter. "Ever had Jebinose coffee before?"

Junior shook his head.

"Then this one's on the house. Our coffee takes some getting used to and you may not want to finish your first cup."

Junior hesitantly nodded his thanks. Try as he might, he could not work up a personal dislike for Jeffers. He sampled the coffee; it had a strong, bitter-sour taste to it and Jeffers' grin broadened as he watched Junior add a few spoonfuls of sugar. He tried it again and it was a little more palatable now.

After a pause, Junior asked, "Just what is it you have against the Vanek, Bill? It's none of my business, I know, but I'm interested."

"You're right about it being none of your business," Jeffers said curtly, then shrugged. "But I'll tell you this much: I don't have anything in particular against them. It's just that they strike me as weird. They get on my nerves with all that talk about wheels and such and, frankly, I just don't like to have them sitting around."

Junior nodded absently. Jeffers was rationalizing and they both knew it.

"What time do they usually start showing up here?" he asked.

"They're usually my first customers of the day."

"But not today, eh?" Junior remarked confidently.

"You didn't beat them in, if that's what you mean. Two of them left just a few minutes before you arrived... bought some food." He stared at Junior curiously. "Something wrong?"

"No, nothing," was the hasty reply. Junior had visibly started at the news but recovered quickly. However, he doubted his ability to hide his surprise and dismay much longer. "Thanks for the coffee, Bill. I'll probably stop back in later on."

"Anytime," he heard Jeffers say as he walked out to the street.

Danzer was fully awake by now. All the shops—they totaled four counting the general store—were open and some of the farmers were driving up and down the street in heavy-duty lorries, some loaded with hay or feed, others with livestock. A pair of locals gave him a friendly nod as they brushed by him on their way into Jeffers' store.

Junior's gaze roamed the street for the robe of a Vanek. He spotted one hurrying up the boardwalk toward him so he advanced to meet him. It was Rmrl.

"At last we have found you, *bendreth*," the young Vanek said breathlessly. He scrutinized Junior's face closely. "I see you already know what we have come to tell you."

Junior gave a confirming nod. "I know. But what I want to know is why? Did the elders go back on their word?"

"No. They kept their word. They told the villagers not to buy from Jeffers but they complained far into the night. The elders held firm for a while but finally had to yield to the pressure."

"I don't understand."

"Our people...they want to buy from Jeffers. They do not want to deprive him of their business."

"Why not?"

"Wheels within wheels, *bendreth*."

"Doesn't what happens to them in that store matter to them?" Junior was totally baffled.

Rmrl shrugged and Junior thought he noticed a trace of resentment in the gesture.

"And you, Rmrl? How do you feel about it all?"

"Wheels within wheels," he repeated and walked away.

Junior was about to go after him but a voice made him turn.

"Bit off a little more than you could chew, Mr. Finch?"

It was Heber.

"What's that supposed to mean?" he asked the older man, who was leaning in the doorway of his office as he watched the offworlder.

"It means that I happened to overhear your conversation with Rmrl. I suppose I could have closed the door, but knowing what's going on in this town is part of my job." For a few fleeting seconds his eyes locked with Junior's, then: "Come inside a minute, Mr. Finch—please."

"Why?" Frustration and bafflement were edging him into a hostile and suspicious mood.

"Well, for one thing, I think I may be able to explain to you why your little plan failed. At least I'll be able to give you something more than 'wheels within wheels.'"

Interested, Junior grudgingly complied.

Heber's office was small and tight-fitting, most of the room taken up by filing cabinets and a huge desk handmade from local wood. A Vanek carving, unmistakable in its style, of a Jebinose species of fowl in a natural woodland setting was prominently displayed on a corner shelf.

"I thought you said there were no Vanek carvings left around here," Junior remarked as he caught sight of the object.

"I meant there were none for sale. That one's a personal gift from one of the elders."

Junior showed his surprise. "A gift?"

"Sure. I have pretty good relations with the Vanek myself. I rather like them. They're quiet, peaceful, and they mind their own business: an all-too-rare quality these days."

"I get the point."

Heber smiled. "There's an ancient saying about 'if the shoe fits…' But I wasn't necessarily referring to you, Mr. Finch. In fact, I have no objections whatsoever to your scheme against Jeffers—except, perhaps, to its overall ineptness."

Again Junior's face registered surprise.

"Since our little chat yesterday, you've been convinced that I'm some sort of a bigot, eh? You've probably got this whole town pegged as being full of bigots, too. It's not, I assure you. We have our share, but let me warn you: overgeneralization can be a serious error on the part of someone trying to institute a few changes."

Junior mulled this over. "Could be I owe you an apology—"

"But you're not ready to say so for sure yet. Just as well. I wouldn't want to hear it anyway." He ran his fingers through a shock of graying hair and indicated a rickety chair. "Let me tell you why your attempt at a boycott failed."

"I'm waiting," Junior said after seating himself.

Sunlight was pouring through the dirty front window and illuminating the cloud of dust motes swirling in the air before him. There was a timeless air about the tiny office, as if it had always been there and always would. Junior found his suspicions and hostilities beginning to fade.

Heber cleared his throat as he took his place behind the desk. "Seems to me you overlooked one major fact: Bill Jeffers owns the only general store within thirty kilometers. His closest competitor is old Vince Peck over in Zarico. So to put it simply: if the Vanek don't get their supplies at Jeffers' place, they don't get any supplies. And if they can't get any supplies, they don't eat."

"I find that hard to believe," Junior said. "The Vanek were here long before Bill Jeffers arrived with his store. How did they eat then?"

"They lived off the land. They combined farming and nomadism instead of rotating crops, they rotated the tribe from one field to the next every year. It wasn't easy, but they managed."

"That's what I figured. And if they managed before, they can manage again."

Heber gazed at him. "Have you any idea what it's like to farm this soil? Terran technology has been strained to the limit to bring in a good crop every year. I don't know how the Vanek ever got by. But the point is this: with the arrival of Jeffers and his store, and the discovery that the income from their statues will buy them all the food they can eat, the Vanek gave up farming. And I don't blame them for not wanting to go back to it. It was a full-time, back-breaking job to get their fields to produce. Now they can fill their bellies by doing what they used to do for recreation: carve little statues."

"They could still go back to it if they had to."

"I suppose they could, but not immediately. The fields are all overgrown now and…and there's the very nature of the race. They're a quiet, introverted, contemplative folk. The excess of spare time they enjoy now is perfectly suited to them. They cherish it."

Heber paused and shook his head. "I'm sure they'd like to sit at one of Jeffers' tables and eat their meal inside just like the Terrans, but the price you're asking them to pay is too great."

Junior leaned back and stared at nothing in particular. It was very probable that Heber was right about the Vanek.

"Then I may just have to feed them out of my own pocket until Jeffers softens up," he said suddenly.

"That would take a pile of money," Heber said with narrowed eyes. "You'd have to ship the food in from someplace else. You got that kind of money, Mr. Finch?"

"I've got it."

There was something in Junior's offhanded affirmation that convinced Heber that the younger man had more than a nodding acquaintance with large sums of money.

"Well, if you're that rich, why don't you start your own general store at the other end of town. You could operate at a loss. Or better still, why not buy Jeffers out? Hell! Just go out and buy the whole town of Danzer!"

Heber straightened some papers on his desk as he let this sink in, then, "Somehow, I don't think you'd find that very satisfying, Mr. Finch. Because I sense that there's more to your actions than a desire to put a stop to a little discrimination at the general store."

Junior tried to hide his discomfort with a shrug. His prior suspicions had been confirmed—under Marvin Heber's slow, rough-cut exterior was an acutely perceptive mind.

"And I wouldn't find that very satisfying, either," Heber continued. "Certain ends of my own would be served by seeing you win this one, but not with a big bankroll. If a victory here in Danzer is going to mean anything to you, to me, or to the Vanek, it must be won with the raw materials at hand. Do you see what I mean?"

Junior nodded slowly. It was obvious what winning this would mean to the Vanek and he was well aware of what it would mean to him. As to Marvin Heber's stake in the affair—he had a vague idea of where he fit in but still couldn't pin the man down. Yet that was of tertiary importance at the moment. His task now was to devise a way to let the Vanek boycott Jeffers's store without making them sacrifice all the conveniences to which they'd become so attached. His brow furrowed, then he jerked upright in his seat.

"Of course! The Vanek have their own income…why couldn't they use it to start a general store of their own? A temporary co-op of some sort that they could operate themselves until Jeffers comes around?"

Heber laughed. "The Vanek as shopkeepers? Ridiculous! A Vanek co-op would fall apart in a week. Their minds just aren't geared to inventories, balance sheets, and so on. And besides, it's not on the Great Wheel. You'd just be wasting your time. And remember, you haven't got much of that."

"Why not?"

"That government anti-discrimination bill—it comes up for a vote in less than two months. Some people who're supposed to know what they're talking about say it will pass, too. So you'd better think of something that'll get the job done your way, or the butt-ins from the capital will come in and do it their way." He punctuated the remark by spitting in the corner.

Junior stood up. "I'll come up with something." He was now sure he knew the reason for Heber's support. He started out but turned as he reached the door. "Thanks, Mr. Heber."

"It's Marvin," he said as he rested his feet on the desk. "And we'll see who thanks who when this thing's over."

THE SKIM MILK SKY of pre-dawn found Junior on the road west out of Danzer. A small flock of black-feathered birds darted above him like a sprinkle of iron filings on its way to a magnet as he stopped for a rest at the halfway point to Zarico. It was a long trip to make on foot but he had no other means of transportation, and the general store there offered him the only possible hope of a solution.

The sun was high when he first caught sight of Zarico and his initial feelings of déjà vu were heightened as he entered the town. It was as if he had traveled in a tremendous circle and wound up back in Danzer. Peck's general store was of the same design as Jeffers' and it too offered a hot lunch.

"Are you busy at the moment, Mr. Peck?" Junior asked as the grizzled old man laid a steaming plateful of stew before him. The store was deserted, and now was as good a time as any to sound him out.

"Not at the moment," Peck replied amiably. "Why?"

"Like to discuss something with you."

"Business?"

"Maybe."

"Find yourself a table and I'll join you in a minute." He disappeared into the back. When he returned, he was carrying an earthen jug and two glasses. Seating himself across from Junior, he filled both glasses about halfway and pushed one across the table. "Nothing like a glass of wine at midday, I always say. Go ahead—try it. It's my own."

Junior did so. The crystal clear fluid was light, dry, surprisingly good. "Very nice. My name's Finch, by the way." Peck nodded and they clinked glasses.

"Well, now," Peck said after a long swallow. "What can I do for you, Mr. Finch?"

"I'd like to talk to you about the Vanek."

"Vanek? We don't have any Vaneks around here. Oh, one or two may pass through now and again, but if you want to know about Vaneks, you'd best go to Danzer."

"I know all I want to know about them," Junior said—which wasn't true. "What I want to know right now is how you feel about them."

Peck finished his glass and refilled it, this time to the brim. "They're all right, I guess. I'm not crazy about their spooky looks but I don't see enough of them to care much one way or the other." He noticed Junior's empty glass so he poured him some more, then drained and refilled his own glass once again.

"Would you mind very much if they bought their supplies here?"

"Hell, no! I'll sell to anyone who's got the money to buy!"

"How about lunch?"

"Sure." He drained his third glass of wine. "Sell them breakfast and even dinner if there's enough of them wanting it."

"Would you let them sit here and eat just as I'm doing?"

Peck paused in mid-pour at this thought, then sloshed the glass full.

"I don't know about that. Vaneks and Terrans don't usually eat together in these parts. Might hurt my business."

"I doubt it. Where else is anybody in Zarico going to go? To Danzer?"

Peck nodded slowly. "I see what you mean."

"And even if you did lose a few customers, I'm going to bring you one Vanek for every Terran customer you've got!" Junior smiled as Peck took a wide-eyed swallow. "That's right. I can double your present business if you'll let the Vanek eat lunch here in the store."

"How're y'gonna get 'em here?" The wine was starting to take effect.

"You must have something around here you use for transportation."

"Sure. I got an ol' lorry out back. It's a wheeled job but it gets around."

"Good. If you let me use that every day, I'll be able to double your profits."

Peck shook his head. "No-no. Won't work. Cause trouble."

"Why?" Junior asked, deciding that now was the time to get aggressive. "Is Bill Jeffers a friend of yours or something?"

"Never met him."

"Then let me give it a try!"

"No. People aroun' here won' like it."

Junior pounded his fist on the table with a ferocity that made the now half-empty wine jug jump. "Who owns this store, anyway?" he shouted. "You gonna let other people tell you how to run your own store?"

Peck straightened his spine and slammed his own fist on the table. "Hell no!"

"Good!" Junior said. He grabbed the jug and filled both glasses to the brim. "Give me a week, and if I can't double your profits in that time, then we'll call the whole thing off."

"I'll drink to that!" said Peck.


THE PLAN WORKED WELL for the first week—profits were not quite doubled but the increase was significant—and Peck extended the trial period. Twice a day, early morning and early afternoon, Junior would squeeze a dozen hesitant

Danzer Vanek into the lorry, then ferry them to Zarico. He would return the first group at noon and the second later in the afternoon, then return the lorry to Zarico, where he'd spend the night. Peck had set up living quarters for him in the back of the store.

Things went quite smoothly until the end of the second week. It was twilight and Junior was about to enter the lorry for the trip back to Zarico when someone grabbed his arms from behind and pinned them there. Then he was spun around. Before his eyes could focus on his assailants, a fist was driven into his abdomen and then into his face. This procedure was repeated until Junior lost consciousness. The last thing he remembered was being dragged along the ground, then nothing.

# V
# OLD PETE

It was nearly a week after their first meeting and Old Pete was in good spirits as he entered Jo's office suite. He had renewed a few old acquaintances around town and had allowed the deBloise matter to slip toward the back of his mind. Jo looked up from her desk as he entered. There was a here-he-is-again sourness in her expression but he didn't let it bother him. She was learning to tolerate his presence—she didn't enjoy it, but put up with it as a necessary and temporary evil.

"You know," he told her, "I just saw a fellow walking down the hall with a rat perched on his shoulder. You taking animal acts under your wing, too?"

"That's no act, and that was no ordinary rat. That man—name's Sam Orzechowski—has managed to tame *rattus interstellus*—"

"Don't try and tell me that was a space rat! Those things can't be trained. If that were a real space rat, it would've swallowed the guy's ear long ago!"

"I checked his background and I can assure you he's all he says he is. Now I have to find some commercial use for the rats. But that's not why I called you here. We've got some information on what's going on with deBloise and Dil."

Old Pete took a seat. "What've you found?"

"Don't know just yet. I put one of the best investigators in the business on the job. He called to say that he's got some interesting news."

"But he didn't say what it was?"

"He never says anything of interest when there's the possibility that the wrong ears might hear it."

Something in her voice told Old Pete that there might be more than a professional relationship between Jo and this investigator.

"When does he arrive?"

"He doesn't," Jo replied with a quick shake of her head. "He never comes to this building. IBA uses his services on a regular basis and frequent visits would give away the relationship. We meet him in a few hours in the casino."

"That's hardly what I'd call a secluded meeting place. It's crowded day and night."

"It's really an excellent place for exchanging information, if you lay the proper groundwork. I make it a practice to visit the casino once a week and he stops in whenever he's in town. That way, no one thinks it strange when we run into each other now and then especially since we're both avid pokochess players."

"Really? So am I. And I haven't had a good game with another human in a long time; playing against a machine keeps you sharp but lacks something when you win."

"It must get lonely on that island."

"Only once or twice a year do I crave the company of others; but I'm never alone—I have me. Fortunately, I'm not one of those people who, when left alone, is faced with the unpleasant realization that there's no one there."

The conversation ranged over various topics without direction until Jo brought it around to one of the trouble spots in her mind.

"Did IBA do any investigating into my father's death?"

Old Pete nodded slowly. "Yes. On two occasions. Neither came up with anything useful. It seems that the head man around the town—I think his name was Heber, or Hever, or something like that—anyway, he seemed to have a genuine regard for Junior and made sure that our people had access to everything they needed for the investigation. He had done a pretty thorough job himself before word even got back to IBA that Junior was dead."

"Those aliens murdered him then?"

"That's what all the evidence says. I still can't quite believe it, though. They've got a special marker for his grave and the vid recording of his funeral that was brought back—"

"I know. I've seen it."

"Then you know that they thought of him practically as a demigod. It makes no sense."

"But you left his body there. Why? Not that I have any morbid need to see my father's remains interred on Ragna; I'm just curious as to why you didn't bring them back."

Old Pete shrugged. "Because his body belonged in that Vanek graveyard more than anywhere else."

Jo made no reply. She made a mental note to look up the copy of her father's autopsy report, then her thoughts slipped back to the day her aunt told her that her daddy wouldn't be coming back; that he'd had an accident on a faraway planet and had died. She remembered trying to hold back the anguish and fear and loss by smothering it with denial, but that didn't work. It was true, she knew. Jo cried then, harder and longer than she had ever cried before. Her aunt held her for a long time, now and then joining her in tears. She was never that close to her aunt again. She could not really remember over crying again since then, either.

Bringing herself back to the present with a start, she rose to her feet. "Time to go. I'll drive."

As the flitter rose from the IBA roof, Old Pete sought to keep the conversation away from Junior.

"I happened to see some of the figures on the currency exchange you started. Not exactly what IBA was intended for, but very impressive."

"Quite the contrary," she said, relishing the chance to correct him. "It's a natural outgrowth of the company's activities. In the course of investigating new markets for clients, we have to keep tabs on the political and economic climates. The monetary policies of local governments are of prime importance, as you well know, so we began indexing rates of inflation, growth of the money supplies, et cetera, for each trade sector. I used some of that data to do a little personal currency speculation a few years ago and did quite well. If a novice like me could make a nice percentage with IBA's index, I figured a currency expert working full time on it could open a new service to our clients. So we hired a couple and we're doing all right."

"You keep much of your own money in that fund?"

Jo shook her head. "I only participate on occasions when I can make a short term gain. If they tell me the Nolevetol *krona* is overvalued, I'll sell them short; if the Derby pound is undervalued, I'll buy a few bundles and wait. Otherwise my money sits in a vault as Tolivian certificates of deposit."

Old Pete nodded approval and said no more. His savings had also been converted to Tolivian CDs long ago. The banks of Tolive were considered an anachronism in many financial circles because they insisted on backing their currency 100 per cent with precious metals. The only coins the issued were 0.999 fine gold or silver, and a "certificate of deposit" meant just that: a given amount of gold or silver was on deposit at that particular bank and was payable on demand. The nominal government of Tolive had only one law concerning monetary policy: all currency must be fully backed by a precious metal; any deviation from that policy was considered fraud and punishable by public flogging.

Old Pete liked the idea of hard money, always had. So did Jo. Apparently she had more in common with him than she cared to admit—

—or with Junior. He was more used to her appearance now. At first sight of her last week, even with her hair darkened toward black, Jo had looked so much like Junior that he had been struck dumb for a moment. But the similarities went beyond mere physical appearance. There was an ambiance about her that reeked of Junior. Anyone who had known the man well would see it in her. He had, of course, expected that, but not to such a degree.

There were differences, too, which were equally startling.

*So like Junior,* he thought, *and yet so unlike him. I really shouldn't be surprised. After all, their developmental environments were so different. And don't forget the opposing sexual orientation.*

As his thoughts began to wander into forbidden ground, he was called back to the present by the sound of Jo's voice.

"There it is," she said, and banked the flitter to the right. "By the way, if you like filet of chispen, they've got a restaurant in the casino that does a superb job on it."

The casino glowed below them like a luminescent fish of prey lurking on an inky sea bottom. Alighting from the flitter onto the roof, they were greeted by an elaborately costumed doorman to whom Jo was obviously a familiar figure. He bowed them through the arched entrance.

The casino consisted of five large rooms arranged in a circular fashion. The elevators from the roof deposited you in the hub and from there you were given free choice as to the manner in which you wished to lose money. Jo headed directly for the pokochess parlor. This was her favorite game, a game of chance and skill in which each player was "dealt" a king, three pawns, and five more pieces randomly chosen from the twelve remaining possibilities. The two players could bet as each new piece was dealt and were allowed to raise the ante whenever a piece was taken during the course of the game.

Pokochess was not too popular with the casino because the house could make a profit only when a guest played one of the house professionals. But the game was the current rage on Ragna and a pokochess parlor in the casino proved to be a good draw. Patrons could use the house tables for a small hourly fee.

Jo stopped at the entrance to the pokochess section and ran her gaze over the room. It came to rest on a nondescript man in his middle thirties sitting alone at a table in a far corner. A shorter, darker man had just left his side and was headed in the direction of the bar.

"There he is," Jo said, a smile lighting her face. She started forward but Old Pete grabbed her elbow.

"That's the man you have working for you?" he asked in a startled tone.

"Yes—Larry Easly. Why?"

Old Pete broke into a laugh. "Because that fellow moving away from him has been working for me—and he's Easly's partner!"

"Really?" They started to make their way toward the corner where Easly sat. "Small galaxy, isn't it?"

Old Pete nodded. "Wheels within wheels, *bendreth*."

"What's that mean?"

"Oh, just an old, old expression that means pretty much what you want it to mean." He threw her a sidelong glance. "You mean you never heard it before?"

"Doesn't sound familiar…where'd it originate?"

"Never mind." He didn't want to bring that up again.

Easly spotted them then, rose from his seat, and came forward. He and Jo clasped hands briefly, formally, but their eyes locked and held on after the hands had parted. Had he wished it, Larry Easly could have been a distinguished-looking man, but the nature of his work demanded that he downplay any striking features. So he made certain that his posture and the cut of his clothes hid his muscular build, that his complexion and the cut of his dark blond hair invited anonymity.

There was a certain squinting quality about Easly's hazel eyes, almost as if the light hurt them. But Old Pete noted that they were constantly roving under cover of that squint, missing nothing.

Larry Easly extended his hand. "We meet at last, Mr. Paxton."

"I knew we would eventually," Old Pete said, "but this is quite a surprise."

Andrew Tella returned then with a drink-laden waiter in tow. After shaking hands with Old Pete and being introduced to Jo, he handed out drinks—scotch to the former, a glass of cold Moselle to the latter—and they all sat down around a pokochess table.

"You can't be as surprised as Andy and I were when we discovered we'd both been requested to investigate the same thing," Easly said with a trace of a smile. His features were soft, gentle-looking, not at all what Old Pete had expected. "But we guessed what had happened and, since Andy got the assignment first, he had the honor of completing it."

Andy Tella cleared his throat and straightened up in his chair. "Since you're both here to learn of the mysterious doings on Dil, I'll get right to them—and believe me, they make some story."

Easly nodded in agreement as he ignited the end of a torpedo-shaped cigar, but said nothing. Clouds of blue-white smoke encircled his head for a brief instant before being drawn away by the ventilation system.

"First step," Tella began, "was to go to the Fed patent office, use a few contacts, and find out if there's been much activity in the way of new patents from Dil. Answer: yes. A spatial engineer by the name of Denver Haas has recently developed something he calls a 'warp gate' and is ready to go into production. I managed to get a quick look at his file, made a copy of it, naturally"—the briefest of smiles here—"and Larry and I went over it."

Easly picked up the story here. "You must understand, of course, that neither Andy nor I have much of a grounding in physics and those papers were pretty damn technical. We couldn't go around asking experts to decipher them for us because we weren't supposed to have a copy. So we bought some teaching trodes and came up with a rough idea of what this 'warp gate' is."

"Let's lay some groundwork first," Tella said, and turned to Jo and Old Pete. "Do you know how the warp unit on the average interstellar ship works?"

Jo shrugged. "It creates some kind of field that allows the ship to leave real space and enter subspace where it can take exaggerated advantage of the normal curvature of space."

"Very nicely put," Tella said with an approving nod. "I've been studying this stuff for the past week and I never could have capsulized it so well. But you've got just about everything there. The warp drive lets you travel under the curve of space; the higher the degree of warp, the longer the jump. That 'some kind of field' is important here, because it determines the degree of warp. Warp fields are a poor imitation of the field around a black hole; Haas has gone a step further. He has managed to link a pair of quantum black holes and generate one helluva warp field between them."

"I knew it!" Old Pete slapped the table. "When I heard fifty years ago that they'd found a way to lock up quantum holes in a stasis field, I said someday somebody's going to find a commercial use for those things! And sure enough, somebody has!"

Jo was pensive. "So he's turned things around, eh? Instead of generating the warp from inside the ship, he generates it externally and lets the ship pass through—for a fee, I assume."

"I suppose so," Tella replied. "Either that or a company buys a gate and uses it exclusively for its own craft. They're going to be hellishly expensive, though. Finding quantum holes isn't too hard, but locking them up in a stasis field small enough to make the holes useful and large enough to prevent anything from accidentally entering their event horizons is pretty tricky. But that's not the whole story. Wait'll you hear this: Denver Haas is rumored to be working on modifications that will theoretically allow his warp gate to operate *inside* a planet's gravity well!"

Stunned silence at Old Pete and Jo's end of the table.

The major drawback to the current on-board warp unit was its inability to generate a stable warp field in the presence of any appreciable gravitational influence, whether stellar or planetary. This necessitated the use of peristellar drive tubes to travel past the point of critical influence for a given planet circling a given star. And this type of travel, despite the use of a proton-proton drive in tubes lined with Leason crystals, was maddeningly slow. But if all that could be eliminated, if all you had to do was shuttle up to the ship, board, and then flash through an orbiting warp gate…

"If that's truly possible," Old Pete said in an awe-tinged voice, "then humankind will be able to begin its golden age as an interstellar race."

Easly and Tella glanced at each other and the latter said, "I never looked at it that way, but—"

"But nothing!" the old man retorted. "The first interstellar trips took decades; the perfection of the warp field made them a matter of days, weeks, or months, depending on where you were coming from and where you were going. We are now talking about hours! Hours between the stars! Think of what that will mean for trade!"

"The thing is, Mr. Paxton," Easly said patiently, "that this guy Haas hasn't perfected those modifications yet."

"He must have if he's going into production as Andy said."

Easly shook his head. "He's going to market with a prototype that can only operate beyond the critical point in the gravity well."

For the second time that evening, there was dead silence at that particular pokochess table. Jo finally broke it.

"You must be mistaken, Larry."

"I assure you I'm not."

"But it simply doesn't make sense. He'll be trying to market a rather expensive device that offers no real advantage over the onboard warp unit."

"Oh, it has advantages," Easly replied. "The gates generate an extremely high-degree warp, high enough so a ship can travel from gate to gate in a single jump. No more jumping in and out of warp, checking co-ordinates, then jumping again. You just follow a subspace beam from one gate to another."

"Not enough!" Jo said. "The big expense in interstellar travel is time, and the Haas gate that takes days to get to saves no time. The warp jumps are inconvenient, but they add little appreciable time to the trip. If Haas can eliminate the trip out past—and back from—the critical point in the gravity well, he'll have revolutionized interstellar travel; if not, then he's only invented an expensive toy."

"Expensive to his backers, you mean," Old Pete added.

"That, too," Jo agreed with a nod. "Star Ways will see to it that he doesn't sell too many gates."

"How can they do that?" Tella asked. "And why?"

Jo signaled the waiter for another round of drinks before answering. "Star Ways is known as the biggest corporation in human history, right? It's a conglomerate with subsidiaries in every sector of Terran space. Everybody knows that. But what is the basis for its growth to its present size?"

Comprehension suddenly dawned in Tella's face. "Of course! The onboard warp unit!"

"Right. The warp gate is an eventual threat to the product that forms the economic basis for the conglomerate. Star Ways is not going to let anything hurt its warp unit sales if it can help it. It will cut prices to the bone until Haas has to fold."

"The Haas warp gate," Old Pete summarized, "is doomed if it goes to market in its present form. It might have a chance if there were no competition from the conventional warp unit sector—some of the trade fleets might decide to invest in gates as their present onboard units depreciated—but it would be a very slow seller. If someone asked me whether or not to venture any money on Mr. Haas, my answer would be a definite no!"

He halted discreetly as the waiter arrived with the fresh drinks, and resumed when the four of them were alone again.

"But the question still remains: what's the connection between Haas and deBloise? There's no doubt in my mind now that Doyl Catera was talking shout the warp gate when he referred to a technological innovation that could make all planets neighbors. But why is it so important to the Restructurists? What do they hope to get out of it?"

"Well," Easly said after carefully weighing and assessing the facts and opinions that had crisscrossed the table since they had seated themselves, "certainly not a return on their investment."

"You mean deBloise and his crew are backing Haas?" Old Pete sputtered, almost choking on a sip of scotch.

"One hundred per cent. But apparently they don't want anyone to know. They've gone to an awful lot of trouble—three or four dummy investment groups, I'm told—to keep their names out of it. Haas probably doesn't even know they're involved. They've done an excellent job, according to my informant; no one could ever prove conclusively that there was a connection between Denver Haas and the Restructurist big shots…and my informant says he'll deny any knowledge of the whole affair if I try to use him as a source."

"Sounds sinister," Joe mused with a glance at Old Pete. "Your conspiracy theory sounds more and more plausible every minute. But the rationale behind the whole thing completely eludes me at the moment."

"I may not know the means," Old Pete offered, "but I know the end: the end of the free market."

Jo wrinkled up her nose in a frankly skeptical grimace.

"You look like you just got a whiff of week-old chispen innards," Old Pete said.

"It's just that it's such an absurd idea. I mean, how can you have commerce without a free market?"

"It can be done. It's not easy, but it can be done. Traders can always find a way. They're the most resourceful members of the species. If a government tries to destroy a free market, as it is often wont to do, by controlling the supply of certain commodities or restricting the free movement of goods, traders and buyers will always manage to get together some way. If the free market is declared void by the government, they make their own. Only then it's known as a 'black' market."

Old Pete paused as he noted the puzzled expressions around him. "I forgot. Your economic education in the outworlds is still very naïve. You lack my advantage of growing up on Earth. I'm all too familiar with things such as excise taxes, trade bureaus, commerce commissions, sales taxes—"

"Sales taxes! What are they?" Tella asked with an amused smile.

"That's a new one on you, is it? You've heard of the income tax, of course. Most outworlds have it in some form or another. That's the way the politicos get your money as it enters your pocket. And when they've taxed that to the limit the populace will tolerate, they go to work on finding ways to get a piece of what's left of your money as it comes out of your pocket. That's called a sales tax: you pay a tribute to the current regime every time you buy something."

Jo shook her head in disbelief. "I find it incredible that any population would put up with such abuse. There'd be rioting in the streets here on Ragna if anyone tried to foist that kind of nonsense on us!"

"Don't count on it. As that famous Earth philosopher Muniz put it a long time ago: 'The masses are asses.' And while I don't subscribe to such a cynical, elitist point of view, I fear he may have been right. I never cease to be amazed at what people will put up with if it's presented to them in a pretty package. These tax schemes are always preceded by a propaganda blitz or by a financial crisis that has been either manufactured or caused by the bureaucracy itself. The 'public good' is stressed and before you know it, the public has allowed someone else to slip his hand into its pocket. As time goes on, little by little the state manages to funnel more and more money through its myriad bureaus and eventually the politicians are running the entire economy."

Jo was still dubious. "Who in his or her right mind would allow politicians to make economic policy? Most of them are small-town lawyers who got involved in planetary politics and wound up in the Federation Assembly. They've had a year or so of economic theory in their undergraduate education, usually from a single source, and that's the extent of their qualifications in the field of economics. How can they possibly have the gall to want to plan the course of an economy that affects the lives of billions of people?"

"They not only have the gall for it; they will claw and scramble over each other in a mad rush to see who can do more of it."

"Okay. Granted, such men exist and some of them are probably in the Federation Assembly. But I'm sure they're outnumbered."

"I'm going to tell you Paxton's First Law," Old Pete said, raising his index finger: "Never trust anyone who runs for office."

"Maybe it's time someone paid a visit to Mr. Haas and got some first-hand information," Easly suggested, getting back to business.

"Good idea, Larry," Jo began. "Why don't you—"

Old Pete interrupted. "I think Jo and I should go see Mr. Haas ourselves. We'll go as representatives of IBA; he's got a product and we want to help him market it. That's our business. What could be more natural?"

Tella and Easly agreed that it was a reasonable approach, but Jo objected.

"Sorry, can't go. Too much work to do."

"You can get away for a while," Old Pete said. "IBA won't fall apart without you. And think of the impact on Mr. Haas when the head of IBA pays a personal visit to his humble abode. Why I'm sure he'll fall all over himself telling us everything we want to know!"

Everyone laughed and Jo reluctantly agreed to accompany Old Pete to Dil. She hated interstellar travel, hated the wave of nausea that hit her every time the ship came in and out of warp. But Dil wasn't that far away and IBA employed a first-rate jump engineer for its executive craft. He could probably make the trip in two jumps and that wouldn't be too bad. She'd bring along some data spools just so the trip wouldn't be a total loss.

The conversation turned to other matters and Old Pete leaned back with a smile on his face and sighed with relief.

# VI
## JUNIOR

Someone splashed water into his face. It was Heber. His expression was grim as he helped Junior to his feet.

"I was afraid something like this would happen."

"You were, huh? Why didn't you let me in on it?"

Junior glanced around as he tried to piece together his whereabouts. He last remembered standing over by the lorry. He had been beaten, then dragged away from it…about half a dozen locals stood around him. Acrid smoke filled the air.

"The lorry!" he cried, and looked past Heber's shoulder. The vehicle was still smoking, though covered with a thick coat of hissing foam.

"Two of Zel Namer's boys did it," Heber told him. "They'd been drinking a bit too much, started feeling mean, and things got out of hand. We've got them locked up for now. I'm just glad they had the sense to drag you far enough from the lorry so's you wouldn't be hurt by the blast."

Junior nodded and gingerly felt his swollen face. "So am I."

The lorry had been parked about one hundred meters from the town center. The locals must have heard the explosion and come running with fire-fighting equipment. His eyes came to rest on a familiar figure: Bill Jeffers stood off to the side, a spent extinguisher dangling from his hand. He sensed Junior's scrutiny and turned.

"I want you to know that I had nothing to do with this, Finch," he said. "Even if you are doing your damnedest to put me out of business."

"You know something, Bill," Junior said in a low voice, "I believe you. And the last thing I want to do is put you out of business. All I want you to do is change a few of your policies."

"You're trying to get me to feed a bunch of half-breeds in my store!"

"I'm not forcing you to do anything," Junior said, maintaining a calm, reasoned tone for the benefit of the other locals nearby who were all ears. "Whatever you decide, the choice will be yours and yours alone. I'm just making it more profitable for you to see things my way."

Jeffers fumbled for an answer. Failing to find a suitable one, he wheeled and stalked away.

"Well, whether it's force or not really doesn't matter much now," said Heber, glancing after Jeffers. "Without that lorry, the game is up."

Junior nodded slowly, grimly. "I guess it is. Peck will never jeopardize another one, and I can't say I blame him."

"Maybe something can be worked out," Heber said. His eyes were fixed on the horizon.

"Like what?"

He shrugged. "I'm not sure, yet. But we can always hope, can't we?"

"Guess so. But hope by itself has a notoriously, poor efficiency record."

Heber laughed. "Agreed. And since it doesn't look like you're going to make it back to Zarico, you'll need a place to spend the night. Come on back to the office and I'll fix you up with a cot."

They walked back to the town in silence. Once in the office, Heber reached down between the side of the desk and the wall and pulled out a folding cot.

"I keep this here for times when it gets too hot upstairs."

"You mean you don't have a temperature regulator?" Junior asked.

Heber snorted. "The human race may be able to travel between the stars but there's no temperature regulator in this building, or in any other building in Danzer. You've got to get it into your head, Mr. Finch, that people out here are just scraping by. You may see a flitter truck now and again but don't mistake it for affluence—it's a necessity for some farmers. We live here at just about the same level as pre-space man back on old Earth. It's a different story in the capital, of course; but Danzer and Copia might as well be on different planets. And speaking of Copia, I've got a call to make."

"Where to?"

"You'll find out. But for now, why don't you just lie down on that cot and get some sleep. Things may look better in the morning."

Junior doubted that but nodded agreement. When Heber was gone, he lay back on the cot and put his hands behind his head, planning to stay awake until Heber's return. He was asleep in minutes.

Someone was shaking him and he opened his eyes. The morning sun was turning from orange to yellow and was streaming through the window into the office.

"Wake up!" Heber was saying. "I've got a vid reporter from the capital waiting to meet you."

Junior jerked upright in the cot. "A vid reporter? Is that who you called in Copia last night?"

Heber nodded. "Yes! And did he jump when I told him what had happened. He seems to think it will make a big story. Wants to meet you right away."

"Damn!" Junior said as he rubbed his eyes and rose to his feet. "Why'd you have to go and do that? You should have asked me about it first."

"What's the matter? I thought you'd be happy."

"Not about a vid reporter, I'm not. They bring nothing but trouble."

"Trouble's already here, I'm afraid," Heber said gravely. "A quick look in the mirror will remind you of that." Junior gingerly touched his swollen, discolored left cheek as Heber continued. "Maybe the knowledge that the vid's got an eye on the town will prevent any follow-ups to last night's incident."

Junior considered this a moment, then shrugged. "Maybe you're right, but I doubt it. Where is he?"

"Right outside. C'mon."

As Junior stepped from the office he saw a compact man in a bright, clean, tailored suit; he was immediately struck by the incongruity of such apparel in the Danzer setting. As the reporter caught sight of him, he snatched up his recording plate and held it out at arm's length. Junior suddenly realized that he must look like hell—his hair uncombed, his bruised face unwashed and unshaven, his clothes slept in.

"Mr. Finch?" said the reporter. "I'm Kevin Lutt from JVS. I'd like to ask you a question or two if I may."

"Sure," Junior said with ill-concealed disinterest. "What do you want to know?"

"Well, first of all, I'd like to get a look at the lorry that was burned."

Junior shrugged. "Follow me." He turned to Heber. "I'll meet you back here later."

Walking ahead as the vid man recorded the scenery, Junior felt ill at ease. He did not relish being probed and questioned about his involvement with the Vanek. It was no one else's business but his own, but Heber seemed to think an interview would help and things couldn't get much worse, anyway.

When they reached the charred remains of the lorry, Junior stood back and watched as the vid reporter set the scene for an interview. He scanned the wreck, then turned his recorder plate on Junior.

"How does it feel to have so narrowly escaped death, Mr. Finch?"

"It was no narrow escape. I was dragged a good distance from the lorry before it was fired. No one tried to kill me, just scare me a little."

Lutt tried another tack. "Just what are your reasons for getting involved in this?"

Junior merely shrugged and said, "Wheels within wheels."

He didn't like Lutt and he was feeling more and more uncooperative by the minute. The big outside world was threatening to push its way into Danzer and the little town could be ruined in the process. And it would all be his fault.

"Did you know there's legislation pending in the capital that pertains directly to such blatant bigotry as this?"

"Heard something to that effect."

"Then why do you feel it necessary to risk your life to do something that the legislature will do for you in a short time?"

"First of all, Mr. Lutt, let me repeat that my life has not yet been in danger, and most likely will not be. And as for your question: I have never depended on any legislation to do anything whatsoever for me. As a matter of fact, it usually winds up doing something to me."

Lutt brushed this off. "You're facing a violent, bigoted town, Mr. Finch. The events of last night prove that. Aren't you just a little afraid?"

Junior almost lost control on that one. In typical journalese, Lutt was lumping Heber and all those like him in with the likes of the Namer boys.

"Get lost, Lutt," he snarled and turned away. He was about to start walking back toward town when a movement in the brush caught his eye.

In a slow procession, the Vanek were coming. As he stood and watched them approach, he noted that Lutt had repositioned himself with his recorder plate held high. When the entire group had assembled itself in a semi-circle around Junior, the chief elder stepped forward and raised his hand. As one, the forty-odd Vanek bowed low and held the position as the elder presented Junior with a begging bowl and a detailed carving of a Jebinose fruit tree in full bloom.

"They'll never believe this at home," Lutt muttered breathlessly, recording the scene from different angles.

"Now cut that out!" Junior yelled at the Vanek.

"But, *bendreth*," said the elder, "we wish to pay you honor. You have been harmed on our behalf. This has never happened before and—"

"And nothing! The whole idea of this little campaign was to get you to assert yourselves and demand the dignity and respect you deserve. I turn around and the next thing I know you're bowing and scraping. Cut it out and stand erect!"

"But you don't understand, *bendreth*," said the elder.

"I think I do," Junior said softly, "and I'll treasure these gifts for as long as I live, but let's forget about gratitude and all that for now. Our main concern at the moment is a replacement for the lorry. Until we can get one, you'll just have to hold out. Borrow from each other, share what food you have until we can get some transportation. Whatever you do, hold to the plan until you hear from me."

The elder nodded and started to bow, but caught himself. "Yes, *bendreth*."

"And don't bow to anyone—ever." He gave a quick wave and started for the town. Lutt trotted up behind him.

"Mr. Finch, you've just made me a famous man. If I don't get a journalism award for this recording, no one will. I'll never be able to repay you for this."

Junior increased his stride and kept his face averted as he replied. The simple unabashed gratitude in the little Vanek ceremony had moved him more than he cared to admit. As he hurried toward town clutching the bowl and the statue, one under each arm, his eyes were tilled with tears.

"You can get lost," he told Lutt.

HEBER SMILED AND SHOOK his head as Junior gave him a quick rundown of what had happened.

"You can't blame them, really," he said. "Every once in a while a Terran will go out of his way for a Vanek, but you're the first one they've ever known to take a beating on their behalf. You'll probably rate a spot on one of the major spokes of the Great Wheel when they tell their grandchildren about you." He paused, then, "How'd you get on with Lutt?"

"Not too well, I'm afraid. How would you feel if you were tired, dirty, grubby, and hungry, and some fast-talking reporter was sticking his recorder plate in your face and asking a lot of stupid questions?"

"Not too much like being friendly, I suppose," Heber admitted.

"And even under the best of conditions I doubt if you'd have liked the timbre of his questions."

Heber shrugged. "I expect some smug generalizations to come out of this, but publicity—even unfair publicity—may save you from another beating."

Junior rubbed his tender jaw. "I'm all for that."

HEBER ENTERED HIS OFFICE the next morning with a news sheet clutched in his hand. Junior was just finishing off a breakfast ration pack.

"Here—read this! It's fresh from the capital."

"Where'd you get it?"

"About half a dozen reporters came in this morning. One of them gave it to me." Heber beamed. "We're all over the front page!"

It was true. The first sheet of the vid service's printed counterpart was devoted entirely to the doings in Danzer. As Junior skimmed the story under Lutt's byline, he saw himself portrayed as a mysterious, close-mouthed crusader against bigotry. And in the middle of the front page was a large photo of the Vanek kneeling in homage to him.

"This is incredible! Lutt has played me up like some sort of fictional vid hero!"

"There's not much else doing on Jebinose, I guess, and you seem to make good copy."

Junior dropped the sheet on the desk in disgust and went to the window. "Where are they now?"

"If I said they were out back, where would you go?"

"Out front!"

"Well, don't worry too much now. They're well occupied down the street at the moment with Bill Jeffers. Probably asking him some very pointed questions."

# F. Paul Wilson

"Oh no!" Junior went to the door and peered out. He could see Jeffers standing in the doorway of his store, surrounded by reporters.

"What's the matter?" Heber asked.

"Does Jeffers have a short temper?"

"He gets hot pretty fast, yes."

"Then I'd better get down there," he said, and was out the door.

As he hurried down the street, he noted that Jeffers was posed in the stance of a cornered animal, his face red, his eyes bright, his muscles coiled to spring. Junior broke into a loping run. It could well be the intention of one of the reporters to provoke the storekeeper into violence—something to make good vid viewing. It wouldn't help the Vanek cause to have the media make a fool of Jeffers and portray him as a violence-prone imbecile; it would only serve to double his obstinance.

"Well, well! 'The Crusader Against Bigotry' has arrived!" Jeffers called and waved a news sheet in the air as he caught sight, of Junior approaching.

The reporters immediately forgot Jeffers and turned on Junior with a flurry of questions.

"I'll talk to you later," he said, elbowing his way by them. "Right now I have something to discuss with Mr. Jeffers."

An overweight reporter in a bright green jumper blocked his path. "We have some questions to ask you first, Mr. Finch." He thrust his recorder plate in Junior's face.

"No you don't," was the tight-lipped reply.

The recorder plate clicked on as the reporter started his interview, oblivious to whatever else Junior had in mind. "Now, first off, just where are you from? Rumor has it that you're an offworlder and I think you should divulge your—"

Without warning, Junior slapped the recorder plate out of the man's hand, grabbed two fistfuls of the shiny fabric of his suit, and shoved him off the boardwalk. Hearing a recorder click into operation behind him, he whirled, snatched the plate, ripped it from the extended hand, and hurled it, too, into the street.

"Now, I said I'd like to speak to Mr. Jeffers. So if you don't mind, wait across the street until I'm finished. It's a private conversation."

"Our viewers have a right—" someone began.

"Look! If you want any kind of an interview at all, you'll wait over there!"

This threat had real meaning for them. They'd had little time with Jeffers and much of that had been stony silence. If there anything was to be gleaned from this long hot trip out to the sticks, it would be in an interview with this Finch character. Slowly, reluctantly, they drifted across to the other side of the street, muttering that they'd rather be off-planet somewhere tracking down the rumor that The Healer was coming to this sector next.

"You should be careful," Jeffers said, watching Junior curiously. "You'll ruin your image."

"I couldn't do that if I tried," he replied with a rueful smile, "just as you couldn't improve yours. They've cast us in our roles and we're locked into them. I'm the hero, you're the villain. My obnoxious behavior just now will be written off in their minds as a personality quirk. If you had acted the same way, it would have demonstrated a basic flaw in your character and people all over the planet would have seen it tonight."

Jeffers made no reply but continued his curious stare.

"Anyway, I guess you can figure out why I'm here, Bill," Junior said finally. "I want to ask you to give in and let's get things back on an even keel around here."

But Jeffers' mind was occupied with something else. "I just can't figure you out, Finch," he muttered, shaking his head in wonder. "Just can't figure you out." Still shaking his head, he turned and disappeared into the darkness within his store.

Junior started to follow, then changed his mind and headed back toward Heber's office, ignoring the waiting reporters. Halfway there, he was stopped by a familiar voice calling him from the street.

"*Bendreth* Finch!" It was Rmrl and he was waving from the cab of a shiny new flitterbus. The vehicle pulled to the curb and Rmrl and a Terran emerged.

"Mr. Finch?" the Terran asked, extending his hand. "I represent a flitter dealer in the capital. Last night we received an anonymous check in full payment for one flitterbus to be delivered to you in Danzer today."

"There's no such thing as an anonymous check," Junior replied as he gauged the size of the bus. It could easily hold thirty or thirty-five Vanek.

"Well, the check wasn't exactly anonymous, but the donor wishes to remain so. I can tell you this, however," he said in a confidential tone, "he's one of the more influential traders on the planet."

Heber, who missed little of what transpired on the street, had come out of his office to see what was going on and heard the last part of the conversation.

"You mean it's free? Free and clear? No strings?"

The flitter dealer nodded. "The donor has reasons of his own, I suppose, but he has asked for no conditions."

Heber slapped Junior on the back. "See! I told you the publicity would do us some good."

"Can't argue with you," Junior said. He turned to the man from the capital. "What can I say? I accept…and 'thank you' to whoever donated it."

"Just sign the receipt and it's yours."

Junior signed and turned to Rmrl. "Let's start the shuttle right now." But the Vanek was already halfway into the cab.


VINCE PECK WAS NOT particularly overjoyed to see Junior again, even if he did bring along a busload of blue-skinned customers with him. But after Junior promised him the new bus as a replacement for the burned-out lorry, the shopkeeper became more tractable. He even made so bold as to offer Junior a salary.

"Yeah," he said, "receipts have been way up since you started shipping in these Vaneks, so I guess it's only fair I should pay you a little something. How's ten credits Jebscript a day sound?"

Junior shrugged. "Sounds okay to me. I'm worth twice that, but you're giving me room and board. And I'd prefer something harder than Jebscript—like Tolivian ags—but that would be inconvenient in this neck of the woods. So we'll call it a deal. We'll count today as my first paying workday. Okay?"

Peck's mouth hung open.

"Why so surprised? Did you think I'd refuse?"

"Frankly, yes. I always thought you do-gooder types weren't interested in money."

"Never considered myself much of a do-gooder, Mr. Peck. Always been fairly interested in money, though. And we have a saying in my family:

'Something for nothing breeds contempt.' If I did all this driving for free, you just might take me for granted. And I wouldn't want that to happen." He regarded his new employer with amusement. "I'm glad you brought it up yourself—saved me the trouble of asking you."

*"You wished to speak to me?"*
    *"Yes, sir."*
    *"Well, have a seat."*
    *"Thank you, sir."*
    *"Now, what's on your mind?"*
    *"I understand you have a problem in Danzer, sir."*
    *"You understand nothing of the sort. I have no problem in Danzer or anywhere else."*
    *"If you say so, sir. However, I can take care of that problem very tidily."*
    *"I'm very sorry, but I have no problems to speak of. And if I did, I'm certainly capable of handling them myself. Good day to you."*
    *"As you wish, sir. But here is my number. I can remedy the problem without any evidence that it was remedied. Remember that: no evidence."*

IT WAS SUNSET. The day's run finished, Junior sat in Marvin Heber's office and savored the evening breeze as it came through the open door and cooled the perspiration on his face.

"Remember when I asked you about a temp regulator a while back?" He and Heber had become close friends since the lorry-burning incident.

The older man nodded.

"Well, I've been thinking. It has its advantages—all-around comfort and all that—but if this little office were regulated, I wouldn't be sitting in this breeze and getting all these fresh smells brought to me for absolutely nothing."

Junior was feeling mellow and very much at peace with himself. "It's really amazing, you know," he rambled, gesturing at the brightening stars. "Out there we've got everything from professional telepaths to genetic architects, and so many people are completely unaware that places such as Danzer exist. And there must be so many Danzers, where people get on with outdated technology and wouldn't have it any other way. I think I'm really glad I came here."

There was a knock on the doorjamb and a young man with an attaché case stood silhouetted in the waning light. "They told me I could find Mr. Finch here."

"That's me."

The man entered. "I'm Carl Tayes and I'd like to speak to you for a moment, if I may."

"Not another reporter, I hope."

"No, not at all. I represent a number of legislators in the capital."

Heber pushed a chair over to the newcomer with his foot. "Sit down."

"Thank you," Tayes said and did so. He placed the attaché case on his lap and opened it. "You've become quite a figure in the last few weeks, Mr. Finch. In that time, you've aroused more planetwide interest in the Vanek Problem than the entire legislature has been able to do in the past few years. But the battle is far from over. Passage of the Vanek Equality Act is not yet assured. To be frank: support is drying up."

"What's this have to do with me?"

"Just this: we would like you to address a few key groups in the capital and urge them to support the bill."

"Not interested," Junior said flatly.

"But you must!"

"I *must* nothing!" Junior said and rose from his seat. "What I'm doing here is contrary to everything in that bill! Can't you see that? If I'm successful here, I'll have proved your Vanek Equality Act to be as superfluous as the men who conceived it!"

Heber listened with interest. He was suddenly seeing a different side of Junior Finch and it answered a few lingering questions.

Tayes was framing a reply when Bill Jeffers burst into the office. He held a pair of ledgers high over his head, then slammed them down on Heber's desk.

"Dammit, Finch!" he roared. "I'm licked. I've just been going over my books and I can't last another day! I give! Bring back my Vaneks!"

"What about eating lunch inside with everybody else?" Junior asked, trying desperately to mute his elation.

"I don't care if they hang from the rafters by their toes and eat lunch! Just bring 'em back!"

"Then they'll be there tomorrow." He stuck out his hand. "No hard feelings, I hope."

Jeffers grasped the hand firmly. "No, and I can't figure out why. If you'd been a different sort of guy, I'd've closed up before I gave in. But you, Finch…I don't know what it is, but somehow I don't mind losing to you."

"Lose? What did you lose?"

Jeffers brow furrowed, then he smiled. "You know, you're right!" He started to laugh and Junior joined him. There was mirth to the sound, but also the tone of immense tension released and dissipating.

Heber leaned over his desk and clapped both men on the shoulder. "This is wonderful!" he kept saying. "This is wonderful!" Then he, too, joined in the laughter.

"Let's go down to my place for something to drink," Jeffers said finally. "I think I need a good drunk!"

"Good idea," Junior said. "Only I'm buying."

"Coming, Marv?" Jeffers asked.

"Right behind you." Heber glanced at the government man, who had been noticeably silent. "Care to join us?"

Tayes shook his head abruptly and snapped his attaché case shut. "No, thank you. I've got to get back to the capital immediately." He rose and hurried off into the dusk.

The other three headed for the store. Walking between the lanky Heber and the mountainous Jeffers, Junior Finch felt like a man reborn. For perhaps the first time in his adult life, he truly felt like a Finch.


*"Ah! So it's you. I've been expecting your call. I knew you'd need me."*

*"Never mind that! Can you… remedy the situation as you said in my office? With no evidence of…anything?"*

*"Yes."*

*"Can you do it tonight?"*

*"Where?"*

*"Danzer, of course!"*

*"Yes, that can be arranged. But first there's the matter of compensation for my efforts."*

*"That's no problem. If you can remedy the situation in the proper way, you will be amply compensated."*

*"Very well. I'll leave immediately. One thing first, however—I must be absolutely sure of this: we are talking about this Junior Finch character, are we not?"*

*"I thought that would be obvious. Tell me…just what is it you're going to do?"*

*"You'll know by tomorrow morning."*

Many hours and many quarts of local squeezings later, the party was interrupted by the opening of the front door to the store. A small, sallow man with a receding hairline stepped inside and looked at the three celebrants.

"Private party!" Jeffers roared. "Store's closed. Come back tomorrow."

"Very well," the little man said with a faint smile.

Junior noted that the stranger's gaze seemed to rest on him for a moment and he shuddered. He couldn't identify what it was exactly, considering his near-stuporous condition, but there was something cold and very unpleasant in that man's dark eyes. He left without another word, however, and Junior went back to drinking.

"Gentlemen," Junior said, struggling to his feet an hour later, "I'm calling it a night."

"Siddown!" Jeffers said. "There's plenny left."

Junior regarded him with genuine fondness. Throughout the entire episode he had been unable to work up any real dislike for Jeffers. The big man was naturally straightforward and honest…just that one blind spot in his character.

"No, Bill. I'm going back to the office to sleep this off. I'm really tight and I'm not used to it. See you both tomorrow."

Heber and Jeffers waved good-by and continued drinking.

At dawn the next morning, a farmer pulled up outside Jeffers' store and was heading for the door when he noticed something in the shadows of the alley next to the building. He walked over to investigate. Junior Finch lay in the dust, a Vanek ceremonial dagger neatly inserted in his heart.

By late afternoon most of the planet had been informed of the incident and Heber found himself besieged by an army of reporters in his office. It was hot, it was muggy, there was no air to be had in that little room, and he felt sick and wished everyone would just go away. He'd grown very fond of that young man in the few weeks he'd known him, and now he was dead.

"The medical report has just come in," he said in a trembling voice that suddenly quieted the babble-filled office, "and it clears the man you were all very quick to suspect." He paused and spoke with studied deliberateness: "The time of death has been fixed and I can vouch for Mr. Jeffers at that time. Is that quite clear?" There was a murmured response, a reluctant acceptance of the fact.

"Now, about the knife. It's utterly ridiculous, of course, to suspect the Vanek. Disregard the fact that there were no human fingerprints or skin cells on the weapon...that can be easily managed with a lightweight glove. For even if the Vanek were capable of such an act, Junior Finch would have been the last person on Jebinose they would have harmed. So, we must look for a Terran murderer. It seems to me—"

The crowd of reporters parted as a young Vanek pushed his way through. Heber recognized Rmrl.

"We have come for the knife, *bendreth*."

"I'm sorry, my friend, but I must keep it for a while...evidence, you know."

Rmrl paused, then: "We have come for the body, too. It is to be buried with our ancestors."

"I suppose that can be arranged when the remains are returned from the capital. There's no one else on the planet to claim it and nobody knows where he came from." As the Vanek turned to go, Heber asked, "Do you have any idea who stole the knife, Rmrl?"

"Stole? It was not stolen."

"Then how was it used against him?"

The Vanek's face twisted into a grimace that could only be interpreted as grief. "We killed him, *bendreth*!"

"I refuse to believe that!" Heber gasped as pandemonium broke loose in the little room.

"It is true."

"But what possible reason could you give for such an act?"

"It is written on the Great Wheel," Rmrl blurted, and pushed his way out.

It took Heber a while to restore order to the office, but when it was finally quiet enough for him to speak: "I refuse for a moment to believe that a Vanek plunged a dagger into Junior Finch's heart! They loved that man. No, there's a Terran at work here and he's holding something over the Vanek to make them take the blame." He came out from behind his desk, suddenly looking very old and tired. "Now all of you please get out of here. I've had enough of this for one day."

The reporters filed out slowly, wondering where to go next. One hung back until only he and Heber were in the doorway. He was young and had said little during the afternoon.

"But I thought Vanek never lie," he whispered.

Heber's expression was a mixture of emotional pain and bafflement, with a touch of fear on the edges.

"They don't," he said, and closed the door.


JUNIOR WAS BURIED by the Vanek the next day with full rites and honors, a ceremony previously accorded to only the wisest and most beloved of their own race.

Marvin Heber and a number of operatives from the capital made a thorough investigation of the incident but could find no evidence that would lead them to the killer.

And as is so often the case, Junior Finch was mourned and praised by many, understood by only a few. His ghost was tearfully, skillfully, and ruthlessly invoked to obtain enough votes to pass the Vanek Equality Act, the very piece of legislation his efforts had proved unnecessary.

# VII
# JO

The trip to Dil took two jumps and six standard days, and really wasn't too bad physically. Emotionally, however, it was wearing. Old Pete was her only company and Jo found it impossible to generate any warmth for the man. She had done her best to get out of the trip—had even hoped that Haas would refuse to see them. No such luck. He was delighted to give them an appointment.

The shipboard time did, however, give her a chance to study her old nemesis, and she found him more puzzling than ever. He was maneuvering her toward something. Pretending to allow her to take the lead, he was actually calling all the plays. But what was the final destination?

And what was his stake in all this? He was out of the company and probably running out of years. Why was he out between the stars with her now?

The pieces didn't fit into a picture that made any sense to her. Everything Old Pete had done had been for her benefit. Why then did she feel she couldn't trust him? Why did she always feel he was hiding something? And he was. Despite countless protestations to the contrary, she knew he was guarding something from her.

Her father's autopsy report was another thing that bothered her. It was incomplete: a whole section was blank. Nothing of any pertinence was missing—the cause of death, a myocardial laceration by a Vanek ceremonial knife, was incontestable—but the blank area gnawed at her. Old Pete had obtained the report but couldn't explain the lapse. Jo would find out sooner or later, though. It wasn't her way to let things ride. Just as it hadn't been her way to sit back and passively collect the annuity from her father's IBA stock.

Jo couldn't remember exactly when she decided to put a Finch back into IBA—somewhere in her mid-teens, she guessed—but it soon grew to be an obsession with her. She studied the history of the company, its solid successes, its more notorious gambles. She grew to be an authority on its workings, maneuverings, and strategies. After tracking down all the printed and unprinted stories of Joe Finch's Earthside and outworld exploits, Jo became infatuated with her grandfather. She was only seven when his flitter crashed, and had vague memories of a very tall man who always had a present or two concealed on his person. And the more she learned about him, the more he grew in stature. By the time she was ready to make her move on IBA, Joe Finch was a giant in her mind.

Old Pete was another matter, however. She knew that IBA had used his theories as a base and probably would not have existed at all without him. He was an integral part of the company's history. She admired him for that, but no amount of admiration could offset the deep conviction that he was responsible for her father's absence. She would need his help, however, if IBA was to have a Finch in charge again.

Surprisingly, Old Pete had gone along with her. After a long conversation during which he quizzed her on the theoretical and practical aspects of IBA's operations, and was suitably impressed, he not only returned her father's stock to her, but gave her proxy power over his own to use as she saw fit when she faced the board of directors. The gesture seemed as out of character then as it did now, but Jo hadn't argued.

The board of directors: seven hard-nosed, tough-minded business professionals; over two centuries of experience in the constant give-and-take of the interstellar markets seated around a conference table, smiling politely and condescendingly as she rose to address them.

The mood around the table was tinged with amusement when she began, but had undergone a startling metamorphosis by the time she finished. The smiles were gone, replaced by expressions of anger, shock, and resentment.

Never would she forget that day. She had been frightened and shaking before beginning her speech, and bathed in perspiration at its finish. Five of the directors tendered their resignations on the spot in an obvious attempt to frighten her into backing down. She called their bluff, and within three weeks the two remaining directors had joined the others. The official reason for the resignations of all seven directors was that the handwriting was on the wall: IBA was on its way to becoming a family company again and this would mean the institution of despotic control over the board. This, being contrary to their concept of the position of the board of directors in the company hierarchy, left them no alternative but to resign.

Privately, they told their friends that they had no intentions of taking orders from a green kid. Especially a green *female* kid.

That had been the deciding factor, Jo knew: her sex. Those men would not work for a woman. It was a matter of pride for them, but the problem went deeper. They had no confidence in a woman's ability to run a company of IBA's complexity.

Strangely enough, Old Pete did not seem to share that view, probably because he was an Earthie. And Earthies, despite all their crowding, their decadence, their bureaucracy-strangled lives, considered males and females equal. In the colonial days, outworlders had held that view, too. Men and women had made the trip out to the stars as equals, had made landfall as equals, and had started the colonies as equals. After a while, however, things changed…especially on the splinter worlds. With little or no contact with the mother planet, the level of technology slipped and the embryo initiators and fetal maintenance units were often among the first pieces of hardware to fall into disrepair.

Children—lots of them—were a vital necessity to the settlements if they were going to survive past the second or third generation, so the colonists returned to the old-fashioned kind of fetal maintenance unit, and the technicians, navigators, and engineers who happened to be female were soon relegated to the roles of baby-bearers and nest-keepers.

Now, centuries later, after the colonies had come into their own as the outworlds, banding together under the Metep Imperium at first, and now under the Federation banner, the attitude remained: a woman's place was in the home.

Jo couldn't—wouldn't—accept that. But her rejection of the prevailing attitudes toward women was not a conscious struggle, nor a crusade. She carried no banners and nailed no theses to the door. After taking over IBA, she was approached by numerous groups pushing for male-female parity but she eschewed them all—partly because she didn't have time and partly because she couldn't really grasp the problem. As far as she could see, women wound up in secondary roles because they accepted them. It would have been easy for her to live off the proceeds of her stock in IBA, but she hadn't been able to accept that. She felt she had a right to lead the company and lead it she would. If anyone objected, he'd better have a good reason or get out of the way. Jo had often been called shortsighted and selfish for this, but her invariable reply was, Excuse me, I've got work to do.

In interstellar trade circles, it was almost unthinkable that a woman should head a major corporation. It had never really occurred to Jo that a woman should not do so. And that was the major difference between Josephine Finch and her contemporaries: others spent their time shouting about woman's equality to man; Jo spent hers proving it.

Word came back that the ship was about to enter orbit, so Jo and Old Pete got their things together and prepared to make the transfer to the shuttle. Dil's name was not well known among the inhabited worlds; it was an industrious little planet but had little in the way of natural beauty and no political notoriety.

Not too far from Dil's main spaceport was the warehouse Denver Haas called home, a large ramshackle affair with a high fence around the perimeter. The most vital and innovative aspects of his warp gate were now protected by Federation patents, but Haas was involved in further refinements and so security remained tight. Jo and Old Pete had to be cleared twice before they were allowed to enter the building.

Haas was obviously not out to impress anyone. The inside of the building was as dingy as the outside, and a lone, harried receptionist-secretary occupied the single desk within the cluttered foyer.

Jo handed the girl a clearance pass. "Josephine Finch and Peter Paxton to see Mr. Haas."

The girl took the pass without looking up, checked the appointments and nodded. Pressing a button, she said, "Finch and Paxton are here."

"Send them in!" replied a gruff voice.

The girl pointed to a nondescript door with a simple "Haas" printed on it. Jo knocked and entered with Old Pete trailing a few steps behind.

The office was an incredible clutter of filing cabinets, diagrams, blueprints, microstats, and miscellaneous notes and drawings on scraps of paper. Denver Haas, a stubby, feverish little man, was bent over his desk, reading and making notes, looking like a gnome king ensconced among his treasures. He glanced up as he heard the door close.

"Ah, Miss Finch and Mr. Paxton," he said, smiling tightly. "You've come. This is quite an honor, even if it is a waste of time for the three of us."

Only one empty chair sat before the desk. Haas rose, gathered some papers off another chair in a corner and threw them on the floor. Pushing the chair around to the front of the desk, he said to Jo, "Sit here," and indicated the other seat for Old Pete.

They did as they were bid and waited for the little man to regain his own seat. He was older than Jo had imagined, with gnarled hands, an unruly shock of graying hair, and, of all things, a beard. With all the permanent depilation techniques available, facial hair was an unusual sight.

"Well, just what is it you wanted to see me about?" he demanded abruptly. "As if I didn't know."

"Your warp gate," Jo stated with her customary directness.

"I thought that was it," Haas muttered, and shook his head. "I've paid a small fortune for what I was assured was the best available security, and here you walk in and talk about my warp gate like you just had it for lunch!"

"Word of something like that gets around," Jo assured him, "especially since this isn't exactly a one-man operation."

Haas's head snapped around. "What do you mean by that? This is my creation! Mine! From the first diagram to the working model—mine!"

"And financed entirely by you, of course."

"What do you know about my financing?" Haas asked in clipped tones.

"Not much. But outside financing causes outside talk, and I keep myself informed on any talk about innovative devices."

"I'll bet you do."

"It's my job. And because it's my job, I've traveled all the way from Ragna to try and convince you that you need IBA. Your device has good potential, but we can make sure you get the most out of it."

"'Good potential,' you say?" he said mockingly with what he probably thought was a sly smile. "It has excellent—it has astounding potential! So what makes you think I need any help at all from IBA?"

"Because you're going to market too soon."

"That is a matter of opinion, Miss Finch."

"It's fact, I'm afraid. Your gate has the potential for use inside a planet's gravity well, but you haven't perfected that aspect yet, and it's that—"

Haas slammed his fist down on his desk and shot to his feet. "How do you know all this! How can you! It's all secret! No one's supposed to know!"

A thought drifted through Jo's mind, like a small winged thing banking off an updraft: What a naive little man. But she refused to allow herself to be drawn from the matter at hand.

"When are you planning to introduce the gate on the market, Mr. Haas? Within one standard year, am I correct?"

Haas nodded, amazed that this young woman could know so much about his affairs.

"And when will the intra-gravity well capability be perfected?"

Haas seated himself again. "Five standards or so," he said hoarsely.

"Well, then. My advice is to wait. It will be extremely difficult to generate much interest in the gate as it stands. You must remember that every interstellar freighter currently in use is equipped with its own on-board warper. These ships have absolutely no use for a warp gate stationed at the critical point in the gravity well; it does little for them that they can't do themselves. The big companies might purchase a few for high traffic use along the major trade lanes, but the smaller companies are going to be hard-pressed to meet what I assume will be a very steep price. In brief, Mr. Hass: without the intra-gravity well capability, your warp gate will never get off the ground."

Haas snorted. "We've already considered all that and dismissed it. There will be an initial flood of orders, no question about it. And when that comes in, we'll be able to produce subsequent gates at reduced cost due to increased production scale." Clasping his hands behind his neck, he leaned back in his chair with a what-do-you-think-of-that? look on his face. "You see? We've taken everything into account."

"Have you? What about Star Ways?"

"What about it?"

"Competition. You don't—"

Haas's burst of harsh laughter cut Jo off. "Competition! The gate is unique! There is no competition."

"If you'd let me finish what I was about to say," Jo snapped with thinning patience, "you might learn something. You don't think that SW is going to sit still and let you make its primary product obsolete, do you? It's going to cut its prices on the on-board warper and it's going to keep those prices down—way down—until you fold. And when you go out of business, SW will come and lease the rights to the warp gate from you and sell it for you. The royalties you'll receive in return will net you enough money to buy a small planet, but your company will be gone." Her voice softened. "IBA can prevent that from happening. Or if not, we'll at least give that big conglomerate a battle the likes of which it's never seen."

"No," Haas said in an intense, low voice as he leaned for rested his arms on the desk. "That will never happen. Star Ways will never get the rights to the gate because I own them *completely!* And I'll never sell or lease or rent or trade no matter what the price. It's not the money any more…" His eyes seemed to glaze, and though he was looking in Jo's direction wasn't seeing her. "It's something more than that. The warp gate is my life. I've worked on nothing else for as long as I can remember. Only recently have I been able to devote my full time to it, but its always been with me. I've worked as an engineer, a designer, even a technician when times weren't so good, but I've always come home to the gate. It's part of me now. I would no sooner lease the gate to another company than I would lease my right arm to another man. The Haas Company will only lease the rights from me; and if the Haas Company can't sell the gate, no one else will. That I promise you."

There was silence in the room. Jo frowned and wondered if deBloise and his associates were aware of Haas's monomania. She could see nothing but financial ruin ahead.

Old Pete's thoughts ran along a different path. He'd been silent since they'd entered the room, watching and admiring the way she handled herself. He'd also been studying Haas and had been moved by the little man's disturbed and revealing statements. A little old man—younger than Pete, yes, but still old—with a dream. His body and perhaps his mind, were becoming unreliable vehicles, but still he drove them toward that dream. A dream! For a person in his or her second or third decade it would be called a dream; for someone Denver Haas's age, it would no doubt be termed an obsession.

Old Pete finally broke the silence. "I wonder what your backers would say if they learned of your attitude."

"They know all about it," Haas replied. "I've always leveled with potential backers." A thin smile briefly straightened the habitual downward curve of his lips. "That's why backers have been a rare species for me. But these fellows— they're with me 100 per cent."

Jo was stunned by the statement. It didn't make sense. "They know, and they're still with you?"

Haas nodded.

"Would you mind telling us the names of your backers?" Old Pete asked.

"Not at all. Be glad to tell you if I knew, but I don't. Oh, I could tell you the names they gave me, but I know they're fronts. For some reason, they wish to remain anonymous—strange, but none of my concern, really. I've searched long and hard to find men with vision such as these. We're in complete accord and everything is legal, so I couldn't care less if they want to remain anonymous."

"They know you want to put the gate on the market as is?" Jo repeated, bafflement wrinkling her forehead.

"Know? They not only know, they've encouraged me to move as quickly as possible. They see no reason to let the gate languish in its present state when it could be earning a good return on their investment while I perfect the modifications." He rose. "And now I must get back to my work. But I do want to thank you both for stopping in: I've always had the utmost confidence in the gate, but you've managed to boost it even higher."

"That wasn't our intention, I assure you," Jo said.

"Well, that's the net effect, no matter what you intended. I was shocked at first by how much you knew about the gate, but then I realized that IBA has far-reaching contacts. The fact that you're interested enough in the gate to come this far in person in order to get in on the kill, that's proof enough for me that its success is guaranteed. Everybody knows that IBA rarely takes on losers."

Jo wanted to say that most of her clients were losers before seeking out IBA's help, but realized the futility of further talk. IBA could have done a lot for him, but under no circumstances could she work with a man like Denver Haas. Shrugging, she rose to her feet and turned toward the door.

"Oh, and there's one little factor you completely neglected in your assessment of the gate's chances on the market," Haas said in a gloating tone.

Jo threw him a questioning glance.

"Military contracts! You forgot all about the military possibilities of the gate! It's perfect for supply and personnel transport on a large scale. He smiled expansively. "Yes, I don't think there'll be any problem in getting those initial orders. We'll just sit back and let them roll in."

"Good day, Mr. Haas," Jo said, continuing toward the door. "And good luck."

Old Pete followed he out, shaking his head sadly.

PREOCCUPIED SILENCE FILLED THE RENTED FLITTER as they headed back to the spaceport. Neither of them noticed a man leave the Haas warehouse after them and enter his own flitter. He was not far behind when they docked their craft in the rental drop-off zone.

"Well," said Old Pete as they entered a lounge alcove to await seats on a shuttle up to their orbiting ship, "I certainly don't know what to make of it."

"I'm in a daze myself," Jo replied. "Especially after his parting shot: military contracts! The man's mad!"

"Obsessed, maybe. But not mad. At least not completely."

"But military contracts! The Federation Defense Force will, I'm sure, be glad to know that such a thing as the warp gate is available, but the prospects of a big order are nil."

"I doubt if the DF will buy a single unit."

"Why do people like Haas allow themselves to get involved in the business end of things?" Jo mused. "He's unquestionably a brilliant designer and theorist—the existence of the gate proves that—but he has no idea of the economic forces against him in the market. We could do a lot for him, you know. Right now I've got a good half-dozen ideas that could possibly get him through the first few years until he worked out the necessary modifications. But as it stands now, SW will wipe him out in no time and deBloise and his crew will lose all their money."

Old Pete grunted. "That's what bothers me: deBloise throwing away a fortune. I've never met that man, Josephine, but I know him. I know him as well as his mother, his father, and his wife know him. I probably know some things about him that even he doesn't know. And one thing's certain: he's not a fool. He's crafty, he covers all exits, and his involvement in this fiasco-to-be is totally out of character."

"Which leaves us with only one possible conclusion," Jo said, glancing at a man leaning against a wall outside the lounge area. It almost seemed as if he were watching them.

"I know," Old Pete replied in a breathy voice. "DeBloise knows something we don't. And that bothers me."

Jo dismissed the watcher as just another bored traveler; this conspiracy talk must be getting to her. "What bothers me more is the thought that the warp gate could be lost to us. I mean, what if Haas's company folds and he really does decide to withhold the gate from sale or lease or whatever. That could be tragic."

Old Pete shrugged. "Tragic, yes. But he'd be perfectly within his rights. According to Andy, the patents are good for at least another couple of decades. The human race would just have to wait it out."

The signal for their shuttle flight flashed and they rode the belt out onto the field. The man who had been standing across from the lounge area went up to the observation deck and watched them enter the shuttle. Only after the craft was airborne did he go below.

He headed directly for the row of subspace transmission booths that are a feature at every spaceport. Entering the first booth, he sealed himself in, opaqued the glass, and began to transmit an urgent message to Fed Central.

## VIII
## DEBLOISE

The barroom was done entirely in wood, something you didn't see much any more on Fed Central. But this section of the club had originally been a tavern in the Imperium days and had been preserved in the original state. The bar itself was the same one patrons had leaned on nearly three centuries ago when the place had been called the White Hart, its solid *keerni* wood preserved under a clear, thick, high-gloss coating through which an idle drinker could still make out doodles and initials scratched into the original finish.

It belonged now to the Sentinel Club, the oldest, most respected, most exclusive club in the outworlds. Membership was strictly male, and restricted to those who had managed to achieve status in the financial, political, and artistic spheres. Elson deBloise reveled in such a rarefied atmosphere, felt a real sense of place and purpose here. He belonged here. There was no comparable establishment on his homeworld where a man of his breeding and wealthy heritage could be among his peers.

He was not among his peers at the moment, however. The hour was a shade early and he was alone at the bar, hunched over a delicate glassful of Derbian orchid wine. The green-tinged fluid was a little too sweet for his taste but was all the rage on Fed Central these days, so he ordered it whenever he was out. Had to keep up with the times, be as modern as the next man, if not more so. Talk about tomorrow, never about the old days.

Because nobody around here thought of the old days as good. LaNague had seen to that: his revolution had changed more than the power structure; it had reached into the hearts and minds of his contemporaries and caused a fundamental alteration in the way they viewed their society. Today, generations later, outworld thinking was still influenced by the lesson of that revolution. So a conservative image had to be avoided at all costs.

"Restructurist" was much preferred as a label. It was neutral in emotional tone and had a certain progressive ring to it. After all, that's what they intended to do—restructure the Federation. DeBloise smiled to himself. Restructure? They were going to turn it upside down and twist it around.

He continued to smile. It was fitting in a way that he should be sitting here in this converted tavern plotting the scrapping of the LaNague Charter. It was said that Peter LaNague and Den Broohnin had spent many an evening in this very room when it was called the White Hart as they conspired to bring down the Metep Imperium nearly three centuries ago.

And what a conspiracy that had been! Despite the fact that deBloise publicly minimized LaNague's contribution to the revolution, despite the fact that the Restructurist movement had for years been engaged in a clandestine campaign to discredit the bizarre society that had spawned LaNague, thereby discrediting the man himself. Despite the fact that the man's ingenious wording of the charter had frustrated Restructurists for generations, he had to grant LaNague grudging admiration. His conspiracy had reached into every level of Imperial society, had stretched from the deepest galactic probe to Earth itself. Utterly masterful!

DeBloise felt he could be generous in his praise. After all, he was the engineer of a conspiracy of his own. True, it didn't have the breadth and depth of LaNague's, and its flashpoint would be nowhere near as brilliant and dramatic, but its outcome would eventually prove to be as crucial to the course of human history. The Haas warp gate provided the key. And when that key was turned, there would be furious protests in some quarters, but nothing that could not be soothed by promises that the invocation of the emergency clause in the charter was merely temporary. All would soon return to normal just as soon as we get this one little matter settled, they would say.

But things would never be the same. A single instance of forceful intervention in the interstellar economy by the Federation was all that was necessary; thereafter, the power of the charter to restrain the Restructurists would be effectively broken. In a few standard years, the charter would be a revered but vestigial document and the Federation would be under Restructurist control.

He could almost picture himself on the high presidential dais after the next Assembly elections. He deserved that seat. He'd worked for it. It had taken many years of searching and planning to find the right issue—volatile enough to energize the Assembly, and yet still manageable as to timing and discretion concerning his involvement. Only he had seen the political potential of Haas's invention; only he had possessed the influence over his fellow Restructurists to convince them to go along with his plan.

Yes, he deserved the presidential seat. And he'd make good use of it once it was his. All economic activity—and thereby all *human* activity—within the Federation would come under his supervision. Bringing the larger corporations and trade services to heel would be no easy matter but it could be done. First he'd start singling out oddball planets like Flint and Tolive and bring them into line through trade sanctions—they'd never willingly accept a Restructurist-dominated Federation. The corporations would naturally protest since they didn't like anyone to close a market to them. When they did, he'd bring the full weight of a bolstered Federation Defense Force against them. And when they tried to bribe him—as he knew they eventually must— he would righteously expose them as the moneygrubbing leeches they were.

And soon…soon humanity would shape itself into a cohesive unit, soon there would be true harmony and equality among the planets, each sharing in the bounties of the others, soon there would begin a new Golden Age for humanity, a Golden Age designed and administered by Elson deBloise.

LaNague had had an opportunity to take a similar course three centuries ago; he'd held the outworlds in the palm of his hand but had refused to grasp them. Instead, he presented them with his charter and hurled them free. Such an act remained far beyond deBloise's comprehension. The human race needed someone to guide it and oversee its course. The great mass of humanity had no thought of destiny. Too many individuals expended their energies in chase of puny, shortsighted goals. They all needed direction—and deBloise was convinced he could provide it.

There would, of course, be those who'd insist on choosing their own course and the rest of humanity be damned. There would always be self-styled individuals who'd selfishly insist on pursuing their own personal values. These would have to be discouraged or weeded out from the vast body of the human race.

He'd also have to contend with that other breed of nay-sayer: the ones who would point to history and say that economies and societies controlled from the top have never succeeded; that the impetus for a society must come from within, not from above.

But he knew that no society in history had ever had a man such as Elson deBloise at its helm. Where others had failed, he could succeed.

A few years ago such thoughts would have been idle fantasies, but now the actual means to achieve them was in his grasp. It was all so exhilarating, almost intoxicating, that even the prospect of today's departure for his homeworld couldn't take the edge off his mood. He checked the chronometer on the wall: he had another hour to kill before his orbital shuttle left the spaceport.

He flagged the bored bartender and indicated his need for a refill. The man dutifully complied and then returned to the far end of the bar. He had tried in the past to strike up a friendly conversation with deBloise—the Sentinel Club paid him well to add the human touch to bar service—but had been ignored each time. So now he kept his distance from Mr. deBloise. And deBloise in turn studied his fingernails as the glass was filled; if he'd been interested in socializing with the likes of the bartender, he would have had his drinks out at the spaceport bar.

He didn't need the extra drink—he'd already had two before leaving Anni's—but decided to have it anyway. The next few days would be spent aboard a Federation liner. The passenger list would contain the names of many elite and no doubt interesting people, some of whom would surely be from his homeworld. And thus he'd be duty bound to play his role of Elson deBloise, sector representative and leader of the Restructurist movement, to the hilt.

The role became trying after a while. That's when he would miss Anni. She was an excellent mistress, socially and sexually skilled, he could let down his guard with her. Yes, he'd miss her the most. Not sexually, however. With the final stages of the Haas plan fast approaching, he'd found himself unable to perform without the use of drugs. The plan dominated his thoughts every hour of the day, sapping his strength and sorely trying his patience.

He smiled again, wondering what the reaction would be if it became generally known that he kept a mistress on Fed Central. A respected sector representative...and a family man, too! It was a common practice in the Assembly and no one paid it too much mind in the cosmopolitan atmosphere

here. But it would be difficult for those provincial clods at home to swallow; they were all firm believers in faithful monogamy, or at least pretended to be. If it came out, someone would no doubt try to score some political points with it on the local level, and his home life would be disrupted for a while; he'd deny it all, of course, and before too long it would all be forgotten. Voters have always had short memories.

No, there wasn't much he could do short of a violent crime or a public obscenity that would significantly erode his support among the yokels back home. He had led the sector into the Restructurist fold with promises of economic rebirth; they expected him to deliver on those promises…someday. Until then, he was the local boy who'd made good and they would follow him anywhere.

But there were always dues to pay. His wife and children remained at home; he wanted it that way. There was, after all, the children's education to think of—it wouldn't do to have them hopping back and forth between worlds—and besides, his wife would help to keep his presence felt on the homeworld when he was off on Federation business. Still, he had to return on a regular basis. The yokels expected it. He had to be seen among them, had to appear at certain local functions, had to play ombudsman for the sector.

And it was all such a bore, really, listening to their petty complaints and trivial problems when there were so very many much more important things that required his attention…like the Haas plan. But, *noblesse oblige.*

There was another reason he disliked going home: a little man named Cando Proska. By the Core, how that monster of a human being frightened him! And as sure as Fed Central circled its primary, he'd be calling at the deBloise office with a new demand. But enough of that! Such thoughts were disturbing.

Another glance at the chronometer showed that it was time to go. He pulled a rectangular disk from his pocket, tapped in a code, and his secretary's face appeared. After telling her to send a flitter to the Sentinel Club to take him to the spaceport, he was about to blank the screen when he noticed that she seemed to be disturbed.

"Something wrong, Jenna?" he asked.

She shrugged. "One of the girls on the second floor came down with the horrors at lunch."

DeBloise muttered his condolences and faded her out. The horrors—he'd almost forgotten about that. The plague of random insanity that had started before he was born and continued to this day was something that everyone in Occupied Space had learned to live with, but it was something that was rarely forgotten. New cases popped up daily on every planet. Yet the Haas plan had pushed it almost entirely from his mind.

He rose to his feet and quickly downed the rest of the wine. The juxtaposition of Haas and the horrors in his thoughts was unsettling. What if Haas got hit by the horrors? The whole plan would have to be scuttled. Worse yet: what if he himself were struck down?

He didn't dare think about that too much, especially since The Healer, the only man thus far able to do anything about the horrors, had seemingly vanished a few years ago. And as each succeeding year passed, deBloise became more firmly convinced that he had been responsible for precipitating The Healer's disappearance.

It had happened on Tolive. DeBloise had traveled all the way to IMC headquarters to talk to the man, to convince him gently to see things in a light more favorable to Restructurism, and had wound up threatening him. The Healer had only smiled—an icy smile that deBloise remembered vividly to this day—and departed. No one had seen or heard from him since. He was probably dead, but there was still this nagging suspicion.

A light flashed above the bar, indicating that someone had a flitter waiting, and deBloise hurried to the roof as if to escape thoughts of the horrors and enigmatic men who could not be bullied or cajoled into line. Thank the Core there weren't too many of those around.

As he took his seat, the flitter driver handed him a coded message disk. He tapped in a combination that only he and a few of his closest associates knew, and five lines of print began to glow on the black surface. The words would remain lit for fifteen seconds, then would be automatically and permanently erased. There could be no recall.

The lines read:

*Haas had two visitors today.*
*Young female named Josephine Finch.*
*Older man unidentified as yet.*
*Both from IBA. Any instructions?*

There had obviously been a leak, but that was not what occupied deBloise's mind at that moment. It was the name Finch. It seemed to mean something to him…and then it came, rushing out of the past.

Of course. *Finch.* How could he have forgotten?

An uneasy feeling settled over him and he couldn't shake it off.

Finch.

There couldn't be any connection, could there?

Of course not. It was just a coincidence. Just an awful coincidence.

# IX
## EASLY

Easly ran the fingers of his right hand up and down the middle of Jo's bare back and wondered idly how she continued to have such a disconcerting effect on him.

Not when they were out in public, of course. Then everything was always cool and professional. They both had their roles and played them well—*lived* them well. She was mistress of a respected business advisory firm; he was master of an information-gathering service. They'd meet now and then for a game or two of pokochess and, if time permitted, perhaps a light meal afterward. They were two self-sufficient and self-reliant individuals who enjoyed each other's company on occasion, but otherwise led separate personal lives. That was in public. And he could handle that easily enough.

But when they were alone, especially like this—in bed, skin to skin, tangled limbs and breathless afterglow, communicating in the tiniest whispers, barely moving their lips and eyes—at times like these he found himself bewildered at the emotional bond that had grown between them. He'd never known a woman like Jo.

And he'd never expected to become emotionally involved with a client. But, then, virtually all of his clients had been male until Jo.

Until Jo. So many things these days seemed to start and end with that phrase.

It seemed like only just the other day that he'd received her message requesting a meeting about a possible assignment. He had hesitated then at the thought of taking her on as a client. He had never dealt with a woman on those terms, and if her last name had been anything other than Finch, he might well have turned her down.

He was glad he hadn't, for he'd found her delightful. Expecting a staid, middle-aged matron, he discovered instead a bright, vivacious creature who could sparkle with the best of them and yet had a laser-quick mind, strong opinions, and unquestionable integrity. Before long he found himself looking forward to their meetings, not just for the intriguing assignments that often developed, but for the stimulus he derived from her company. He would search for ways to increase the frequency of their meetings, and to prolong them once they were together.

Eventually, they met for other than business reasons and quickly graduated to the sexual intimacy of lovers. Here, again, Jo surprised him. For one so cool and seemingly detached across a pokochess board or a dinner table, she exhibited a passion and a lack of inhibition between the sheets that to this day continued to leave him gasping.

An enigma, this woman. Easly couldn't decide whether she was a core of steel with a woman's exterior, or a vulnerable little girl hiding behind a metallic patina. Sometimes she seemed one, sometimes the other. He was forever off balance, but delightfully so.

One thing was certain: this woman was a friend. She was a companion; she complemented him, rounded him off, made him feel somehow more complete when he was with her than when he was not. Especially at a time like this when they had each other totally to themselves.

She was a *friend*, and he wasn't used to having friends who were women. Until Jo.

He had told Jo that once, and she'd haughtily called him a typical product of the outworlds. On the surface, he resented being called typically anything, but inwardly he was forced to admit she was right. His view of women had been typically and rigidly stereotyped: they were frail, lovable creatures, good for homekeeping and bedwarming, requiring affection, protection, and occasionally a good swift kick; their capacity for original thought and practical behavior in the outside world was strictly limited.

He'd never verbalized these concepts, of course; he owed himself credit for that. But he also had to admit to being surprised whenever a woman exhibited prowess in any field of endeavor outside the home, thus eminently qualifying him for the title, "Typical Product of the Outworlds."

Until Jo.

In the past his relationships with women had been fleeting and superficial. Intentionally so. Women were for huddling with, for satisfying mutually urgent physical needs, but not for spending serious time with. There were more important, more intriguing, more demanding things calling him.

Until Jo.

Easly knew he would never be the center of her life; nor she the center of his, for that matter. They each had "the business" as the major recipient of his or her attentions. It was a subject that had never come up in discussion and probably never would. It was understood. Neither of them was the type of person who lived for other people.

Yet they were close—as close as each could be to another person. But despite that emotional proximity, Easly was aware that there was an important part of Jo closed off to him. Somewhere within her psyche he sensed a hot, high-pressure core of…what? Something raging and ravenous there, locked away from the world and, perhaps, even from Jo herself. There were times in the too few nights they could spend together when he'd awaken and find her rigid beside him. She'd be asleep, her eyes closed, but her teeth would be clenched, her hands would be squeezing his arm, and every muscle in her body would be straining as if against some invisible force. Then she would suddenly relax and a thin film of cool perspiration would sheen her skin.

"What's your secret?" he whispered to her.

"Mmmh?" Jo lifted her head and opened her eyes.

He shook her playfully. "What dark mystery is enshrouded within you? C'mon…tell me!"

She rolled onto her back and threw her right forearm across her eyes. She was naked, quite unselfconsciously so. "Sacre bleu! Tu es fou!" she moaned, lapsing into Old French, the second language of Ragna.

After a moment or two of silence, she uncovered her eyes and rose up on one elbow. "You're really serious, aren't you?"

Easly nodded, holding her eyes with his.

"Some nerve!" she snapped. "You've never even told me what planet you were born on, and don't tell me Ragna 'cause I know you weren't born here."

"How can you be so sure?"

"You don't speak French."

"Maybe I just pretend I don't."

"Maybe you pretend a lot of things, Larry. Maybe that isn't really your name. But before you try your deductive powers on me, better do a little talking about yourself!"

Sitting up, Easly leaned his shoulders against the headboard and reached for a cigar. He favored the dry-cured type, toasted crisp in the ancient Dutch method. He picked a torpedo shape out of a recess in the wall behind him, squeezed the tip to ignite it, and was soon puffing away. Regarding the white ash, he said, "Nice aroma. Reminds me of a story. Want to hear it?"

"I'm ready to settle for anything by now," Jo replied sharply. "Stop fooling with that foul-smelling roll of dried leaves and start talking."

"Soon as I get comfortable." He drew his legs into the lotus position and leaned back, puffing leisurely. "Can't do this in that float bed of yours," he remarked. Easly used to have a deluxe, anti-gravity float bed with laminar air flow and all the other accessories. But he'd found himself waking every morning with a stiff back.

"Okay. Where shall I begin? How about the name of the planet on which the story takes place?"

"Good start!" came the sarcastic reply.

"The planet is Knorr and the story concerns a love triangle of sorts. The woman's name was Marcy Blake and the man's was Edwin—Eddy—Jackson—typical names for Knorr since most of the original colonists there were of English extraction. Marcy was young, beautiful, and had inherited a personal fortune of a couple of million Knorran pounds. She was unattached, too; which might seem strange, considering her appearance and wealth. But anyone who knew her personally did not think it strange at all: besides being of borderline intelligence, Marcy's personality was totally obnoxious. She was an incredibly boring woman whose voice and manner always managed to set people's teeth on edge.

"Eddy Jackson was as handsome as Marcy was beautiful, as crafty as she was stupid, and as poor as she was rich."

Jo interrupted: "And so he decided to marry her, have her killed, and inherit her fortune. What else is new?"

"Just have a little patience, my dear. You're jumping way ahead of me. Eddy toyed with the idea of marrying her but never quite had the courage to take the plunge—which will give you an idea of what Marcy's personality was

F. PAUL WILSON

like. He did keep company with her now and then, however, just to keep his options open. And he noticed that she made a few visits to the neurosurgical center in Knorr's capital city. A little bribe here, a little bribe there, and he learned that Marcy had a unique, idiopathic degenerative disease of the central nervous system. The prognosis was death in two years or so.

"*Then* he decided to marry her, especially since Knorr's common law provided certain advantages in the area of survivor's rights. Eddy figured he could put up with anything for two years, after which he would be a bereaved but wealthy widower.

"So he figured. But marriage seemed to have a beneficial effect on Marcy's condition. Two years passed. Then three. By the time their fifth anniversary rolled around, Eddy was near the breaking point. Marcy had controlled the purse strings for those five years, keeping Eddy on a strict allowance, and talking, talking, talking. He finally confronted her physicians, who informed him that the disease seemed to have undergone a spontaneous remission. If her progress continued at its current rate, she would probably have a normal lifespan."

"That's when he decided to kill her," Jo stated confidently, but Easly shook his head.

"No. That's when he decided to leave her, money or not. He took what money he had saved out of his allowance and traveled to the city to see what kind of luck he'd have in the casinos. He was sure he could parley his winnings into a good-sized stake, and then he'd say good-by to Marcy.

"Naturally, he lost every cent and had to return home in disgrace. And then, a miracle—or what seemed like one. Eddy entered the house and noted the faintest aroma of cigar smoke; it was particularly strong in the bedroom. Cigar smoke! Neither he nor Marcy smoked at all, and few of their friends did since tobacco wasn't plentiful on Knorr. He asked Marcy if anyone had stopped by over the weekend and she very innocently said no…too innocently, he thought.

"Eddy was flabbergasted. Incredible as it seemed, Marcy was cheating on him! Infidelity, as I'm sure you know, is the rule rather than the exception on the Sol system planets. But on outworlds like Knorr, it remains scandalous. Not that he cared—it was just a question of *whom*. The *why* of it was conceivable: she was undeniably attractive and, he supposed, bearable in small doses.

"He decided to learn the identity of her lover and even went so far as to tip a rookie flitter-patrol cop to watch the house and see who came and went when Eddy wasn't there. He planned to threaten Marcy with exposure and disgrace once he had his proof, and allow her to buy his silence with a nice chunk of her fortune.

"But the patrolman reported nothing: no visitors to the Jackson home. Eddy's allowance wouldn't cover the expense of a detective, so he resigned himself to the unhappy conclusion that Marcy's affair must have been a one-time thing—after a single intimate meeting, Marcy's lover had probably come to know her well enough to know that he didn't want to know her any more."

Easly paused to blow some smoke rings, then he turned to Jo. "*That's* when he decided to kill her."

She yawned. " 'Sabout time."

"His plan was very tight, very simple, and very workable. He borrowed a gambling buddy's flitter, made a copy of the by-pass key (Knorran flitters use a thumbprint for ignition, but everyone keeps a by-pass key in case someone else has to drive it), and arranged to have this buddy meet him in the city for a night at the tables. At one point during the evening, he intended to excuse himself from the room, run for the casino roof, and roar off in his friend's flitter. With his running lights out, he'd land in the dark backyard of his home, go inside, kill Marcy, grab some valuables, then race back to the casino. He'd have an alibi: he was at the casino all night; the roof attendant would truthfully say that the Jackson flitter never left its dock; and the crime was obviously a, robbery-homicide.

"Not a perfect plan, but as I said: tight, simple, workable."

"But it obviously didn't work," Jo said. "Otherwise you wouldn't be telling me all about it."

"Right. But it almost worked. He came in the house and grabbed a vibe-knife from the kitchen and called for Marcy. She was on the upper level and asked him why he was home so early. As he rode the float-chute up, he said he got bored with the games and decided to come home. She was wearing only a filmy robe and her back was to him as he walked into the bedroom. Without hesitation, he spun her around and plunged the vibe-knife into the middle of her chest. Its oscillating edges sliced through cloth, skin, bone, cartilage and heart muscle without the slightest difficulty; and Marcy Jackson, *nee* Blake, died with a strangled, gurgling sound.

"It was probably just then that Eddy noted an odor in the room; and his olfactory sense was probably just about to label it for him when he heard a voice behind him.

"You killed her!' it said in a shocked whisper.

"Eddy spun around to see the rookie cop—the one he had tipped to keep an eye on the place—emerging from behind a drape. He was half-dressed; there was a half-smoked cigar in his left hand, and a blaster pistol in his right. The last thing Eddy saw before he died was a searing white light at the tip of the blaster barrel."

"Cute," Jo said in an unenthusiastic tone. "But hardly original. Especially that part about hiding behind the drape."

"Where would you have hidden in his place?"

Jo shrugged. "Whatever happened to this rookie?"

"He got in a lot of trouble. At first he tried to tell his superiors that he'd heard Marcy scream and went in to investigate, but soon the history of his detours into the Jackson home whenever Eddy was out and things on the beat got slow came to light, and he finally told the whole story."

Jo suddenly became interested in the rookie. She sat up and faced Easly. "What'd they do to this cigar-smoking character?"

"Oh, not much. A trial would have been an embarrassment to the force; and, they rationalized, even though he shouldn't have been in the Jackson home at all, he was on duty at the time he blasted the murderer. The conundrum was finally resolved when it was decided that the best thing the rookie could do was resign from the force and set up future residence on a planet other than Knorr. Which is just what he did."

"Tell me something," Jo said. "Why is it you named only two of the characters in the triangle? Why does the rookie remain nameless?"

"His name isn't important, just the fact that he was a young, inexperienced rookie who foolishly allowed himself to get involved in a compromising situation."

"How come you know so much about him?"

Easly puffed on his cigar: "Professional interest."

"And where is this rookie now?"

"Speaking of professional interest," Easly said with a quick cough, simultaneously shifting his body position and the subject of conversation, "how're you getting along with Old Pete?"

"Why do you ask?"

"You don't trust him—I can tell."

"You're right. And as days go by, I trust him less and less. Remember that autopsy report on my father I told you about—the one with the blank area?"

Easly nodded. "Sure."

"Well, I contacted the Jebinose Bureau of Records and their copy is incomplete, too."

"Maybe it's just a clerical error. Things like that do happen, you know. There wasn't anything of consequence missing, right?"

"No. Just the analysis of the urogenital system. But I checked the company records and found vouchers for Old Pete's trip to Jebinose after the murder. He was there about the time the report was filed. And when he tells me he can't explain that blank area, I don't believe him. I have this feeling he's hiding something."

Easly chewed on the end of his cigar for a moment, then: "Tell you what, since you got nowhere with Haas, why don't I send someone to Jebinose to investigate deBloise's background. And while he's there he can check into this autopsy report."

Jo bolted upright in the bed. "Jebinose? What has deBloise got to do with Jebinose?"

"It's his homeworld."

"Jebinose?" She pressed her palms against her temples. "I knew he represented that sector, but I never realized that was his homeworld!"

"I thought everybody knew that."

"I've never had much interest in where politicos come from, who they are, or what games they play." She lowered her hands and turned narrowed eyes upon Easly. "Until now. Larry, I want you to go to Jebinose yourself. Dig into deBloise's past for whatever you can find. And while you're there, dig up whatever you can on the death of one Joseph Finch, Jr."

Josephine Finch had just become personally involved in Old Pete's conspiracy theory.

# X
## JO

Jo sat behind her desk and thought about rats. Or tried to. She had just completed a short meeting with Sam Orzechowski, the man with the trained space rats, and had informed him that she'd only found partial backing for him. He'd seemed disappointed but was willing to keep on waiting. He had no choice, really: IBA was the first company to take him seriously since he had come up with his rat control method years ago. But Jo felt she should have been able to do more for him by now...if only this warp gate affair would get out of her mind and let her get back to work.

She expected Old Pete momentarily. He'd said he wanted to see her—something about planning the next step. He was so persistent on deBloise. She had tried to drop the subject and let it go as a foolish gamble on the politician's part, but Old Pete wouldn't let her. And even if he had, the problem would have stayed with her.

It was that damn recording from the Restructurists' conference room. It raised too many questions that wouldn't let the problem go away. Besides... deBloise was from Jebinose.

Old Pete strolled in. "What's new?" he asked, sliding into a chair. He always said that, even if he'd seen you only a few hours before. It was his way of saying hello.

"Nothing," she said. That incomplete autopsy report still bothered her.

"I was afraid you'd say that. Looks like we don't know much more now than we did at the start."

"Not true," Jo replied. "We now know who Haas is and we know that he's developed something that will eventually revolutionize interstellar travel. We also know that Elson deBloise and the Restructurist inner circle have placed a huge sum behind Haas and the warp gate."

Old Pete's smile was grim. "And we can be certain that the motives behind their actions are purely political. In my years of study of deBloise's life, I've yet to find any action on his part that was not designed to further his career and increase his political power. His mind is homed in on one goal and he allows nothing to sway him from pursuit of it. Nothing!"

"That leaves us with the obvious conclusion that there's a political plot connected with the Haas warp gate."

"Which is right back where we started," he grunted.

"But the way they're going about it, they must know that the gate will be driven off the market before Haas can perfect the improvements that will make it economically viable."

"And if Haas means what he says—and I believe he's absolutely sincere about withdrawing the gate permanently from the market if it fails commercially—we'll have lost the greatest boon to interstellar travel since the original warp field was developed back on old Earth."

Jo leaned forward and rested her chin on folded hands. "You know, I have this horrible suspicion that they want the gate to be a commercial failure, that they know Haas will withdraw it from the market then, and it will be lost to us until the patents run out or somebody else figures out a different way to get the same result."

"I can't see the sense in that at all."

"Why else would they be encouraging Haas to rush the gate to market?"

"Don't know. Maybe there is something to that remark about military contracts. Maybe deBloise has cooked up something with one or two of the higher-ups in the Fed Defense Force."

"A military coup?"

"No." Old Pete sighed. "That's patently ridiculous, I know. But the military could be involved just the same."

Jo shook her head slowly, confidently. "The military's not involved."

"I suppose you're right," he admitted. "The gate could be of tremendous value in a war, but there is no war. I mean, who're we going to fight? The Tarks?"

"You never know." Her tone was serious.

"Don't be silly, Jo," he laughed. "We may not be on the best terms with the Tarks—as a matter of fact, we've never been on good terms with those scoundrels—but there's no such thing as a war in sight, despite the wails of the more panicky members of the Fed Assembly. And don't go thinking of the Tarks as a potential market for the gate, either. They'll buy one as a model, then pirate the design and build their own. The Tarks are a blind alley, I'm afraid."

"Perhaps you're right. Anyway, on the deBloise end, I sent Larry to Jebinose to do some direct investigation on him. And while he's there, I told him to look into my father's death."

She watched Old Pete's face closely for a reaction. She saw surprise and…was it fear?

"Why Jebinose?" he said, the words coming in a rush. "I thought you'd send him to Fed Central. That's where all deBloise's machinations take place."

"Maybe he's more careless at home."

Old Pete suddenly seemed anxious to leave the room. "Let me know the very instant he turns up anything."

"Oh, you can count on that," Jo replied in a low voice as the door closed behind him. She'd never seen Old Pete so upset. What secret lay dormant on Jebinose that he feared disturbing?

Never mind that now. Larry would find out. Right now another part of her brain was screaming for attention. Something Old Pete had said before had closed a circuit…something about a war with the Tarks when they were talking about Haas and his—

She leaped to her feet and began to pace the floor. She knew deBloise's plan. All the pieces that hadn't seemed to fit had suddenly fallen together. And the Tarks were the key. Old Pete's reference to them had brought a vast conspiratorial vista into sharp focus and Jo was struck by the genius and delicacy and deviousness of what she saw. She was terrified, too.

The entire interstellar free market was threatened.

She pressed a stud on her desktop. "Find Bill Grange—tell him to drop whatever he's doing and get up to my office immediately!"

The market. To some people it was the place where stocks and bonds were traded; to others it was the local food store. But these formed only a minuscule part of the market. For the market was life itself, and the free market was free life, the active expression of volitional existence. It was billions of billions of daily transactions: the purchase of a loaf of bread, the selling of an asteroid mining firm along with all its equipment and planetoid leases; every interaction and transaction—be it social, moral, or monetary-between every sentient being in Occupied Space added to its endless flux and flow.

The free market was neither good nor evil, selfish nor generous, moral nor immoral. It was the place where rational minds met for a free exchange of goods, services, ideas. It played no favorites and bore no grudges. It had its own ecology, regulated by the inexorable laws of supply and demand, which were in turn determined by the day-to-day activities of every intelligent creature who interacted with another intelligent creature. If demand for a species of product or service dried up, that species became extinct. When new demands arose, new species sprung into being to satisfy them.

The market's urge toward a balanced ecology was indomitable. It could be warped, skewed, stretched, contracted, puffed up, and deflated by those who wanted to control it, and thereby control its participants; but not for too long. It always sought and found its own level. And if manipulators—invariably governmental—prevented it from finding its true level for too long, a great mass of people suffered when it finally burst through the dams erected against it.

LaNague had taught the outworlds that bitter lesson. But three hundred years had passed since then and it was quite possible that history was ready to set the stage for a repeat performance. The Restructurists were fortunate to have a remarkable man such as Elson deBloise at their head in their drive for control of the Federation and, from there, control of the market.

But the market had Josephine Finch. The market was inviolate as far as she was concerned. It was an integral part of human existence, especially Jo's existence. Her professional life was spent in taking the pulse and prognosticating the course of the market and she would do her best to see that no one meddled with it.

Right now, the only way she could see to put a stop to deBloise was to cripple Star Ways, the biggest interstellar conglomerate in Occupied Space. Hardly a realistic option, but it was all she had.

Bill Grange was IBA's resident expert on Star Ways and his knowledge would be a critical factor in Jo's plan. Of course, it would save her an intolerably large amount of time and effort if she could go up to someone in charge of Star Ways and tell him that a monstrous political plot was afoot and that his company was going to be used as a scapegoat. But you couldn't do that with a conglomerate, you couldn't deal person-to-person with it. So Jo would have to induce co-operation from Star Ways; she'd have to jab at it, stab at it, slice away at its appendages until it was forced to do her bidding. And she'd relish every minute of it.

For there was no love lost between Josephine Finch and the interstellar conglomerates. They disturbed her sense of fair play. It was not that they broke any of the rules of the free market—they sold to those who wanted to buy and bought from those who wished to sell. But there was something about them that...offended her.

The conglomerates were faceless monoliths. Nobody seemed to be in charge. There were boards of directors and committees all composed of people; they hired and directed the work of other people; products were turned out which were sold to still other people. Human beings were intimately involved in every function of the conglomerates, yet the final result was a structure devoid of all human qualities. It became a blind, impersonal leviathan lumbering through the market, obliterating anything that got in its way—not through technical skill or marketing expertise, but through sheer size.

And it was not size itself that Jo found offensive, although that was part of the problem. Despite the fact that people made all the decisions for them, their huge size prevented their humanity from showing through. Smaller companies each seemed to have their own personality. Conglomerates strode through the market, the testing ground for all human endeavor, like giant automatons.

Yes, they were huge, and their size and diversification inured them and insulated them from immediate changes in the market. But no insulation is perfect. The conglomerates were not invincible. If a subsidiary company was ailing, there was a great financial pool from which it could draw. But there were limits to any pool. And if more than one subsidiary were in trouble...

Leviathan could be wounded and caused to retreat if attacked at multiple vulnerable sites.

Jo only hoped that Star Ways had a few vulnerable sites.

The door opened and Bill Grange walked through. He was tall, gaunt, graying, fifty-four years old—he liked to say that he and IBA had been born the same year. He had been with the firm nearly a decade when Joe, Sr., died and had stayed on through all the turmoil that followed. He had been neither for nor against Josephine when she took over IBA; all he wanted was someone in charge who could get the company going again. If she could do it, he was all for her. If she loused it up, he'd walk. As it stood now, there wasn't much he wouldn't do for Josephine Finch.

"Something wrong, Jo? The message sounded urgent."

"I need some information on Star Ways," she said, taking her place behind the desk again, "and I need it now."

Grange visibly relaxed at this statement and took a seat. He probably knew more about Star Ways than many of its board members. He knew it from dealing with it on a daily basis in the current market, and he knew it from a historical perspective. The conglomerate was centuries old, born in a small company on old Earth celled Helene Technical, which happened to develop the first commercial interstellar warp unit. The old name was quickly scrapped for the more picturesque Star Ways, and the new company severed its ties with Earth, relocating on the planet Tarvodet—a tiny world but one that afforded mammoth tax advantages.

It became a huge, successful corporation. Through imaginative marketing, tricky financial maneuvers, and the old tried-and-true business practice of hiring the best and making it worth their while to stay on, SW moved into other fields, buying up subsidiary companies and becoming the first interstellar conglomerate. Other conglomerates had developed since, but Star Ways Corporation was still the largest.

"What do you want to know? I could talk all day."

"I'm sure you could. But I want to know where, in light of what's going on in the current market, SW can be hurt. If it can be hurt at all."

Grange's eyebrows lifted. "Hurt Star Ways, eh? Not so hard these days as it might have been when you arrived on the scene."

"Oh, really?"

"Yeh. SW's mortgaged to the hilt and overextended in all quarters. It needs some new blood on those boards, and when the financial reports come out"—he chuckled—"there'll be a lot of screaming from the stockholders."

"I wasn't aware of this."

"It's not public knowledge yet, but that's what our informants tell us. And I've seen it coming for years. But don't worry. Star Ways will pull through just fine—minus some dead wood at the top."

Jo mulled this over. It was encouraging. "Give me some specific weak points."

"I can think of three right off the top of my head: General Trades, Stardrive, and Teblinko. General Trades has always generated a lot of income on luxury items, but has lately run into hordes of competitors and lost part of its share of the market.

"Stardrive is a different story. That's their tube drive subsidiary—SW's oldest subsidiary, as a matter of fact. When they picked that up, they were able to outfit ships for both interstellar and peristellar travel—that's when they really started to grow. Stardrive Inc. has always had competitors, but lately a little company by the name of Fairleigh Tubes has been giving it a real run for its money." He grinned. "Does that name sound familiar?"

Jo nodded and returned his smile. "Certainly does." Fairleigh Tubes was an IBA account.

"Then we come to Teblinko Corporation, the pharmaceutical firm Star Ways acquired a few years back—that's been a real problem lately. They had to pour a lot of money into it to get it moving, and it's only now just starting to pay off. Once Teblinko starts consolidating its gains, it'll be less crucial to SW's over-all profit picture; but right now it's touch and go.

"If you're still looking for more cases, I can—"

Jo held up her hand. "That'll do for now, I think." She paused. "Teblinko's biggest competitor is Opsal Pharmaceuticals, right?"

Grange nodded. "We did some work for them in the past."

"How come they're not with us now?"

"Don't need us. They're doing fine, so we put them in the inactive file." He grinned again. "But with the way Teblinko is moving up, I expect to be hearing from them soon."

Jo nodded absently, making mental notes.

"What's this all about, if I might ask?"

Jo considered bringing Grange in on it, then vetoed the idea. If she told him what deBloise was planning, he'd think she was paranoid; and if she explained what she wanted to do to Star Ways, he'd be fully convinced that she had crossed the line into overt schizophrenia. No, better keep it to herself.

"Just working out a theoretical problem," she told him. "And you've been a big help. Can I call on you again if I need some more information?"

"Of course," Grange replied, taking the hint and rising. He was too canny to be fooled by Jo's lame explanation—you weren't told to drop everything and get up to the head office because of a theoretical problem—but he was sure he'd be filled in on all the details if and when he came to be involved.

He turned at the door. "It occurs to me that you might not have a certain factor in your theoretical problem, a factor that has the potential to put Fairleigh way ahead of Stardrive: the Rako deal. If that ever comes through—"

Jo's eyes widened. "Rako! Of course! You know, I'd forgotten all about that. Thanks, Bill."

When he was gone, Jo ordered the complete files on Fairleigh Tubes and Opsal Pharmaceuticals. She also asked the same questions she had asked Bill Grange. The information came up. It agreed with Grange that General Trades and Teblinko were the weak links in SW's chain of subsidiaries. But Stardrive, the subsidiary Grange had emphasized, was conspicuous by its absence.

Jo wasn't surprised. Bill Grange approached the market with an intuitive sense that could not be programmed into any machine, no matter how sophisticated.

The records department informed her that the Fairleigh and Opsal files were now keyed to her viewer and she could activate them anytime during the next two hours. This was part of the IBA security routine. Client files were available only to authorized personnel on specific request and only for a strictly limited time period. Most contained sensitive and confidential information that would be invaluable to a competitor.

Current information on Opsal was scanty. It was a reputable firm with a long-standing history of high quality pharmaceutical production. Teblinko was coming up in the field and pushing Opsal, but the older company was maintaining its lead by virtue of its superior distribution system.

Not much help there.

She moved on to Fairleigh. The peristellar drive tube market was a stable one. The proton-proton drive had remained the best real-space propulsion method for centuries and the Leason crystal had remained the only practical lining for the drive tubes for an equal amount of time. Emmett Leason, an extra-terrestrial geologist, first identified the crystal on one of the three tiny moons of Tandem. When he could not determine the melting point of the crystal by conventional means, he knew he had something.

Someone eventually devised a means of coating the inner surface of a proton-proton drive tube with the crystals and found that the new lining prevented the tube from vaporizing as had all the previous prototypes. An experimental means of transportation suddenly became the norm.

Leason crystals became a hot item among prospectors but it was soon discovered that natural deposits were rare. While these were being mined down to bare rock, the laboratory boys were hard at work developing a synthetic substitute. They were successful, but the man-made crystals were hellishly expensive.

And that was how the drive tube market stood. The patents on the synthetic process were long defunct and anyone who wanted to make Leason crystals was welcome to do so. But that didn't make the process any cheaper. As the human race expanded and colonized more new worlds, the demand for p-p tubes grew steadily, and more and more companies entered the market. Still, no one was able to reduce significantly the cost factor in synthesizing the crystals, so they remained the major contributor to the tubes' high price tag. It was thus the dream of every company to stumble upon a mother lode planet of natural crystals.

Fairleigh had found such a planet: Rako. But there was a hitch. As a matter of fact, there were a number of hitches.

One of them was the Tarkan Empire.

Jo frowned. The Tarks were popping up more and more lately. There would no doubt be a clash someday—a big one. But not in the near future. The Tarkan Empire was ruthless and active and probably took the loose, formless structure of the Federation as a sign of weakness. One day it would overstep its boundaries to test the Federation's mettle. The empire's economy was rigidly controlled and centralized and such economies needed periodic armed conflicts to rejuvenate themselves. Free markets tended toward the other extreme: wars meant killing, and killing meant a reduction in the overall total of available customers.

She activated her intercom. "Get hold of Mr. Balaam at Fairleigh for me."

The smiling, distinguished face of Harold Balaam soon filled her vid screen. He had held the president's seat of the drive tube company, which kept its main office on Ragna, for the past decade. He and Jo enjoyed an excellent working relationship.

After the usual amenities, Jo asked, "How's the Rako situation going, Hal?"

The smile faded. "Don't ask. It's costing us a fortune and we're getting nowhere. I'm afraid I'm going to be forced to pull the team if we don't start getting some results soon."

"Anything in particular holding you up?"

"Yes. The Rakoans themselves." He gave her a brief summary of the situation.

"Sounds like you need a public relations man out there."

Balaam grunted. "Know of a PR company that has any experience with degenerate aliens?"

"Not exactly," Jo laughed, "but if I can have an authorization from you, I may be able to send somebody out there who can help."

Balaam considered this for a few seconds, then nodded. "I think we can commission a trouble shooter through you. You haven't steered us wrong yet…and if you come through on this, you can name your fee."

"The usual contingency percentage will be fine. Just beam the authorization over as soon as possible and I'll get right to work on it."

When the screen was blank, Jo leaned back in her chair. She needed someone to send to Rako immediately, someone with good judgment, a quick mind, and the ability to improvise. That was Larry. But he was on Jebinose and so she'd have to settle for whoever was next in line. Perhaps "settle" wasn't fair. Larry had the utmost confidence in Andy and that should be sufficient endorsement for anyone.

She hoped he was available. She was going to send him out to the far edge of the human sector of the galaxy.

# XI
## DEBLOISE

It was a corner office, and when the windows were set at maximum transparency the view was impressive. Copia, the capital city of Jebinose, was a showcase for the planet. The average outworld could claim one large city and it was usually located near its major—and sometimes only—spaceport. Into this city was poured all the technical skills and available funds the inhabitants could muster. Some cynics denounced the efforts as hypocritical window dressing, but to most inhabitants of the planet it was very important to put on a pretty face for visitors, important to leave an impression of prosperity and well-being.

Copia was designed to leave such an impression. The rest of Jebinose might be economically and culturally backward, but Copia had a medical center, a psi-school, a university, a museum of Vanek artifacts, and a huge sports arena.

DeBloise's office overlooked the northern quarter of Copia; its outer corner pointed toward the graceful spire that marked the university campus. Delicate violet and yellow-striped tendrils of Nolevetol deng grass intertwined across the floor, forming a thick, soft, living rug. Exotic plants climbed three corners of the room; a huge desk, its entire top surface made of solid Maratek firewood, filled the fourth.

DeBloise sat behind that desk. Holographs of his wife and two children were prominently arrayed before him, but his eyes were on the latest in the morning's long procession of visitors and supplicants.

Henro Winterman, a leader of one of the sector's larger merchant combines, didn't fit deBloise's image of a merchant. Merchants should be porcine and endomorphic; this one was lean and lupine. And vaguely arrogant. But his pompous air carried a wheedling undertone. Winterman's group and others like it had formed a strong pro-deBloise base in the sector's business community. They had helped significantly in elevating him to initial prominence in interstellar politics, but he had gone on from there without their help. And at this point Winterman was not too sure of his footing with the man who was now so closely identified with the Restructurist movement.

"It seems that my associates are growing just a little bit impatient, sir," he said with the perfect blend of impudence and deference. "We've actively backed you for a good number of years now and we don't seem to be getting anywhere. The sector continues to wallow in an economic slump and, very frankly, sir, none of us is getting any younger."

"So?" deBloise said with raised eyebrows and a completely neutral tone.

Certain economic considerations had been implied when they had offered their support for his initial campaign to go to the Federation as a Restructurist. Somewhat less than two standard decades had passed since then and apparently some of the merchants thought the bill was past due. It irritated deBloise to the point of fury that Winterman should have the audacity to approach him in this manner, but he checked himself and limited his reply to the noncommittal monosyllable. The time had not yet come when he could loose his rage on Winterman, but that time was coming…it was coming. Until it arrived, he could not allow anything to erode his power base.

"Well," Winterman said slowly when it became obvious that deBloise was waiting to hear more, "my associates and I are quite concerned about the indigenous economic integrity of our sector."

DeBloise had to smile at that: *Indigenous economic integrity.*

What an ingenious phrase! It meant nothing, really, but was infinitely malleable. DeBloise had used a number of similar phrases and catchwords on his way up; they were indispensable to the political process when it was necessary to create an issue.

Interpreting the smile as encouragement, Winterman hurried on. "We know the Restructurist movement is sympathetic to our goal of eliminating outside commercial interests from the sector, and we know it's just a matter of time before the movement achieves dominance in the Fed Assembly and gives us the backing we need, but there is a bit of an economic lag in the sector and we were wondering how long—"

"Not too much longer, Henro," deBloise said with hearty confidence and one of his best public smiles.

But beneath the smile he was snarling. He saw the merchant as a filthy, greedy, moneygrubbing parasite and knew exactly what he and the other members of the merchant combine meant by the "indigenous economic integrity of the sector": they wanted a monopoly on all trade in and out of the sector. None of the members was skilled or talented enough to achieve that goal either as an individual or as part of a collective. So—they were looking for a little Federation muscle to help them. But the LaNague Charter prohibited any and all interference in the economy by the Federation. Thus their support of deBloise and Restructurism. Strange bedfellows, indeed.

Speaking continuously as he moved, he rose and expertly guided Winterman out of the office. With his hand on the man's shoulder, he assured him of his deep sympathy and concern for his predicament and of his firm intention to do all he could for him just as soon as the Movement made some headway toward changing the charter. He also made a point of reminding him that if that day was ever to come, it would require the continued support of such model citizens as Henro Winterman and his fellow merchants.

DeBloise glanced questioningly at his receptionist as the waiting room door slipped closed behind Winterman.

"You're ahead of schedule, sir," she said, knowing what was on his mind. "That reporter isn't due until ten-point-five."

He nodded and returned to his inner office. A mirthless smile warped his lips as he waited for the chair to adjust to his posture in a semi-reclining position. It never ceased to amaze him how much a part greed played in politics. That, at least, was something he was well insulated against, thank the Core. The deBloise name had been synonymous with wealth on Jebinose for generations; his personal fortune was more than he could hope to spend in two lifetimes.

No, Elson deBloise had more important concerns than money, but that didn't mean he would renege on his promise to use whatever power he achieved after the Haas plan came to fruition to aid Winterman's crowd. He'd be delighted to help them gain a stranglehold on trade in the sector, absolutely delighted.

And soon, as Restructurist control of the Federation increased as it inevitably must after they achieved their beachhead—the Jebinose trade cartel and others like it would find themselves under direct supervision of the newly restructured Federation. The real power over the human sector of Occupied Space would then be where it belonged—with the new Fed president, Elson deBloise.

Money as an incentive? Never! Then what was his incentive? DeBloise's mind had developed numerous diversionary tactics to deal with that question. Most of them were quite ingenious. But every once in a while his defenses collapsed and the inescapable truth leaked through: rich and influential men entered politics for one reason…power. Lower class nobodies became politicos with the power motive in mind, too, but it was often diluted by a drive for prestige and the financial advantages that so often attend the acquisition of public office. Being moneyed and respected at the start, however, left only power as a goal.

*The quest for dominion over other men's lives was not necessarily an evil thing if, after achieving that dominion, it was used toward certain beneficial ends.*

DeBloise had repeated this to himself so many times that by now he actually believed it, and the thought that a good many people might not share his vision for the human race did not bother him in the least. He would override their opinions and in the end they would see that it was all for their own good.

As his mind reflexively skittered away from any in-depth analysis of the moral implications of his life's work, his eyes came to rest on the holographs of his wife and children on the desktop.

His daughter was on the left: a pretty brunette with some wild tendencies. These were presently being curbed—he wanted no bad publicity involving his family.

Rhona, his wife, was in the middle. She too was a brunette, although she weighed more now than she did in the holo. Their offspring has been limited to two—one of each sex—at deBloise's insistence; it made for a perfectly balanced family portrait. Rhona had been the eldest daughter of another rich Jebinose family, and two fortunes, as well as two people, had been united at their wedding. They were husband and wife now in name only, however. They slept in separate quarters at night and led separate lives by day; only on public record and in the public eye were they married. Both seemed content with the situation as it was.

He had never loved Rhona. At one time he thought he might someday grow to love her, but as his rise in politics began to accelerate, the discrepancies between the public deBloise and the private Elson widened. And he found that he preferred the role of the public deBloise, a role he could not play with any conviction in Rhona's presence. She'd known him since adolescence, knew all his fears, fantasies, and idiosyncrasies. In her eyes, he would never be the wonderful man who was the public deBloise, and so he avoided her.

The homely face of his son, Elson III, filled the third and final holo. He was proud of Els—just fourteen, president of his class and active in the Young Restructurists Club. He encouraged his son in these activities, for he'd found them invaluable in his own youth. Through being a class officer and the head of committees, you learned how to handle people, how to get them involved in projects, how to get them to work for you.

His son would start at the university next year, and that brought back a swarm of memories for deBloise. He had never planned on going into politics, aiming rather for a long life devoted to being very idle and very rich. Something during his years of higher education had sparked him, however. He didn't remember exactly what it was, perhaps some of those Restructurist-oriented professors who were so openly critical of the Federation, spending entire class periods in an overt attempt to sway developing minds toward their point of view. Perhaps young Elson deBloise had sensed a path to power within the philosophy of political interventionism.

He entered the political sphere soon after graduation, not as a Restructurist, however. Restructurism was irrelevant then as a philosophy in lower-echelon politics on Jebinose. His name and his position made him welcome in the inner circles of the local machine where he quickly identified the movers and the shakers. He made the right connections, spoke up for the right causes at key affairs, and finally gained enough leverage to be nominated to the Jebinose Senate.

Even as he made his maiden speech before that august body, he was planning the moves that would take him to Fed Central. Jebinose was not yet in the Restructurist fold, was not in any fold, for that matter. The planet was situated near some of the major trade lanes, yet did little trading. There was little there to interest anyone: no drugs, technological hardware, or chemicals—just those damn Vanek artifacts, and a single shipload could handle a year's output.

So, traders rarely stopped at Jebinose. It was a fact of life. But coupled with the current slow, steady decline of the planet's economy, that fact of life held great potential as a political issue of interstellar scale. To transform it into such an issue would require some fancy footwork and what his advisers referred to as "the old reverse."

This is how it would work: It was obvious to anyone vaguely familiar with Jebinose and elementary economics that major traders didn't stop there because it had a simple agrarian economy with nothing to trade. To make an important political issue of that, you merely inverted the situation: Jebinose had a poor, simple agrarian economy because the traders refused to stop there; if the traders could be made to stop and deal with Jebinose, the planet would undergo an industrial and economic boom. And that's why Jebinose needs a Restructurist working for her at Federation Central.

You couldn't spring this on the populace *de novo*, of course. You had to spend a few years laying the groundwork in the media, dropping phrases like "functional trade sanction" whenever asked about the Jebinose economy, and continuing to utilize the phrase until it was picked up by others. After it had been repeated often enough, it would be accepted as matter-of-fact truth. And if they could accept that amorphous phrase, then they would have no trouble swallowing "the old reverse."

Used properly, that would be the issue to launch him into interstellar politics. But until the foundation had been properly laid, he must cast around for local issues to keep himself prominently displayed before the public.

And that was when some minor public official suggested that there was too much discrimination against the Vanek in the rural areas where they lived. DeBloise and the other Restructurists in the Jebinose Senate jumped on the idea, and the Vanek Equality Act was soon making its way through the legislature. Elson deBloise, more than anyone else, had staked his political future on that bill. He toured the entire planetary surface speaking on it. If it passed, he would instantly become the fair-haired boy of Jebinose politics and would immediately introduce his manufactured trade issue in a bid for the Jebinose seat at the Federation Assembly. If it hit a snag, it would set his timetable back five, perhaps ten years.

It hit a snag.

And that's when Cando Proska introduced himself.

Since then he had never had a good night's sleep on Jebinose.

"That reporter is here, sir," said his receptionist's voice.

DeBloise shook himself back to the present and assumed a more upright posture.

"Send him in."

A nondescript man of average build with dark blond hair and eyes that seemed to be bothered by the bright, natural light of the office strolled through the door and extended his hand.

"Good day to you, sir. I'm Lawrence Easly from the Risden Interstellar News Service and it's an honor to meet you."

XII

EASLY

Easly's credentials as a news service reporter were the best money could buy. It was a useful identity, allowing him to roam and ask embarrassing questions. It secured him an interview with deBloise himself within the span of one local day—it was difficult for any politico to turn down free exposure in the interstellar news media.

He had done all the research he could on the way out from Ragna, and now he had the rest of the day on his hands. Danzer wasn't too far away, so he rented a small flitter for a quick run to the little town. Jo had told him about her father's murder there and he wanted to have a look...for her sake.

And for his own. Easly had approached the Junior Finch aspect of the Jebinose trip as he would a typical missing person case. His routine in such was to learn all he could about the individual in question before starting the leg work; he liked to feel as if he knew the quarry before initiating the search. In Junior's case he had found that unsettlingly easy.

Old holovid recordings in the Finch family library were the starting point. There weren't many. None of the Finches was crazy about sitting still for cameras, it seemed. He did manage to find one, a long one, recorded at what must have been a family outing shortly before the death of Jo's grandparents in the flitter crash. The viewing globe filled with woods, grassy knolls, a pond, and for a short while, Junior Finch sitting under a tree with a five- or six-year-old Josephine perched on his lap. They were posing and the family resemblance was striking, especially since Jo's hair had been lighter then.

But Easly's eyes had drawn away from the child who had grown to be his lover and come to rest on Junior. He felt as if he were looking at a slightly distorted reflection of the adult Josephine, recognizing parallels that went beyond build, facial features, complexion. There was a whole constellation of intangible similarities pouring out of the globe: the relentless energy forever pushing to find new channels, the undefined urgency that so typified Jo's character as he knew her today percolated below Junior's surface even in the midst of pastoral tranquillity.

But not until the camera had panned to the right, placing Junior on the periphery of the visual field, did the uncanny similarity between Jo and her father strike him full force. Junior stood leaning against a tree, staring at nothing, his arms folded, his mind obviously light-years away from the family picnic. It startled Easly because he'd caught Jo hundreds—thousands!—of times staring off into space that same way, steeped in the same private world.

There were other recordings, and on the trip to Jebinose Easly had studied them, watching Junior's every move. He found something immensely appealing in the man's quiet intensity and became increasingly involved in him...fascinated, infatuated, haunted by the shade of a man he had never met, yet felt he had known most of his life. It bothered him.

The tragic course of Junior's life saddened him, and annoyed him as well. What made a grown man drop a top position with a respected firm like IBA, a firm presented with interesting, challenging problems on a daily basis, and travel to a place like Jebinose?

He smiled as a thought came to him: probably the same thing that made a nineteen-year-old girl forsake a life of ease and luxury to singlehandedly challenge the IBA board of directors and outworld conventions as well. He then realized why he felt so close to Junior Finch: Josephine, for all the adulation and admiration she lavished on the memory of her grandfather, had grown into the image of his son.

And now he was gilding toward the death-place of that son, her father. She had given him three names: Bill Jeffers, Marvin Heber, and a Vanek named Rmrl, or something like that. The first would be easy to find if he still ran the store.

He missed Danzer on the first pass, but circled around and followed a dirt road back into the center of the tiny town. Jeffers' name was still on the sign above the general store, so he made that his first stop.

Jeffers wasn't there at the moment, but a clean-shaven, heavy-set young man who professed to be his son asked if he could help.

"I'm looking for Marvin Heber," Easly said. "Know where I can find him?"

"He's dead. Died sometime last spring."

"Oh, I'm sorry to hear that."

"You a friend of his?"

"Not really. A friend of a relative of an old friend of his—you know what I mean." Young Jeffers nodded. "I was supposed to stop in and say hello and see how he was. Oh, well."

He strolled out onto the boardwalk. It was hot and dry outside and a gust of wind blew some dust into his face. He sneezed twice. Hard to believe people still lived like this.

He still had some time left to check out this Rmrl. Jo had told him that the Vanek tribe had set up a vigil of sorts on the spot in the alley next to Jeffers' store where Junior had died; it was the one place where he could always be sure of finding a Vanek, no matter what the time of day.

Today was no exception. Easly rounded the corner of the store and there, cross-legged in the center of a crude circle of stones, humming and jiggling the coins in his cracked earthen bowl, sat a lone Vanek beggar.

"Wheels within wheels, *bendreth*," he intoned as Easly approached the circle.

"Sure," Easly replied, stopping with his shoes a few centimeters from the stones. "Can I speak with you a minute?"

"Speak, *bendreth*."

He squatted and looked at the beggar. Pupils dilated from a long watch in the shade of the alley gazed out at him from beneath hooded eyelids but appeared to be focused on something other than Easly, something neither of them could see. The blue-tinted skin of the face was wrinkled and dusty. This was one of the older Vanek.

"I want to know about Junior Finch," Easly said in a low voice, after glancing around to be sure that he and the beggar were alone in the alley.

The Vanek's mouth curled into a poor imitation of a human smile. "He was our friend."

"But he was killed."

The smile remained. "Wheels within wheels, *bendreth*."

"But who killed him?"

"We did."

"But why?"

"He was our friend."

Easly was getting annoyed. "But why would you kill a man you say was your friend?"

"He was different."

"How was he different?"

"Wheels within wheels, *bendreth*."

"That doesn't tell me a damn thing!" Easly said, his voice rising. "You've said you killed him. Just tell me why."

"He was our friend."

"But no one kills somebody because he's a friend!"

"Wheels within wheels, *bendreth*."

Easly made a guttural sound and rose quickly to his feet. If he thought the beggar was deliberately trying to be evasive, he would have understood that and accepted it. But this was apparently the way the Vanek mind worked.

Or was it?

"Do you know Rmrl?" he asked abruptly.

The Vanek's pupils contracted noticeably, and for an instant he actually looked at Easly rather than through him.

"We all know Rmrl," he replied.

"Where is he at the moment?"

"Among us." The eyes resumed their indeterminate gaze.

"How can I find him?"

"Wheels within wheels, *bendreth*," the beggar said, and jiggled his alms bowl.

Easly growled and strode away without leaving any coins. How could he hope to glean any coherent information from a member of a half-breed alien race that killed the man who tried to help it, then made a shrine of sorts out of the place where they murdered him? The whole trip had been a waste of time. He hadn't even enjoyed the scenery.

He spent the early part of the next morning gearing himself up for his meeting with deBloise. This was the prelude to his investigative work: getting a feel for the man. And for that he needed personal contact. His object was to find out anything at all that might be useful against him—anything. Jo seemed to be playing for keeps on this one.

He arrived at Sector Representative deBloise's plush homeworld offices a little early and watched the receptionist until she motioned him into the next room.

DeBloise stood and waited for him behind his desk. He had a bigger build than Larry had expected—probably muscular once, now tending slightly toward puffiness—but the dark hair and the graying temples were familiar, as was the cordial smile fixed on the face. Easly reflexively disregarded the comfortable, friendly exterior; his research had shown beyond a doubt that there was a core of diamond-hard ambition hiding beneath.

"Well, Mr. Easly," deBloise said after they shook hands, "what do you think of our fine planet so far?"

"Very nice," Easly lied as he took the indicated seat.

"Good. How can I help you?"

"The Risden Service is doing a series of reports on human-alien relations, and the most intimate such relationship, of course, exists here on Jebinose with the Vanek."

DeBloise nodded. "It must be remembered that the Vanek are not totally alien; they are a mix of human and alien. But I can see why they would be of prime interest in such a series. Where do I fit in, however?"

"You were one of the principal sponsors of the Vanek Equality Act, were you not?"

DeBloise inclined his head.

"Well then, that makes you a principal figure in modern Terran-Vanek relations, and your files would be of invaluable assistance to me. Might I have access to them?"

DeBloise considered this; there was extraordinary potential here for a massive amount of good press. "I could give you selective access. I'm sure you understand that I couldn't possibly open all my files to you."

"Of course. Whatever you think best. Now, there's also another important figure in Terran-Vanek relations: Joseph Finch, Jr., I believe."

There was a barely perceptible cooling of deBloise's attitude at the mention of Junior's name. "I'm afraid I didn't know him at all. Never met him."

"But that was quite an impassioned speech you made about him on behalf of the Equality Act after his death. I heard a recording—very moving, even after seventeen years."

"Thank you," deBloise replied with a bland smile. "But one didn't have to know him personally to be moved by his death. I knew what he was trying to do: he was trying to bring equality to those less fortunate than he; he was trying to bestow a little dignity on the Vanek; he was going out on a limb for a fellow rational being. I understood him perfectly, and I'm willing to wager that if he were alive today he'd be very active in the Restructurist movement."

Easly nearly choked, but managed to keep a straight, attentive expression. "What about the Equality Act, sir? Would it have passed without Mr. Finch's death?"

"Definitely. Not with such resounding unanimity, perhaps, but it would have passed. It was an idea whose time had come. That bill, by the way, was pending before Finch came to Jebinose."

"And on the reputation you earned with the passage of the Equality Act, you went on to successfully run for a planetary representative seat at Fed Central, is that correct?"

DeBloise paused and scrutinized his interviewer. "Are we talking about human-alien relations or my political career?"

"The two are somewhat intertwined, don't you think?"

"Somewhat."

This writer, Easly, had a manner about him that deBloise did not care for…made him feel as if he were under a microscope. He'd have to run a check on the man before he let him anywhere near his files.

The intercom chimed and waited to be recognized. "I thought I told you not to disturb me for the next few minutes," deBloise said.

"I'm sorry, sir," the receptionist said, "but Mr. Proska is here and wishes to see you immediately."

The casual observer would have noticed nothing. But Larry Easly's training enabled him to pick up certain cues immediately. His attention became riveted on deBloise.

The man was terrified. At the mention of the name "Proska," his body had become rigid; there was the slightest blanching of the skin, the slightest tightening of the mouth. To a trained observer, Elson deBloise was transmitting acute fear. His voice, however, was remarkably calm when he spoke.

"Tell him I'll see him in a moment," he said to the air, then turned back to Easly. "I'm very sorry, but some urgent business has just come up and I'm afraid we'll have to cut this interview short. I'm leaving for Fed Central in a few days but will probably return within a standard month. Please check with my secretary and make another appointment."

"But your files—" Easly began

"We can attend to that next month." DeBloise rose. "But right now, you must excuse me."

Easly muttered a thank-you and made his exit. He was bitterly disappointed—those files were crucial to his investigation. As he reentered the waiting room, he saw only one occupant besides the receptionist. A small, sallow, balding man sat with his hands on his knees, and rose as Easly left the inner office. Easly was about to classify him as a timid nonentity until he caught a glimpse of the man's eyes as he passed. There was not a hint of timidity—nor love nor fear nor hatred nor mercy, for that matter—to be found there.

This was undoubtedly the Mr. Proska who struck such fear into the heart of the powerful, secure, influential Sector Representative Elson deBloise. It was suddenly very obvious to Easly that Mr. Proska had some sort of hold over deBloise; finding out just what that was might prove useful.

"Excuse me," he said to the receptionist after the door to the inner office had closed behind Proska. "Wasn't that Harold Proska?"

The receptionist smiled. "No, that was Cando Proska. Perhaps you know his brother."

"Does he have a brother?"

"I couldn't say." She shrugged. "I believe he's an old friend of Mr. deBloise's. He stops in now and then. But I really don't know a thing about him."

"I must be thinking of someone else," he said, and sauntered out of the waiting room.

An old friend, eh? he thought as he walked across the hall and stepped into the down chute. He fell at the rate of one kilometer per hour until he passed the "Ground Floor" sign, then grabbed the handles and pulled himself out of the chute and into the lobby. No old friend of mine ever scared me like that!

Pondering his next move as he stepped out into the late morning sunlight, Easly suddenly remembered that he was on a Restructurist world. And all worlds within the Restructurist fold had a policy of maintaining what they called a Data Center, a centralized bank where vital, identifiable statistics of all natives and permanent residents were kept on file. The information stored usually included date of birth, place of birth, parents' names, education, employment record, present location, and so on.

Easly flagged a flittercab and headed for Copia's municipal complex. He idly wished that all planets had Data Centers—it would certainly make things easier for someone in his line of work—but then banished the thought when he realized his own vital statistics would be listed.

The Data Centers were a natural outgrowth of Restructurist philosophy, which viewed humanity as a mass and approached it as such. As a result, the government on a Restructurist world was highly centralized and geared its actions toward what it decided were the common denominators of the collective. To determine those common denominators—to "better serve the public interest," as it was wont to put it—the government had to know all about the public in question.

Thus the Data Centers. And since all men were brothers, all should have access to the data. This was the Restructurist version of a truly "open society."

Individuals like Larry Easly and Josephine Finch and Old Pete posed a thorny problem for Restructurist theory, however: sometimes consciously, most often unconsciously, they refused to accept the common denominator for themselves and persisted in sticking their heads above the level of the crowd. They thought brotherhood was a nice idea but they didn't think it could be institutionalized. And they never ceased to be amazed at the amount of garbage other people would swallow if the sugar coating were laid on thick enough.

The flittercab dropped him off before a complex of Neo-Gothic abstract buildings that housed the municipal offices of Copia. From there it was no problem finding the Data Center. Slipping into an empty booth, he punched in the name Cando Proska. If the little man had been born on Jebinose, his name would definitely be listed. If he were an immigrant, there was still a good chance to locate him here.

A single identity number flashed on the screen. Easly punched it in and hoped for the best.

PROSKA, Cando     Lot 149, Hastingsville
Male
Age: 44 Jebinose years
Height: 1.58 M     Weight: 68.2 Kg
Parents: Carter & Dori Proska
     (Both deceased)

Developmental environment: SW SECTOR. COPIA
Religion: NONE
Political affiliation: NONE
Marital status: UNATTACHED
Offspring: NONE
Education history:  COPIA PSI-SCHOOL, AGE 5-10
               COPIA SECONDARY, AGE 11-16
Employment history: CLERK, JEBINOSE BUREAU OF
        STANDARDS, AGE 19-27 (VOLUNTARY TERMINATION)
Current employment status: NONE

There could be little question that this was the man: height, age, weight, it all seemed to fit. He noted with interest the fact that Proska had dropped out of psi-school at age ten. That was certainly unusual because there's no such thing as losing a psi-talent—you're born with it and it stays with you the rest of your life. The purpose of a psi-school is to hone and develop a native talent; therefore you have to be able to demonstrate psionic ability before being accepted into such a school.

And you didn't quit. People with psi-talents were always in demand; even those with the most mediocre abilities were assured a good income for the rest of their lives. Proska had been a student there for five years, which meant he had some psionic talent. Why did he drop out?

And why hadn't he put the talent to use? He had spent eight years at the bottom rung in a government office that even in the best of times was notable only for its nuisance value. Then he quit again. No employment for the last seventeen years. Also strange.

Not much information, but Easly was satisfied with it as a starting point. And as a little extra bonus, something had clicked in the back of his mind as he was reviewing the information; he couldn't place it right now—his brain often made correlations without immediately informing him—but he knew from experience not to push it. Sooner or later it would come to the surface.

He decided that a quick look at Proska's living quarters was in order and wrote down the address. It was a calm, sunny day so he rented an open flitter and took it up to a high hover level where he could put the vehicle in a holding pattern and consult the directory. The autopilot code number for the aerial co-ordinates of Lot 149, Hastingsville, was F278924B. Easly punched it in, set the speed at slow cruise, and leaned back to enjoy the ride.

It took longer than he anticipated. Instead of heading him toward inner Copia, the autopilot took him northeast and outward. He had originally expected to find himself over one of the poorer areas of the city, but now he was entering a suburb.

The flitter stopped and hovered over a sprawling mansion located in the center of an obviously well-to-do neighborhood. He allowed the flitter to lose altitude so he could get a better look. The house consisted of four octagonal buildings connected in an irregular line and built at varying levels. The landscaping had been extensive: the rest of the lot was covered with an intricate pattern of color-co-ordinated shrubbery. A "149" on the landing platform confirmed the address.

Not bad for a man who hasn't worked in seventeen years, Easly thought. Not bad at all.

As he dropped lower, a number of bright red lights began to flash from the roof and landing pad, a warning that clearance was required from below before he would be allowed to land. Easly veered off and followed the fenced perimeter of the property all the way around. His trained eye picked up traces that indicated the presence of a very effective and very expensive automated security system.

He was about to make another pass over the house when his peripheral vision caught sight of a moving object to his left: another flitter was approaching. He gave the guide stick a nudge and moved off in the opposite direction at an unhurried pace. The other craft seemed to hesitate in the air, then landed at Proska's residence. There were two men inside—he was almost positive they were deBloise and Proska—and they did not leave the vehicle right away.

Cursing himself for his carelessness in renting an open flitter, he picked up speed and altitude and set a course in the general direction of Copia. Of course, he did have an excuse or two: he had made the erroneous assumption that Proska would be living at a low socioeconomic level, and that his home would be somewhere in the capital city where an extra flitter in the air would go completely unnoticed.

But Hastingsville was not in Copia; it was in an exurban area where his hovering craft was like a vagrant leaf in a well-kept swimming pool.

If deBloise had recognized him, then Easly's cover was most certainly in jeopardy. His policy in any situation such as this was to assume the worst. That being the case, the wisest thing he could do at this point was to get off-planet immediately.

But there was one more thing he had to check before leaving. He looked up the aerial co-ordinate code number for the psi-school in Copia, punched it in, and sat back to review what he knew so far as the autopilot took over.

Proska was blackmailing deBloise. That much was obvious. Easly had no idea what the lever was, but it had to be a big one. Proska had no doubt squeezed the mansion and a generous annuity out of deBloise's personal fortune in return for his silence. But there was more going on besides simple blackmail. DeBloise was in actual physical terror of the little man.

The reason for that could, perhaps, be found at the psi-school.

The flitter stopped over an imposing, windowless, cuboid structure. Easly landed and walked inside. He waited until someone who looked like a student strolled by.

"Excuse me," he asked a boy who looked to be about ten standard years of age. "Who's the dean?"

"Why, Dr. Isaacs, of course."

"How long's he been dean?"

The boy shrugged. "How should I know? Check the plaque over there. You should be able to figure it out from that."

Easly approached the indicated wall where a silvery metal plaque listed all the deans and their period of tenure since the school's founding. A man named *Jacob Howell* had been dean thirty-four years ago. That was the man he wanted.

The vidphone directory gave him the address and phone code of a Howell, Jacob, who lived in Copia. Easly went to a booth, punched in the code, and waited. The face of a thin, elderly man lit up the screen after the third chime.

"I'm sorry to bother you, sir," Easly said, "but are you the Dr. Jacob Howell who used to be dean of the psi-school?"

"One and the same," the old man said with a smile. "What can I do for you?"

He held up his bogus identity card. "I'm doing a series of articles on psi-schools for the Risden News Service. The piece I'm currently working on concerns psi-school dropouts, and I understand there was a dropout when you were dean. Now, I was wondering if you could tell me—"

"Why, of course!" Howell beamed. "I'll be glad to help. Come right over and we'll talk about it."

"I really haven't got too much time left on Jebinose," Easly protested. "If you could just answer—"

"I'll be home all day," the man said, smiling. "You can drop by anytime." With that, he cut the connection.

Easly debated his next move. Howell obviously wanted to get him over to his home. Why? Was he lonely? Or didn't he want to discuss anything over the phone? Or was there another reason?

He decided to go. There were a few unanswered questions here that would nag him incessantly if he did not make at least one attempt to answer them.

"Ah! So you decided to come after all!" Jacob Howell said as he opened the door to his modest apartment. It was immaculate. The walls were studded with plaques, degrees, and testimonials; the furnishings were simple and functional. A holo of a middle-aged woman was affixed to the wall above the vid screen.

A quick glance around and Easly had a capsule description of the man: a retired academic, a widower, somewhat compulsive in his habits, lonely. He welcomed Easly warmly. Any company, even that of strangers, was better than sitting alone.

"Please have a seat and let me get you a cool drink," Howell said.

Easly demurred and tried to get to the point. "There was a student named—"

"No names, please," Dr. Howell said, raising both hands before him. "I was dean of the psi-school for nearly forty years and only one child dropped out. I will discuss the matter with you freely, but without the use of a name."

Definitely compulsive, Easly thought.

"I assure you the article will not name names, but I do need to know some specifics."

"Of course. Well, I've been going over the incident in my mind since your call. It's not something one would easily forget. Nasty business, that."

"What do you mean?"

"Well, little Can—" He stopped short. "I mean, the boy we're discussing got into an argument with another little fellow—it was in the telekinesis lab, I think—and the other boy died right there on the spot. It was a shocking incident. The boy you're interested in—let's call him 'Master X,' shall we?—apparently blamed himself and refused to set foot inside the school again."

"What did the other boy die of?"

Howell shrugged. "We never found out. His parents were from the farm region and were devout members of the Heavenly Bliss sect—we had a lot of them on Jebinose, you know—and they refused to allow an autopsy. It's part of the Heavenly Bliss canon that the human body not be willfully mutilated, neither before birth, during life, nor after death."

"There are plenty of non-invasive methods of determining the cause of a death."

"These were employed, of course, and nothing beyond a previously known congenital heart defect was uncovered. That was assumed to be the cause of death. It was probably the excitement of his argument with Master X that triggered it, and of course one couldn't lay any blame on the little fellow. But you couldn't convince him of that, however. He considered himself responsible and never wanted to come back."

"Congenital heart defect?" Easly's tone was dubious. "That's ancient history. Nobody walks around with something like that any more."

"He does when his parents refuse to consent to surgery...mutilation, you know. If the same thing happened today, there would be an autopsy, Heavenly Bliss sect or not. But we weren't as well organized then as we are now. I wish we could have insisted on an autopsy, then little Master X would have been spared such a burden of guilt. I seem to remember that he showed promise. Such a shame."

"Would you happen to know what he's doing nowadays?" Easly asked.

Howell shook his head. "No, I never kept track of him. To be perfectly frank with you, I tried to forget the whole matter as soon as possible."

Easly digested what Howell had told him for a few minutes, then rose. "Thank you for your time, Dr. Howell. You've been most helpful."

"You mustn't leave yet!" Howell said, leaping to his feet. "There's a lot more I can tell you about psi-schools. I can prepare an early supper and fill you in on many operational details that may prove very useful as background material."

"Some other time, perhaps," Easly said, reaching for the door. "I'm on a very tight schedule now, really."

"Stay and have a drink, at least."

Easly begged off and slipped out the door. As he walked down the hall he could feel the lonely old man's eyes on his back. He felt guilty. All Dr. Howell wanted in return for his information was a little companionship. But companionship meant time, and time was something in short supply at the moment.

The sum total of Larry Easly's instincts and training was prodding him to leave Jebinose immediately, but he shrugged it off. He was hooked now and couldn't run out just yet. He had the tantalizing feeling that all the pieces were here and that a nice coherent picture would be formed if he could arrange them in the proper light. He started laying them out for examination.

DeBloise was terrified of Proska; Proska was a psionic talent of some sort. Those two could be accepted as fact.

Now for a little extrapolation: A little boy at psi-school had died during an argument with Proska and Proska had refused to return to the school because of guilt. Why so much guilt? Unless he knew he had killed the other boy!

Could Cando Proska kill with his mind? Was that why he inspired such fear in deBloise? Was it that plus some very sensitive knowledge that had enabled him to extort a house and probably a yearly income from deBloise for the last seventeen years?

Seventeen years...the Vanek Equality Act had passed almost seventeen years ago—

The subconscious correlation his mind had made back at the Data Center suddenly bobbed to the surface: Junior Finch was murdered on this planet seventeen years ago!

There were too many seventeens involved here to be written off as mere coincidence: deBloise's political career took a sharp upward turn seventeen years ago with the passage of the Vanek Equality Act; Junior Finch was murdered while working among the Vanek seventeen years ago; Cando Proska, a man who might have the ability to kill with his mind, stopped working for a living seventeen years ago and started blackmailing deBloise.

It all fit!

No, it didn't. The Vanek killed Junior…they admitted it openly. And Vanek never lie. Or did they? It was also generally conceded that Junior's death merely increased the margin by which deBloise's pet Equality Act was passed. So deBloise had nothing to gain from Junior's death. Or had he?

By the time he reached the roof, he knew where he was going. Not the spaceport…he had just two more stops to make before the spaceport: The first, his hotel room; the second, Danzer.

IT WAS DARK by the time he reached Danzer and there was a different Vanek sitting cross-legged inside the circle this time. A small flame sputtered before him and cast a wan glow on his features. This one was younger-middle-aged, Easly guessed—with a spot of dark blue pigmentation on his forehead. This Vanek would no doubt be as informative as the last one, but Easly had secured a small vial of gas from his hotel room, something to give him a conversational edge over the Vanek.

"Wheels within wheels, *bendreth*," the beggar greeted him.

"Wheels within wheels, yourself," Easly muttered as he squatted before him.

"Have you come again to meditate on our friend, Junior Finch?"

Easly started. "How did you know I was here before?"

"We know many things."

"I'll bet you do. Right now I'd like to meditate on someone else. I us name is Cando Proska. Know him?"

The beggar's eyes remained impassive. "We know Mr. Proska, but we do not fear his power."

The directness of the response surprised him. "What power?"

"The Great Wheel imparts many powers in its turning. Mr. Proska possesses an unusual one."

"Yes, but just what is his power?"

The beggar shrugged. "Wheels within wheels, *bendreth*."

Here we go again, Easly thought, and reached for a cigar. But there was a subtle difference here. Yesterday's beggar had an air of tranquility about him; he had sensed an innate passivity about that one. Today's beggar was something else entirely. Outwardly, he looked like a quiet, removed, contemplative sort. But Easly sensed that this was a thin veneer under which churned a very purposeful being. There was power here, and determination. This creature was not at all like a Vanek should be.

He took his time lighting the cigar. By the time the tip was glowing a bright red, both he and the beggar were enveloped in a cloud of strong-smelling smoke. This was the effect he desired, for he had removed the small gas vial along with the cigar and now had it palmed against his thigh and pointing toward the Vanek. A flick of his index finger opened the cock and the colorless contents streamed out.

Easly held his breath and waited for the vial to empty. It contained a powerful cortical inhibitor that worked as a highly effective tongue-loosener on humans. The gas, kelamine, was not entirely odorless, however, thus the improvised smoke screen. He had taken a considerable risk by traveling with kelamine. It was illegal on most planets—Jebinose included—and mere possession could result in imprisonment. There were no physical or mental after effects, but its use was classified as "chemical assault."

A vial was kept hidden in his luggage at all times for use in extreme circumstances. This was such a circumstance. He could only hope that the half-breed Vanek nervous system was human enough to respond to the gas.

When the vial was empty, he slipped it back into his pocket and allowed himself to breath again.

"What is Proska's power?" he asked again.

"Wheels within wheels, *bendreth*," came the standard reply.

Easly cursed softly and was about to get to his feet when he noticed the beggar begin to sway.

"I am dizzy, *bendreth*. I fear it is the smoke you make."

"Very sorry," Easly said with the slightest trace of a smile. A mild dizziness was the drug's only side effect. He ground the cigar out in the dirt.

"Perhaps you misunderstood my question," he said carefully. "I want to know what kind of power Mr. Proska possesses."

"It is a power of the mind," the Vanek said, and put a finger to his forehead.

Now we're getting somewhere!

\* \* \*

IT WAS FULLY an hour later when Easly returned to his flitter and took to the air. Even with the help of the kelamine, it had been hard work to pull any concrete information out of the Vanek; their minds work in such a circumspect manner that he almost had to start thinking like one before he could get the answers he wanted.

But Easly had his answers now and his new-found knowledge made him set a course for the spaceport at full throttle. His luggage was still at the hotel, and as far as he was concerned, it could stay there. There was only one thing he wanted now and that was to get off Jebinose.

His expression was grim as he dropped the flitter off on the rental platform and went to secure a seat on the next shuttle up. The mystery of Junior Finch's death and Proska's diabolical psi-talent had been cleared up. He shuddered at the thought of running into Proska now. The little man was no mere psi-killer as Easly had originally suspected. No, what Cando Proska could do to a man was much worse.

Larry Easly was frightened. He had faced danger before—in fact, at one point during an investigation last year, someone's bodyguard had placed the business end of a blaster over his left eye and threatened to pull the trigger— but it had never affected him like this. This was different. This was an unseen danger that could strike anywhere, at anytime, without the slightest warning. And there was no possible way to defend himself against it.

He didn't know the range of Proska's power. Did it require a certain proximity to its target to be effective, or could he just sit in a room somewhere and strike out at will? Every shadowy corner posed a threat now. His palms were clammy, his stomach felt as if something cold and sharp was clawing at it, and the skin on the nape of his neck crawled and tingled.

He was almost giddy with relief when the read-out at the reservation desk told him he had a seat on the next orbital shuttle leaving in one quarter of a standard hour.

On his way to the shuttle dock, he passed the subspace communication area and thought it might be a good idea to get a message off to Jo...just in case something happened to him.

He entered one of the large, transparent booths, closed the door behind him, and seated himself at the console. The locus computer informed him that it was midday at the IBA offices on Ragna. Not that it mattered: the subspace laser was the fastest means of communication yet developed, but it was still a one-way affair. Delay between transmission and reception could range from minutes to hours. And Easly was not waiting around for a reply anyway. The message would be automatically recorded at IBA and Jo would replay it at her convenience.

Easly noted the vid receptor before him and realized he was in a deluxe booth that sent a combined video and aural message. He shrugged and tapped in the IBA locus. All he wanted to do was get the message off, then get up to the shuttle dock. The extra expense was the least of his worries. A red light went on and he slipped his credit ID disk into a slot. The disk popped out and the light turned green. A two-minute transmission had begun.

Jo WAS SURPRISED to learn that she had a subspace call from Larry. He would only contact her like this under emergency conditions, so she ordered an immediate replay on her office vid screen. She started to smile as his face appeared, then remembered that he could neither see nor hear her. His voice was stern:

"This is a personal and confidential message for Josephine Finch—her eyes only. Please record the following without monitoring." He waited a few seconds, then his tone softened.

"I'll have to make this quick, Jo, and more cryptic than my usual since I don't know who else will see this before it gets to you. First off, as to your close relative's end, it's not at all what it seemed to be. The man you sent me here to investigate may well be intimately involved. And there's a wild card: a psi-talent who...who..."

Jo saw Larry's face go slack as his voice faltered. He swayed in front of the screen, fighting to keep his balance. Utterly helpless, Jo had to sit and watch in horror as his eyes rolled up into his head and he sank from view.

Picture transmission was not interrupted, however, and Jo anxiously watched the passers-by, hoping that one of them would glance in and realize that something was wrong with Larry. One man did stop and peer through the glass. He was short, sallow, and balding. His hard little eyes seemed to rest on the spot where Larry had fallen but he registered no surprise, made no move to help.

He merely smiled and turned away.

# XIII
## TELLA

Andy Tella had a strict personal rule against taking blind assignments. He not only insisted on knowing the immediate objective but the final one as well. This attitude had ultimately led to his failure as a Defense Force trooper: he hadn't been able to muster the reflexive obedience required to function successfully in a military unit.

He was bending his rule somewhat for the current assignment, however. The immediate objective was quite clear: secure the export contract for the Rakoan Leason crystals; do it in accordance with Federation conventions on relations with alien races...but do it. The ultimate objective remained vague, and that bothered him.

His first impulse had been to turn the assignment down. He knew nothing about dealing with aliens, knew nothing about Leason crystals other than the fact that they were used to line drive tubes and were extremely valuable, and had no desire to increase his knowledge in either area. But the request had come from Josephine Finch and she said the job was important and of a highly sensitive nature. It pertained to the deBloise caper, but she wouldn't say just how.

On faith alone, he had accepted the assignment and was now a passenger aboard IBA's own interstellar cruiser as it slowed into orbit around a cloud-streaked, brown-and-blue ball called Rako. The days on ship had been spent in encephalo-augmented study of everything known about the planet and the humanoids who inhabited it. Rako was a water-oxygen world circling an F3 star situated along the mutual expansion border of the Terran Federation and the Tarkan Empire. It had been discovered six and a half standard years previously by a Fairleigh Tubes exploration team on a follow-up mission after spectrographic analysis of its primary suggested the possibility of deposits of natural Leason crystals. They found them—huge fields of them.

They found something else, too. The planet was inhabited. They came upon evidence of intelligent life long before they found the Rakoans, however. Dead cities—dank, decaying, alloy-and-polymer corpses, some almost completely overgrown with vegetation—dotted the planet, indicating a sophisticated level of technology at one time. But no natives. It was initially suspected that a plague or biological catastrophe had wiped them out and the members of the exploration team breathed a sigh of relief—intelligent life forms on Rako would complicate matters by preventing them from claiming the planet for Fairleigh.

They decided to take a look at one final derelict city that appeared less overgrown than most of the others from the air. And that's where they found the last of the Rakoans. Besides their height—some of the adults were almost three meters tall—the most outstanding feature of the otherwise humanoid mammals was their thick, horny epidermal layer which was constantly flaking off. They had three fingers and an opposing thumb, wide-set eyes, and a shapeless nose that drooped over a lipless mouth equipped with short, flat, block-like teeth—a sure sign of a vegetarian.

And they were dying.

Not from disease, but from a birth rate that produced one healthy child for every twenty-three adults of the previous generation. The result was a very steep geometric regression in the planet's population—from an estimated five billion to roughly thirty thousand, most of them gathered in this single city.

That was one complication for the Fairleigh team. Then the Tarks arrived, claiming they had discovered the planet previously and were only now getting around to mining it. That was a transparent lie. The Tarks had long ago pirated the process for synthesizing Leason crystals and would have immediately begun stripping Rako of its natural deposits—with or without native permission—if they had been the first there.

The Federation stepped in then. It reminded the Tarkan Empire of the expansion treaty it had signed with the Fed nearly two standard centuries before. One of the major articles of the treaty outlined the accepted procedures for dealing with worlds inhabited by intelligent creatures. Since Rako fell into this class, the question of who discovered it first was irrelevant. The Empire and Fairleigh Tubes would have to make competing offers for a trade contract with the Rakoans, with the strong proviso that consent from the Rakoans be informed consent.

The Federation made it clear to the Tarks that it was quite willing to enter into armed conflict to protect the interests of Fairleigh and the Rakoans. Fairleigh, in turn, was advised to abide strictly by the conventions or Fed protection would be withdrawn from the company—not only on Rako, but throughout Occupied Space.

So the Terrans, the Tarks, and the leader of the Rakoan remnant got down to dealing. And that's where the third complication arose.

The Rakoans wanted more than money and technology in return for their crystals. They wanted a future for their race.

"I suppose you're well on your way to a solution by now, eh, Doc?" Tella said, fully aware that the answer would be negative.

He sipped a cup of hot tea as he sat across a table from Avery Chornock, the head of the research team on Rako. Chornock had disliked him on sight, and Tella sensed this. But he chose to ignore it, preferring to play the part of the brash, young, bonus-hungry company trouble shooter to the hilt. For that's how Chornock had labeled and pigeonholed him after reading his authorization from the Fairleigh home office.

"We're nowhere near a solution, Mr. Company Man," the lank, aging scientist rumbled. "And under present conditions, it's highly unlikely we'll ever get near one."

"What more could you want? You've got a full research team of your own choice here; you've got a subspace link to the Derby University computer, which is packed with every available scrap of information on human and non-human reproduction; and you've got an open-ended budget for any hardware you should need."

"Not enough!"

Tella considered this. If Dr. Avery Chornock, the number-one expert on alien embryology and reproduction in the Federation, was at an impasse, what could he contribute?

"What more do you need?"

"I need to be back in my lab at Derby U. investigating live Rakoan subjects. We've done all the cadaver work we need and I've exhausted the possibilities of field work on live subjects. I need to get a few males and females back to my lab for definitive studies and then I might—I said, might, mind you—be able to come up with something."

"None of the Rakoans will volunteer, I take it?"

Chornock nodded. "That is correct."

"Maybe they're scared of you."

"No. These people aren't scared of much. It's got something to do with their religion." He made a disgusted noise. "They'll all be extinct in a few generations and all because of some imbecilic superstition!"

One of the lab technicians stuck his head through the door. His expression was anxious.

"Vim is here."

Chornock twisted abruptly in his seat. "Are you trying to be funny or something?"

"Of course not!" the technician replied in an offended tone.

"Well, don't just stand there. Send him in."

The head disappeared and a Tarkan male entered a few seconds later. Tella had seen holos of them before, and had seen them on the vid, but this was the first time he had ever viewed a Tark in the flesh. There was quite a difference: the doglike face with its short snout and sharp yellow incisors was the same, as were the stubby-fingered hands, the barrel chest and the short, dark, bristly fur; but no vid recording or holo had ever managed to convey the sheer brute strength that seemed to ripple under the creature's exterior...nor the pungent odor that surrounded it like a cloud. It stood close to two meters tall and weighed 100 kilos easily.

A second Tark entered and stayed slightly behind and to the right of the first.

"Please have a seat, Dr. Vim," Chornock said, rising.

The Tark to the rear made some growling noises and the first Tark replied in kind. Then the second Tark spoke to Chornock in oddly guttural, but grammatically perfect Instel.

"No time, I'm afraid. I've been recalled."

"Oh no! This is terrible! Why?"

Again, the growling exchange between the two aliens. It was now obvious to Tella that the first Tark was Vim and that he didn't speak the Terran interstellar language. The translator turned back to Chornock.

"Too expensive, it seems. My superiors have interpreted our lack of progress as a sign that this race is doomed. They have decided to wait until its final members die off. Then there will be no need to make arrangements to pay these primitives for the crystals."

"Do you agree?"

"I do not see much hope for a solution under these conditions," the translator said after another exchange. He paused while Vim said some more, then continued. "Before I leave, may I say that it has been a privilege to share the same soil with you. I would have much desired to work at your side in this matter, but that was forbidden, as you know. I look forward to seeing more translations of your excellent papers. Good-by."

With that, the pair of aliens turned and left.

Chornock sat in silence for a few long moments. "A decent fellow, Vim. I know he's deeply disappointed."

"Didn't show it," Tella remarked.

"Tarks cannot afford to show displeasure with their superiors' decisions; from what I understand, such behavior tends to shorten their lifespan—if you catch my drift. But he's disappointed. The Rakoans pose quite a challenge. We could clone out new ones, of course, but their leader says that's an unacceptable solution. He wants true, natural biological reproduction reestablished on a scale that will ensure the future of the race. I can't blame him, but I'm afraid I can't help him either."

"They're sterile?" Tella asked. Chornock had lost some of his hostility as he talked about the Rakoans; he was almost likable.

"Sterility would be much easier to deal with. No, there are plenty of active gametes in both sexes—they just won't combine as they should. But I'm sure Vim's also disappointed about leaving the *bassa* behind."

"What's that?"

"A very fascinating grain rust with curious antibiotic activity: when an extract of the rust is ingested in sufficient quantity, it irreversibly incorporates itself into the metabolic pathways of any and all the bacteria in the body within one standard day."

"So?"

"So, when the extract is withdrawn, the bacteria die. The patient must be immediately reinoculated with his own enteric organisms, but the Rakoans seem to have the technique perfected. There doesn't seem to be any evidence of resistance, either."

"What about host metabolic pathways? Don't they get changed?"

"Apparently not—probably because the nucleoproteins of a larger animal don't replicate at anywhere near the rate of a bacterium's, so there just isn't time for the rust extract to insinuate itself into the metabolism. But I suppose if one made a steady diet of the rust…" He let the thought trail off.

Tella used this opportunity to make his exit. He rose. "Well, time for me to get to work."

"And just what kind of work might that be, Mr. Company Man?" Chornock asked, his surliness coming to the fore again.

"Convincing these aliens to send a few volunteers back to Derby with you, for one thing. Who can take me to them?"

"I'll let Sergeant Prather take you over—just to make sure you don't try anything foolish. You'll probably find him in the courtyard behind this building."

PRATHER WAS RUNNING his daily check on the a-g combat unit that stood in a sheltered corner of the courtyard. It towered a full four meters in height. Once inside, a seasoned trooper could clear a forest, level a city, or hide at the bottom of a lake for a month. Prather was the Federation Defense Force representative on Rako. A cruiserful of troopers waited in orbit. Just in case.

The sergeant was preoccupied and ignored Tella's request for a tour around the city. But Tella knew how to break through the soldier's barrier of military professionalism.

"Doesn't look like they've changed the unit much since I was in the Force."

Prather's glossy shaved head snapped up. "You were in the Force? When?" Tella was suddenly a real person to Prather.

"Eight standards ago. Infantry, like you. Used to be pretty damn good in one of these things."

"Howcum you're out?"

Tella shrugged. "Didn't get along too well with the brass. You know how it is."

"Yeah," Prather agreed with a nod. "They get to some people more than others. But you say you used to operate a unit like this?"

"Almost like it; this must be a newer model."

Tella stepped back and looked at the combat suit. It was squatter than the one he'd trained in, and looked lighter. Except for the prominent Federation star-in-the-ohm insignia, the unit's surface was a dull black from the anti-gravity plates in the feet to the observation dome on the shoulders, but only because it wasn't activated. In action it could assume any color scheme for instant camouflage.

"It's the latest. Easy maintenance, for which I'm glad at the moment. With the Tarks calling it quits on the research, there's no telling what they might try."

"You don't really think they'd try anything against Chornock and his crew, do you?"

"They wouldn't dare. They know we're fully armed up there," he said, jerking a thumb at the sky, "and they know I'm down here with my unit. We made sure they knew about that—although we were careful to hide the unit from the natives; they might not understand that this monstrosity is here for their protection. What I do worry about is the Tarks trying some sneaky way of wiping out the Rakoans so they won't have to wait for them to die of natural causes."

Tella was at once sickened and amazed at the simple, direct logic of such a solution. And if the Tarks were only one half as ruthless as their reputation, ways and means had no doubt long been formulated to bring about such an end.

"Well, I'm sorry, Sergeant," Tella said, turning away, "but I've got to get over to the Rakoan section of the city. And if you won't take me, I'll just have to find my own way."

"Now just wait a minute there…Andy, isn't it?" Tella nodded. "My first name's Bentham—Ben—and I don't see why I can't take a few minutes out to show an ex-trooper around the city. Let me get this lubricant off my hands and we'll be on our way."

It was Tella's first good look at the city. The Rakoans obviously had a thing for spires—every building he saw tapered to a graceful point. And there was a strange quality to the streets in the way they twisted and turned and interconnected around the buildings; almost as if the buildings had been set down wherever the constructor's fancy indicated, and the roads put in later as a sort of afterthought. The small, open flitter did not have to make many turns before Tella was hopelessly lost.

"You know where you're going, Ben?"

"Sure. I make the trip every day to keep an eye on the natives and make sure the Tarks aren't up to anything. You'll know we're there when we get there."

Tella puzzled over that last remark until they rounded the corner of the next building. There in a clearing stood a building without a spire. It was a low dome, remarkably crude in comparison to the other architecture of the city, and around it stood a circle of Rakoans, male and female, shoulder to shoulder.

"What's going on?"

"That's the temple of Vashtu, the ancient god of Rako. At any time of the day or night you can find five hundred and twelve natives standing around it as a guard. Why that particular number?" he asked, anticipating Tella. "If you remember that the Rakoans have four digits on each hand, it's no surprise that their number system has a root of eight."

Prather let the flitter glide toward an ungainly old Rakoan who was strolling toward the temple carrying a long wooden staff.

"That's Mintab, the leader of what's left of the natives. If you want to talk to someone, it might as well be him. He's the mouthpiece; his people make all their decisions as a group. And don't try to pull anything over on him—he's a sly old bird."

Mintab spotted the flitter and stood waiting as Prather grounded it; he joined the two humans as they debarked. It was an unholy trio standing there beside the vehicle: the tall, shaggy-skinned, floppy-nosed Rakoan, the short, dark, stocky Tella, and the glossy-scalped Prather.

The trooper introduced Tella as the-man-who-wants-to-buy-the-rocks. Although he addressed Mintab in the Rakoan tongue, Tella's crash encephalo-augmented course in the language during the trip out allowed him to understand what was being said. Speaking Rakoan, however, was a different matter—there were too many nasal intonations that were impossible to reproduce without practice—but he could manage to make himself understood if he kept it short and chose his words carefully.

"The furry ones have left," Mintab said, turning his gaze on Tella. "When will your people remove your doctor?"

"Soon," Tella replied in halting Rakoan. "No answer here. Must take some people away for answer."

"I have tried to convince my people of this but they will not listen." He glanced over to the encircled dome. "Don't judge us too harshly. Our manner of living was not always so primitive. Our dead cities tell you that. We once flew through the air and talked across the oceans. But there are no longer enough of us to maintain that level of technology. As our numbers collapsed, so did our means of production, and thereafter we ran out of precision parts. We are now reduced to this."

"But why won't your people cooperate?"

Mintab started for the dome. "Come. You will see."

The circle of Rakoans parted for the trio as Mintab led them into the crude structure.

"You are entering the temple of Vashtu, Giver of Light and God to us, his chosen race," he said. "Before you is his shrine."

In the center of the gloomy temple stood a huge statue; a good seven or eight meters in height, it was hand-carved out of a jadelike stone and showed one creature standing over the slumped form of another.

"It looks…old," Tella remarked lamely. The lighting, the postures, and the sheer size of the work gave it an eerie power.

"It is ancient. We do not know when it was carved, but throughout our recorded history it has been the focus for my race's religion…now more than ever. It depicts Vashtu triumphant over the fallen M'lorna, God of Evil and Darkness."

Tella moved closer. Vashtu was Rakoanoid with a sunburst for a face; he held a staff with a huge scarlet gem affixed to the end. The creature at his feet was indistinct, however.

"I can't see M'lorna."

Mintab motioned him toward the doorway where the light was slightly better. A carving on the wall showed a biped creature with a huge single eye where the head should be, and pincerlike hands. Its body was covered with alternating green and yellow stripes.

"That is M'lorna."

"But I still…do not understand…why your people will not help us help them."

"It was in this very place," Mintab said, "that Vashtu defeated M'lorna in the days when our world was new. But M'lorna was proud and swore that he would return and destroy the temple of Vashtu. The great Vashtu gave my people the mission of defending the temple when M'lorna returns.

"Generations ago, when our cities teemed with healthy millions, we forgot Vashtu and turned our minds and hearts to other matters. We left the temple unguarded. And for this dereliction, Vashtu has allowed our numbers to decrease. Soon there will not be enough of us to adequately guard the temple. And then M'lorna will come and destroy the temple at his leisure. When that happens, we will have failed Vashtu and he will cast our spirits adrift among the stars."

"But…" Tella searched for the phrasing and couldn't find it. But Mintab seemed to know what he wanted to say.

"None will leave the planet. A race that was once ruled by reason is again enslaved to superstition: They fear the day of the Dark One is near and feel they must be here. I have tried to tell them that Vashtu will understand that they left Rako for the good of the race, so that it might go on protecting the temple. But they insist it will be taken as a sign of further desertion of our sacred trust." The alien paused; then, "I would leave myself but I am beyond the age when I would be of use."

Tella could not read Rakoan expressions, posture, or vocal tone, but there was a very definite air of hopelessness about Mintab as they walked back into the waning sunlight.

He and Prather were halfway back to the Terran camp at the edge of the city when the idea struck him. It was daring, even by his own standards, and would either land him the crystal contract or land him in a Federation prison. He decided to check with Jo first.

On landing, he went directly to the communications setup and sent a carefully worded vocal message to Jo on Ragna. It went out via subspace laser and he decided to spend a little more time with Prather while waiting for a reply. He had given no details about what he planned to do, but had hinted that it was legally risky; he had also mentioned the antibiotic properties of the *bassa* and wanted to know if she could find a use for it.

Prather was back at work on his combat unit when Tella found him.

"Do they still have manual controls on the camouflage?" he asked the trooper. "I used to pull some fancy tricks when I was in the force."

Prather nodded and showed him the controls. There hadn't been any significant changes in the past few years; the console still had a familiar feel. Tella activated the skin, then adjusted the tint and pattern controls. Prather stepped back and began to laugh as the combat unit lit up like a red and white barber pole.

"Where'd you learn to do a thing like that, Andy?"

"This is just one of the many things that endeared me to my superiors during my four years in the force. Whenever I got bored I'd figure out a new way to dress up my unit. Even figured out a few pornographic ones if you're interested."

The communications operator came out then, saying he had a brief message from Ragna for Mr. Tella. Andy took the player and listened to the recording of Jo's reply. Her voice was clear but sounded strained:

> *Andy, I'm rushing off to Jebinose. Your success on Rako may be more crucial now than even before, especially if what you say about this bassa is true. As of now, you not only represent Fairleigh Tubes, but Opsal Pharmaceuticals as well, and can make tentative arrangements for them should the Rakoans decide to sell bassa. If you're successful, notify the interstellar news services without delay. Good luck."*

Tella handed the player back to the operator, then climbed back into the combat unit. "Tell me if this reminds you of anything, Ben."

He made some adjustments on the console, then closed the observation bubble over his head. The body, arms, and legs of the unit began to glow in green and yellow stripes while the observation bubble took on a brilliant blue-white color with a large black spot in the middle.

Prather's voice came through the earphones: "You know, Andy, that looks a lot like that God of Evil over in the temple. Whatsisname…?"

M'lorna," Tella whispered and activated the anti-grav plates.

THERE WASN'T MUCH LIGHT LEFT, but he didn't think he'd get lost. After all, he had no intention of trying to follow the streets. He climbed for altitude and headed in the general direction of the dome. It was easy to spot from the air and he circled around in order to approach it from the far side.

It was dark where he landed at the edge of the park, but infra-red lenses and image intensifiers gave him a day-bright picture on his screen.

Let's make this short but sweet, he thought, and started the unit on a slow walk toward the dome.

He was almost halfway there before one of the natives spotted the towering and all-too-familiar figure shambling out of the darkness. There was an instant of panic, then a great shout went up as the guardians quickly formed a barrier between M'lorna and the temple of Vashtu. Rakoans of every description—male, female, crippled, and infirm—poured onto the clearing from all sides to reinforce the living wall before the Dark One. Tella watched Mintab scurry inside the temple, then activated one of the lasers.

A beam of green light lanced out and scored a groove along the outer wall of the dome to his right, then arced over the doorway and grooved the left wall of the dome. And then M'lorna was among the Rakoans.

They smashed, bashed, slashed at him with fists, feet, rocks, clubs, and knives to no avail. Their proud defiance faded as they saw the God of Evil and Darkness wade inexorably through their ranks like a farmer through a grainfield. M'lorna was at the entrance to the temple of Vashtu, his ancient enemy, and nothing could stop him.

But before the Dark One could enter, a struggling, staggering Mintab emerged, holding high the jewel-tipped staff that had rested in the hands of Vashtu in the shrine. M'lorna halted abruptly and, as Mintab moved forward with the staff, gave ground. Then, before the eyes of the assembled faithful of Vashtu, the God of Evil and Darkness rose slowly, silently, and disappeared into the blackened sky.

"You're under arrest, Tella!" said Prather as Tella extricated himself from the unit. The sergeant's face was scarlet, and he held a gravity cuff under one arm.

"What's the charge?"

"How does assault on an alien population sound for a start?"

"What makes you say I assaulted anyone?" Tella knew he was in trouble but was not going to allow himself to be trapped into any admissions.

Prather smirked. "I monitored your screens from the moment you left.

I saw every move you made; even made a recording of it. You're in trouble, friend. You're going up to the cruiser for safekeeping, and from there you're going to Fed Central to face charges."

"But first he's going to make an abject apology to Mintab and the Rakoan people for desecrating their shrine!" said Chornock as he stormed into the courtyard. "He has completely destroyed whatever good will I've managed to build up with these people and I demand that he make an apology before he leaves!"

After a lengthy debate, Prather reluctantly agreed to ferry Chornock and Tella over to the Rakoan section of the city, but the trip proved unnecessary: Mintab was waiting for them by the flitter.

"My people will now go with the doctor to his homeland," he said without preamble. He stood tall and impassive in the dark, but his respiratory rate seemed to be more rapid than usual.

"B-but..." Chornock stammered.

"My people are celebrating now. They have successfully defended their temple and deserve to congratulate themselves. In the morning, however, we shall begin to make arrangements with this man to trade for the stones." He indicated Tella.

"I'm afraid Mr. Tella will not be here in the morning," Prather said.

"We will deal with no one else," Mintab shot back. It was a statement of fact.

Chornock and Prather glanced at each other, then shrugged. "Very well. He will be here in the morning."

"And *bassa?*" Tella asked, feeling relief flood through him; he was off the hook. "Will you trade *bassa?*"

"Of course. What we shall ask in return is continued work toward assuring the future of our race." His eyes bored into Tella's. "With help, my people will surely be here to protect the temple on the day M'lorna really comes."

Tella suddenly felt as if someone had rammed a fist into his solar plexus.

"Excuse me," he said in his native tongue as he backed away from the alien. "I've got a number of very important subspace calls to make."

# XIV
## JO

Traveling in a state of mental and emotional anesthesia, Jo barely remembered the trip between Ragna and Jebinose. One shock had followed another and it was only after the commercial liner she had boarded had gone into orbit around her destination that she began taking notice of her surroundings again.

Immediately after seeing Larry collapse during his subspace call, she had placed a call of her own to the spaceport on Jebinose. The administrator there informed her that an unidentified man had been rushed to Copia Hospital—alive but unconscious. Her next call was a message to the hospital stating that the man from the spaceport was to be given all necessary care and that all bills would be paid in full through a given account number at a sector bank.

Then came the next shock: after deciding to go to Jebinose herself and to take Old Pete with her—she didn't want him out of her sight—she discovered that he had departed for Jebinose days before. There could no longer be any doubt in her mind that Old Pete was involved in her father's death...and perhaps involved in whatever had happened to Larry.

Jebinose twirled below her now, looking like any other innocent, Earth-class planet. But Jebinose was different. Jebinose had killed her father and injured her lover. Jo was reluctant to board the waiting downward shuttle. She feared the planet.

Thoughts of her father tumbled into her head; sharp, clear memories that time couldn't blur. There had existed an indescribable bond between them that had been intensified after her mother's death to the point where at times she almost thought she knew what her father was thinking. She hadn't understood then why he had left her with her aunt and uncle and gone off to another planet. It had crushed her. She couldn't fully understand it now, but at least she could accept it. Her acceptance in no way, however, diminished the inner tension between the love she still felt for her father and the residual anger and resentment at what she considered a callous desertion.

She looked again at the planet outside the viewport and felt a pressure within her. She wanted to strike out at something, someone, anything. She was like a dying giant star that had collapsed in on its iron core and was waiting to go supernova. But she held on. You couldn't hate a planet. There was a human hidden somewhere on Jebinose who was responsible for what happened to Larry. She knew what he looked like—she had replayed the recording of Larry's subspace call over and over on the way out from Ragna until that balding head, sallow skin, and pair of merciless eyes were seared upon her memory. She fingered the tiny blaster in her hip pouch. She would find him…

She would find Old Pete, too. And what an explosive confrontation that would be. It was all his fault, really. If he had only stayed on his island in the Kel Sea, if he had only stayed out of her life, if he had only kept his suspicions to himself, she and Larry would probably be at the casino now playing a round or two of pokochess.

True, his suspicions had not been unfounded—there was most certainly a plot against the Federation and he deserved credit for recognizing it long before anyone else. But that could not absolve him from whatever he was covering up on the planet below.

The steward was signaling her that it was time to board the shuttle. With a deep breath and clenched fists, she turned from the viewport and walked toward the lock.


THE SPACEPORT OUTSIDE COPIA doubled as a port for intra-atmospheric travel as well and was jammed with people at this hour. Jo felt very much alone despite the crowd eddying about her. She didn't even have her own name to lean on—she was traveling under an assumed identity and had paid for her ticket in cash on the chance that someone might be looking for a traveler named Finch or one from IBA.

As she stepped out of a dropchute from the upper level, Jo saw her first Vanek, unmistakable in his dusty robe with his blue-tinted skin and braided black hair. He sat silent and cross-legged with his back against a column in the middle of the wide, crowded, ground floor mall. His left hand was folded inside his robe and his right held a cracked begging bowl in his lap. A few coins gleamed dully from the bowl. Passers-by took little notice of him and the Vanek, in turn, seemed oblivious to the activity around him. His hooded eyes were apparently fixed on something within.

Jo stopped and stared at the beggar momentarily. So here was one of the half-breeds who had killed her father. Perhaps the very one. Looked harmless enough.

With a quick shake of her head and shoulders—almost as if she felt a chill—she started walking. There were too many things to do before warp lag caught up with her to waste time sight-seeing. She passed within arm's length of the Vanek without another glance she certainly wasn't going to give him anything for his bowl—and didn't notice his eyes snap open and follow her as she moved away. She was about to round a corner when she heard a crash behind her.

Startled, she turned to see the Vanek beggar on his feet, statue still, staring at her with wide dark eyes. His earthen bowl was shattered on the floor, some of the coins still rolling away on end in random directions. The travelers passing through the mall slowed their comings and goings to watch the tableau.

Then the Vanek moved toward Jo, his step faltering, hesitant. Drawing to within a half meter of her, he stopped.

"It's you!" His voice was a hoarse, high-pitched whisper.

He reached out a spindly arm and touched her hand. Jo recoiled from the dry, parchment touch.

"It is truly you! The Wheel has turned full circle!"

He whirled abruptly and hurried away.

When he was out of sight, Jo shrugged uncomfortably and continued on her way. The momentary spectators around her did the same. Soon, only two small boys remained at the scene, picking spilled coins from among the shards of the forgotten begging bowl.

SHE FOUND A PUBLIC VIDPHONE BOOTH and called Copia Hospital. The Vanek incident moments earlier lingered in her mind. There was an eerie quality about the whole thing. He seemed to recognize her. Could he have somehow perceived the relationship between her and Junior Finch? She shrugged again. Who knew what went on inside a Vanek head anyway?

A middle-aged woman in traditional medical white appeared on the screen. "Copia Hospital," she said.

"I'd like some information on a patient named Lawrence Easly," Jo told her. "He was admitted as an emergency three nights ago."

"I'm sorry, but that is considered privileged information and not for release. If you wish, you may contact the patient's physician directly—"

"I was given to understand," Jo cut in, "that he was alive three days ago. Can you tell me that much?"

"I can tell you that he is stable and that's about all," the woman said, sensing Jo's concern. "Does that help any?"

"Yes, it does," Jo replied, relieved. That meant he was holding his own.

A sign on the wall outside the vidphone area glowed "Subspace Calls" and she followed the blinking arrow. The booths were located halfway down a long, low mezzanine that ran between the mall and the service area. Jo stood and surveyed the six deluxe booths. All were identical and it would have been virtually impossible to identify the booth she sought had she not noticed the tool cart sitting outside the furthest one.

A closer look revealed a man in coveralls crouching on the floor of the booth, peering through an inspection port.

Playing a hunch, Jo opened the door. "Find out what hurt that guy yet?" she asked.

The serviceman looked up. "Nothing in here hurt anybody, lady. Everything's in top shape." His attitude was defensive.

"I've got a few questions about these booths—" Jo began.

"Look, lady," he said with some annoyance, "I'm not supposed to say anything. If you've got questions, go ask them down at the main office. Addams Leasing—it's in the directory."

"Okay. I'll do just that."

She rented a flitter, punched in the code number of the company's main office, and sat lost in thought while Copia passed unnoticed beneath her. It stopped automatically above her destination and she brought it down for a landing on the roof.

Inside, a lean, hawkish man awaited her behind a counter. "May I help you?" he said in unctuous tones as she approached.

"Yes. I'd like some information on your subspace call booths."

A sign on the counter identified the man as Alvin Mirr and he brightened visibly. "Ah! You wish to lease some?"

"No, I just want to ask somebody a few questions."

Mr. Mires attitude cooled abruptly. "Oh. In that case, you can find all you want to know in this." He brusquely flipped a pamphlet across the counter at her and started to turn away.

"Listen, you!" Jo flared, flinging the pamphlet back in his face. "One of my employees—who happened to be in excellent health until he stepped into one of your booths—has spent the last three days in the local hospital, and whether or not you find yourselves up to your ears in a lawsuit may very well depend on the answers I get here today!"

Mr. Mirr suddenly became very accommodating. "You must be referring to that unfortunate incident out at the spaceport. We're terribly sorry about that, of course, but I can assure you unequivocally that our callbooths are absolutely accident-proof. Especially our deluxe models—they're shielded in every way with the finest insulation. Why, we even have a psi-shield on each and every one. We haven't overlooked a thing. And something else I should—"

"Wait! Stop!" Jo said, interrupting the torrent of explanations. "Did you say the callbooths have psi-shields?"

"The deluxe models, yes," he nodded. "For the utmost in privacy. The caller can even opaque the glass to guard against lip-readers if he so desires."

"But why a psi-shield?"

"Some very important and sensitive communiqués regarding high-level business and political matters go out from those booths. Our customers want to know that every effort has been made to ensure their discretion. They want to know that even a telepath can't eavesdrop on them."

Jo considered this for a moment. "Does it work in both directions?" she asked after a pause.

"I don't under—" Mirr began, a puzzled expression flickering across his face. Then, "Oh, I see what you mean. Yes, the psi-shield is non-directional: there's a damper effect on either side of the booth wall."

"Thank you!" Jo said and turned and headed for the root.

Next stop was Copia Hospital. She punched in the number and thought about psi-shields. Before collapsing, Larry had mentioned a "wild card," a psi-talent who was somehow involved—involved with her father or involved with deBloise, he never said. Then there was that horrible little man who looked into the booth after Larry went down. She wondered...maybe Larry was supposed to die in that booth and maybe the psi-shield saved his life.

But that would mean she was dealing with a psi-killer and such people were not supposed to exist. Of course, the psi-killers lurking about Occupied Space would certainly like everyone to think so. There had never been a confirmed case, but Jo was sure that somewhere a psi who could kill with his mind existed...in all of humanity's trillions on all the inhabited planets, there should be at least one—more than one.

One thing she knew: Larry uncovered something here, something potentially damaging to deBloise or his plans. There was even an intimation of deBloise's involvement in her father's death in that foreshortened call. But how could that be?

Unless Old Pete was the link.

The flitter slowed and hovered. Copia Hospital waited below.


Jo HAD NEVER BEEN inside a hospital before and she did not find the experience a pleasant one. It was as if the big building existed apart from the rest of society, isolated in its own time and space. The subculture here consisted of the physically ill and those who cared for them. Nothing else seemed to matter.

A nurse guided her to Larry's private room where she happened to catch his doctor on afternoon rounds. Most of the medical care as well as most of the scut work in the hospital could have been handled by machines at greater speed and at much less expense. But the fully automated hospital had been tried long ago...and found wanting. Patients simply didn't do well in them. There appeared to be significant psychophysiological benefit to be derived from personalized care by another human being, rather than a machine. And so the. physical presence of the attending physician at intervals, and the ever-present nursing staff, remained an integral and indispensable part of the hospital routine.

"At first we thought he was another case of the horrors," the doctor said. He was a heavy-set, swarthy man who spoke in clipped tones and wasted neither time nor words. "But we have ways of testing for the horrors, and this is definitely something else."

Jo was surprised at Larry's appearance—he looked so healthy. He lay quietly in the bed, breathing easily, a calm, untroubled expression on his face. He looked for all the world like a man taking an afternoon nap. But no one could wake him.

"The horrors," the doctor was saying, "is an unwillingness to respond to any external stimuli. The conscious and subconscious portions of the brain receive the stimuli but block response as part of the pathological process. Mr. Easly's problem is different: he seems to be suffering from complete deafferentation."

"You'll have to explain that term, doctor." Jo was listening attentively but her eyes had not moved from Larry's face.

"Well, it means that all—and I mean *all* external stimuli are being blocked from his conscious mind. For a crude analogy, think of a computer with all its inputs disconnected."

"And what could cause something like that?"

"Can't say. Was he a stable personality? We could be dealing with a psychotic state."

"He was about as stable as they come," Jo said, glancing at the doctor. "Could this…deafferentation, as you call it, be some sort of defense mechanism?"

The doctor's smile was condescending. "Highly unlikely. And if it were, it isn't a very good one. It's like sticking your head in the sand: it doesn't do much for the rest of the body."

"It does if someone's aiming at your head," Jo muttered. She caught a puzzled look from the doctor and changed the subject. "How long before he comes out of it?"

"Impossible to say at this point—tomorrow, a week, a year, I don't know. But he will come out of it."

"You're sure?"

"As sure as I can be with no past experience in this kind of thing. Our tests this morning showed a slight decrease in the level of deafferentation; we repeated them just before you came in, and if those show a further decrease, we'll be able to estimate the rate of improvement and give you a prognosis." So saying, he turned and left the room.

Jo returned her attention to Larry and the sensation of an impending internal explosion returned, more forcefully than ever this time. Larry should not be like this—he was such a strong, capable man, it was obscene to see him lying in a comatose state, utterly helpless. And there was nothing she could do to help him.

She grasped the top rung of the guardrail at the side of the bed and squeezed until her knuckles turned white and emitted little popping sounds of protest. She wanted to scream in frustration but held back. She would save it for the time when she caught up with the man who did this.

Eventually, she made herself relax with slow, deep breaths. She released the guardrail and paced the room with her arms folded across her chest. She was almost herself again by the time the doctor returned.

"He's making excellent progress," he said in a matter-of-fact tone. "Should be out of it in six or eight hours if he continues his present rate of reafferentation."

Jo's heart leaped. "How will he be when he wakes up?"

The doctor shrugged. "How can I say? Anything I tell you will be pure guesswork. He could be alert and well rested, like a man awakening from a good night's sleep, or he could be irreversibly psychotic. We'll have to wait and see."

The nurses were changing shifts then and the new head nurse came in as the doctor was leaving.

"Sorry," she said, "but visiting hours are over."

"Not for me," Jo said.

There was something in her tone that made the head nurse hesitate. She glanced at the doctor.

"Let her stay," he said. "It's a private room and she won't be disturbing anybody."

The nurse shrugged. "As long as you chart it as done by your authority, it makes little difference to me."

When they were gone, Jo dropped into a chair, then flipped a switch and watched as part of the outer wall became transparent. The sun was setting in gory splendor, she closed her eyes and let its bloody dying light warm her face until it was out of sight behind he neighboring buildings. A noise behind her made her turn.

The door was opening and through it passed a procession of five cloaked and hooded figures. The last to enter closed the door behind him and then all pulled back their hoods at once to reveal blue-gray skin, high-domed foreheads, and long black hair in a single braid.

Vanek!

Jo rose to her feet as the first visitor approached her. He appeared to be identical in features to the other four except for a spot of darker blue pigment to the left of center on his forehead. Although there was nothing menacing in their actions, Jo felt uneasy…these were the creatures who freely admitted murdering her father.

"What do you want?" she asked, and cursed her voice for the way it quavered on the last word.

The one who appeared to be the leader stopped before her and bowed at the waist. His four companions did likewise. Holding this position, they began a sonorous chant in the old Vanek tongue. There was a queer melodic quality to the sound that Jo found oddly soothing. As they held the final note, they resumed an erect posture.

The leader then withdrew his hands from beneath his robe. The right held a cracked earthen bowl, the left a delicate carving of a fruit tree in bloom.

"These belong to you," he said in a sibilant voice. Jo could not read his expression clearly. There was deep respect there, but it was overlaid with a mixture of awe and vindication.

She took the gifts and tried to speak, but found she could not. She knew they originally had been given to her father and holding them in her hands suddenly made her feel close to him again.

"The evil one is near," the leader said. "But he will not harm you again. I will see to that."

"Evil one!" she said, finding her voice at last. "Who is he? Where can I find him?"

"Wheels within wheels, *bendreth*," was the answer.

Then the five Vanek pulled their hoods up and filed out the door without another word. Dazed by the entire incident, Jo simply stood in the middle of the room and watched them leave. With the click of the closing door, however, she shook herself and hurried after them.

The hall was deserted. A nurse rounded the corner and Jo stopped her.

"Where did those Vanek go?" she asked.

The nurse cocked her head. "Vanek?"

"Yes, five of them were in Lawrence Easly's room just now."

"My dear," she said with a short laugh, "I've spent half my life working in this hospital and I've never seen one Vanek in these hails, let alone five! They have their own medicine." Her brow, furrowed momentarily. "Come to think of it, though, there have been an awful lot of them outside the hospital lately. I guess they could sneak in, but I don't know why they'd want to."

"But what about the room monitor?" Jo had noticed a vid receptor plate high on the wall opposite the foot of Larry's bed. "Didn't anyone see them on the screen?"

"We only monitor the patient's bed with that," was the terse reply. "Now if you don't mind, I've got work to do."

Jo nodded absently and returned to the room. She placed the bowl and statue on the night table and pulled a chair up next to the bed. This was where she would spend the night. She was tired, but somehow she doubted she would be able to sleep.

## XV
## DEBLOISE

Elson deBloise tapped in Proska's vidphone code and waited. He was calling from a public booth. In all the too-many dreadful years of his association with Proska, this was only the second time he had ever called him, and he was not going to entrust the ensuing conversation to his office phone. After the events of the past few days, there was no telling who might be listening in on that.

He waited for Proska's face to appear. How he hated and feared that little monster. How he wished he had never oozed into his office that day—was it really seventeen years ago?—and offered to put Finch out of the picture without force or violence. If only he hadn't—

The screen lit up with Proska's grim, pinched features.

"Well, well!" the little man said with genuine surprise. "What have we here? An eminent sector representative calling me on my humble vidphone! Such an honor!"

"Never mind the feeble attempts at humor—it doesn't become you. And there's nothing humorous behind this call."

"Well?"

"I've got an errand for you," deBloise said and watched carefully for Proska's reaction. He was going to cherish this—after seventeen years of catering to the monster's every whim, at last he had a demand for him.

But Proska remained impassive, only the slightest flicker of his dark-eyed gaze revealing anything untoward in the conversation. He waited in silence until deBloise was forced to go on.

"You failed. The booth was psi-shielded, and a source at the hospital informs me that the investigator you were supposed to eliminate will regain consciousness before morning."

"Investigator? I thought you told me he was some sort of a reporter."

"That's what I thought. That's what customs thought. His identification was completely phony. I had a few of my contacts check with the Risden Service and they never heard of him. The name he used, however, was legitimate: he is Lawrence Easly, a private investigator who does a lot of work in the business sector."

"Business? Why would he be checking up on you?"

"I don't know. I didn't say he was exclusively an industrial spy. Besides, I've been aware that I've been under some sort of surveillance for a number of years now and perhaps he's been behind it."

"But to what end?"

"Very possibly he works for someone with political ambitions who's preparing for the day when he meets me head-on and wants to store up a little dirt in advance."

"A potential blackmailer, then."

"Yes. Competition for you."

Proska's smile was not a nice thing to see. "No one could know what I know, could they, Elson? Or if they did know, they couldn't prove it like I can."

"That doesn't matter right now! If I'm exposed…if even a hint of what happened in Danzer should leak out, I'll be ruined. And that'll mean the end of your meal ticket. So I expect you to go over to the hospital and finish the job!"

"Dear Elson, how you've changed! I remember the horror and revulsion you expressed the first time I demonstrated my little specialty to you. And now you actually want me to use it twice on the same man!"

Proska's mocking observation stunned deBloise and his mind suddenly leaped back seventeen years to the day a lowly civil servant stood in his office—smaller and more sedate than the one he occupied these days—and told him he could "take care of the problem in Danzer." DeBloise had summarily dismissed the man, but the memory of his eyes and his expression when be spoke remained with him.

And when Tayes returned from Danzer a few days later with the news that Jeffers had capitulated and that the Vanek Equality Act would be as good as dead once word got out, deBloise knew he had to act immediately if he was to save anything. He contacted the little man and sent him to Danzer.

The next morning, all of Jebinose was shaken by the news that the man who had been pushing the Vanek cause in Danzer was dead. And that the Vanek had confessed—as a group—to his murder. So it was a natural reaction for deBloise to laugh in Proska's face when he showed up that afternoon demanding "compensation" for his services.

Proska did something to him then…something horrible…a little taste of his "specialty," as he liked to call it. And then he took him to the oldest, most run-down part of Copia, picked out a besotted derelict, and showed deBloise what happened when Cando Proska loosed the full force of his power on a man. But that wasn't the end of the show. Next stop was Proska's dim little flat where deBloise watched in horror as a vid recording showed him telling Proska to put an end to Junior Finch's meddling in Danzer. He was watching a copy. The original would be released to the public should any mishap, even slightly suspicious, befall Proska.

Cando Proska had been bleeding him ever since. And the thought of what Proska could do to him, politically and personally, had haunted him ever since, waking him in the night sweating, panting, and clawing at the air.

"I never realized then what you intended to do," he said hoarsely, snapping himself back to the present, "or what you could do."

"Would it have made any difference?" Proska sneered. "Finch showed the VEA to be a useless political charade. I saw that coming; that's why I came to you. Because once he succeeded, support for your Vanek Equality Act would have evaporated. And if the VEA went down, so would you! You remember how you looked on that recording—you were ready to do anything. Anything!" His tone suddenly became businesslike. "Speaking of the recording, it now resides on Fed Central, addressed to the Federation ethics committee."

DeBloise's face blanched and his voice shook. "Proska, I'd like to—"

"I know what you'd like to do, that's why the recording is where it is."

DeBloise struggled for control and finally regained it. After a long pause, he said, "Are you going to finish the job?"

"Certainly. But I need a way to get into the hospital without attracting too much attention. I require a certain proximity, you know."

"That can be arranged. I'll have my source at the hospital contact you. I'm leaving for Fed Central tonight. I hope everything is settled before my ship has made its first jump."

"Don't worry. I'll take care of everything."

# XVI
## JO

Jo was dozing lightly in a chair when the new head nurse came in during the changeover to the third shift and startled her to wakefulness.

"Sorry if I surprised you, dear," she said with a warm smile. "Just making my rounds."

She was older than most of the other nurses and seemed to have all her moves down to an almost unconscious routine. She checked the vital-signs contacts and gave Larry a long, careful look. Apparently satisfied, she smiled and nodded to Jo, then left.

The door was opened again a few moments later by a middle-aged orderly. He was short, sallow-skinned, and balding. He seemed unduly surprised to see Jo sitting by the bed.

"I'm sorry, miss," he said in a low voice, "but I'm going to prepare the patient for some final tests and you'll have to step out for a few minutes."

Jo shot to her feet and started to reach for her pouch, then changed her mind. "What? Must I?"

"I'm sorry...hospital rules."

"All right," she said resignedly, and started for the door, swaying slightly with fatigue.

When she passed behind the orderly, however, her whole demeanor changed. Her right hand shot into her hip pouch and pulled out a small but very deadly blaster. She had it pointed at the orderly's head and was squeezing the trigger when his peripheral vision caught the movement. He turned—

—and Jo had no body. At least that's the way it seemed. All tactile and proprioceptive impulses from her extremities and torso had been cut off. She was a head floating in the room. It was a sickening sensation. She could still use all her facial muscles and could move her eyes. Could she speak? She was afraid to try, afraid she'd only be able to scream. And she didn't want to do that, not in front of this creature.

"Not a fair play at all," he said mockingly. Jo's arm was still extended in front of her, the blaster still in her hand. He reached out casually and took it from her grasp. "Why would you want to blow a poor orderly's head off?"

Jo took a deep breath. At least she thought she did; there was no sensation of her chest expanding. She wasn't sure she could keep herself from gibbering with fear, but she would try to speak.

"I…" Her throat seemed to be closing; she swallowed and tried again. "I wanted to keep you from finishing what you started the other night."

Eyes wide, the little man moved closer. "How do you know about that?"

"I was on the receiving end of the subspace call he was making when he collapsed. You walked up, looked in, and walked away. I knew you were responsible."

"So," he said slowly, glancing between Jo and Easly, "it seems I made *two* mistakes the other night. Not only did I forget about the psi-shields on those booths, but I walked into the field of the visual pickup. I'm either getting old or I'm getting careless." He held up the blaster. "Tell me, would you have really used this on the back of my head?"

Jo tried to nod, but her neck muscles wouldn't respond. "Without the slightest hesitation." Her right arm remained extended with her hand a few tantalizing centimeters from the blaster, but she could not reach for it. The arm would not respond! It was as if it no longer belonged to her. She gave up trying and hunted for ways to keep the man talking. Maybe the head nurse would come back.

"Can you think of a better way to handle a psi-killer?" she added.

"Is that what you think I am?" he said with an amused leer. "A psi-killer? How quaint!"

"Aren't you?"

"My dear, to compare my capabilities to those of a psi-killer is to compare the transmitting power of a subspace laser to an ancient crystal radio."

Right then and there, Jo knew she was dealing with a monstrous ego.

"What can you do that's so special?"

His eyes danced as he looked at her, and suddenly she was—

—*nowhere. There was blackness, a total absence of light. There was silence, a total absence of sound. There was a total negation of sensation: she did not soar, she did not float, she did not fall. The blackness had no depth, nor did it press in on her. There were no dimensions: no time, no depth, no length or width—she couldn't even call herself a locus. She was nowhere and there was no way out. She began to panic. There were no reference points. If only she could find something to latch onto, to focus her mind on, she'd be able to hold her sanity. But there was nothing but nothingness. Her panic doubled. Then doubled again. Before too long it would overwhelm her consciousness and she'd be irretrievably insane. She—*

—was back in the hospital, a head floating in the room.

"Like it?" he asked, still smiling and watching her closely. "That's my specialty and that's how you'll spend the rest of your life. But first, some answers, please. We know this man is a detective—did you hire him?"

It was a while before Jo could speak. She was totally unnerved. She'd say anything to delay being sent back into nowhere, but right now she couldn't speak. He waited patiently. Finally:

"Yes. I hired him years ago to see what he could get on Elson deBloise." She would lie, but slowly and carefully.

"Why deBloise?"

"I represent a number of pro-Charter groups who think the Restructurists are getting too powerful. They want leverage against deBloise."

"Ah! Political blackmail!"

"The name of the game. But we never expected to run into anything like you," she added, trying to maneuver the conversation back around to what was undoubtedly the man's favorite subject: himself.

He bit. "And you never will! Even if you should walk out of this room and live for another thousand years, you will never meet another like Cando Proska! I was ten years old when I first found out I could hurt someone with my mind. I killed a boy that day. The knowledge of what I had done, and could still do, nearly destroyed me then. But no one believed I was responsible."

Although his eyes remained fixed in Jo's direction, he was no longer seeing her. "I never tried to use my power again, never had another contact with psionics until I was eighteen. I was walking through one of the seedier sections of our fair city one night when a young man about my age pointed a blaster in my face and demanded money." He paused and smiled. "I killed him. It was so simple: I just wished him dead and he dropped to the pavement.

"Suddenly, I was a different person!" he said, his eyes focusing on Jo again.

He was relishing the telling of his story—he had the power of life and death over anyone he chose, but no one knew it. He could not gloat in public and he desperately craved an audience.

"I began experimenting. I used the flotsam and jetsam of the city—the zemmelar zombies, the winos, the petty thieves, people no one would miss. I didn't understand my power then, and I still don't, but I know what I can do. I can shock a person into brief unconsciousness, or kill him instantaneously. Or"—again a pause, again a smile—"I can throw him into permanent limbo: not only complete deafferentation, as they call it, but complete de-*efferentation* as well. No neurological impulses can enter or leave the conscious mind. It is the most horrifying experience imaginable. You just had a taste of it and can appreciate how long your sanity would last under those conditions."

He began to pace the room. "I bided my time doing bureaucratic drudge work until I could find a way to make my special talents pay off. My patience was rewarded when I found I could help out Elson deBloise by working my little specialty on a troublemaker in a town called Danzer. If you were a native you'd have heard of the man—Junior Finch."

Had Proska been watching Jo at that moment, he would have realized that he had struck a nerve. Jo closed her eyes and clamped her teeth down on her lower lip. All fear was suddenly gone, replaced by a mind-numbing coldness. But in the center of that coldness burned a small flame, growing ever brighter and hotter. The sensation of an impending explosion was returning, building inexorably.

"I've heard of him," she managed to gasp after the slightest hesitation. "But I thought the Vanek killed him."

"Oh, they did!" Proska said with a laugh. "They said they did and the Vanek never lie. Perhaps you'll appreciate the story. The man, Finch, was posing a real threat to deBloise's political career. We came to an agreement: In return for certain financial considerations, I would take Finch out of the picture. I went to Danzer that night, waited for him to leave a little celebration he was having, and then intercepted him in an alley. He had been drinking, yet even in an alcoholic haze he gave me more resistance than all my previous experimental subjects combined. But I succeeded, as I always do. He was little more than a drooling vegetable when I left him, an apparent victim of a very severe case of the horrors. And that was the turning point of my life."

Jo was sick and nearly blind with fury at this point, but utterly helpless to do anything. Her voice was almost a sob. "But the knife—the Vanek knife."

"Ah!" he said, too enraptured by his own narrative to notice Jo's tortured expression. "That was the final and perfect touch! One of Finch's Vanek friends apparently happened on him in the alley and somehow realized what had been done to him—they have much greater depth of perception than pure Terrans. A knife in the heart is a true act of friendship to someone I've put into limbo. The death worked out very well for deBloise—his legislation passed with great fanfare and his political future was set. He gave me a little trouble by crediting the Vanek with ending Finch's interference, but I gave him firsthand experience in the range of my power, and he suddenly became quite agreeable. As an insurance policy, I have proof of his first-degree involvement in Finch's death ready to go to the Federation ethics committee should anything suspicious happen to me. All in all, my life is quite comfortable nowadays as a result of our arrangement."

He moved close to Jo now, his face inches from hers. "But so much for history. My hold over deBloise is weakened if anyone else knows what I know. Therefore, it is my sad duty to see to it that you and your detective friend never know anything again."

The room dimmed but did not disappear. Jo was ready for him this time and held on to reality with every fiber of her consciousness. Her mind was being fueled by a most formidable force: hate.

Proska's voice seemed to come from far away. "You put up a good defense," he said with amusement. "The last one to give me this much of a fight was Finch."

"Maybe it runs in the family," Jo heard herself say.

"What do you mean?" His tone was puzzled and the onslaught against her mind slackened ever so slightly. She screamed:

*"JUNIOR FINCH WAS MY FATHER!"*

The emotional bomb that had been building within Jo detonated then, and the force of the explosion coursed along the psionic channel that Proska had opened between them. It was an awesome thrust: the grief, the anger, the repressed self-pity that had accumulated within Jo since the death of her father had at last found a target. It merged with the fresh rage and fury sparked by Proska's coldblooded recounting of the destruction of her father's mind, and lashed out with one savage, berserk assault.

Proska reeled backward and slammed his palms over his eyes. His mouth opened to scream but no sound came forth as he toppled to the floor and lay flat on his back, unconscious.

Jo suddenly was aware of her body again. Her arms, legs, and torso were hers once more, but the legs wouldn't support her. Her knees buckled and she hit the floor. Consciousness began to slip away, but before it was completely gone, she saw a hooded, blueskinned head poke inside the door and peer about the room.

When Jo next opened her eyes, she found herself looking into the face of the night nurse. It took a few heartbeats to orient herself, then she looked across the floor to where she had last seen Proska. He was gone. So was her blaster.

"Where is he?" she asked, raising herself to a crouching position.

"Where is who?"

"That man! The one who was on the floor over there!"

The nurse smiled. "I'm afraid you might be just a little bit overtired, dear. You should take better care of yourself. You might have been lying on the floor here half the night if Mr. Easly hadn't buzzed."

"Larry!" Jo cried, leaping to her feet.

Larry Easly lay quietly in bed, his hands folded on his chest, a tired smile on his face.

"Hi, Jo."

Relief and reaction flooded through Jo as she crossed to the side of his bed and grasped both his hands. There were tears on her cheeks...for the second time in seventeen years, she cried. It was a joy to see Larry conscious again, to see life in his eyes and hear his voice. But there was something else...mingling in the relief was a curious, unfamiliar lightness of spirit, as if she had been purged of all doubt and grief and fear. She felt reborn, released from the past.

Except for Old Pete. There was still that reckoning to come.

"I'll leave you two alone a minute," the nurse said, "then he's got to go to neuro for retesting." She closed the door behind her.

"I'm okay, Jo," Larry said in a faint voice. "Just weak. So weak, it was all I could do to press the buzzer when I came to and saw you lying on the floor."

Jo's head snapped up. "Did you see anyone else on the floor?"

"No. Who do you mean?"

"Proska."

Larry's eyes widened. "You know about him?"

"He was here! He tried to do to me what he did to my father and almost did to you." She hesitated. "Were you in…limbo all this time?"

"No," he said, shaking his head vigorously. "But I know what you mean. A Vanek explained to me what Proska could do. No, I was unconscious. I don't remember a thing between the booth and this room. But where is he?"

"I don't know. Something happened when he tried to do whatever it is he does, and we both collapsed. He was on the floor last time I saw him." She glanced at the wall clock. "And that was two hours ago!"

"Well, I've only been conscious for about a quarter hour and he wasn't here when I came to." He tried to lift his head but the effort was too much. "That means he's free. Jo, we've got to get off Jebinose. Proska is the most dangerous man alive! I can't walk yet, but I'll go on a stretcher!"

The nurse returned then. "Time to go. The neuro crew's waiting for you."

"The only place I'm going is deep space!" Larry said with what little vehemence he could muster.

Ignoring him, the nurse flipped open the top of a small console at the foot of the bed. "You're going to neuro. Doctor's orders. Besides, you're too weak to go anywhere else." She tapped in a three-digit combination, then closed the console cover.

The bed began to roll toward the door and Larry looked around helplessly.

"Jo?"

"It's okay," she said. "I'll wait for you here." She was not looking at Larry anymore. Her eyes were riveted on a figure standing in the shadows out in the hall.

When the bed had disappeared down the hallway to the left with the nurse in tow, Jo went and sat in the chair by the window.

Old Pete entered. Jo's blaster was in his right hand and he crossed the room and laid it on the night table beside her.

"You won't be needing this," he said.

"You sure?" Jo's voice was flat, hard. Her eyes were on the wall.

"Proska is dead. He will probably be found shortly after sunrise in the park across the street. His hands and feet have been tied to a tree; the top of his skull has been removed and his brain has been smashed at his feet."

Jo looked at Old Pete's face and saw in it a sense of infinite satisfaction. "You?"

He shook his head. "No. The Vanek. They removed him shortly after he passed out here and then Rmrl came to my hotel room. He returned your blaster and led me out to view their handiwork."

"But I thought the Vanek never took any initiative—never acted on their own or anyone's behalf."

"They don't. Or at least they didn't until now." He took a deep breath and shivered. "For beginners, they sure don't fool around."

"How do the Vanek know you?"

"I met Rmrl seventeen years ago when I was looking into Junior's death."

"Is he the one with the blue spot on his forehead?"

Old Pete nodded. "He's the one who delivered the *coup de grace* on your father and he's been waiting in silence all those years for the Great Wheel to turn full circle and exact its vengeance on Proska. Your arrival prompted him into action. He was no longer a typical Vanek after his close association with Junior Finch, and when word of your arrival spread among the Vanek—"

"How did they know who I was?"

He avoided Jo's eyes. "They…knew. And Rmrl was determined to prevent the same thing that happened to Junior from happening to you. So he and a few of his friends decided to take Proska out of the picture, permanently. He had to die…there was no other way to handle him."

"I hope they catch up to deBloise, too!"

"They have no quarrel with him."

"They should—Proska told me that he went after my father at deBloise's direction."

Old Pete's voice was a whisper. "Then it's true!"

"What…?"

"It's true! DeBloise is involved. I've had that feeling in my gut for seventeen years and could never prove a thing! That's why I've kept such close surveillance on him all this time!"

"And what about Proska?"

"Never knew he existed until this morning when Rmrl told me all about him and showed me his remains."

There was a long silence. When Jo finally broke it, her voice was low but carried a sharp edge.

"Do you really expect me to believe that?"

"It's true."

She rose slowly to her feet and faced him. She wanted to believe it. She wanted everything over and done with and settled so she could get on with her life. But there were still too many dark areas concerning the old man.

She spoke the question that had hovered unasked between them since Old Pete entered the room.

"Why are you here?"

"On Jebinose? I came to see if I could help Larry. After all, I've been here before and—"

"Lie! You came here to cover something up—or to make sure it stayed covered. What is it?"

"Nothing!" He spoke the word without conviction, as if he knew he would not be believed.

"Another lie! The only connection between you and Jebinose is my father—and he's dead. You're somehow involved in that and I want to know how!"

"Never! I'd never do anything to hurt Junior. How can you say that?"

"The Vanek told me, 'He will not harm you again.' Did he mean you?"

"No! He meant Proska!"

"Impossible! Proska didn't even know I existed until tonight. How could he hurt me 'again'?"

Old Pete blanched and said nothing.

Turning to the night table, Jo picked up the blaster and pointed it at the old man's head.

"Tell me now or I swear by all I believe in I'll burn a hole in you! What was your involvement in my father's death?"

Her eyes told him that she was not bluffing. She had tasted vengeance tonight and was not going to stop until all accounts were settled. Old Pete began to tremble. He found a seat by the far wall and slowly lowered himself into it. Looking up, he held Jo's angry glare and spoke in a dry, cracked whisper.

"Junior Finch isn't dead and he wasn't your father."

The words lay on the air like dead fish on a stagnant pond. Finally, Jo shook her head as if to clear it.

"What are you saying?" She was nearly insane with rage. "Do you think you can get yourself out of this by concocting some wild—"

"It's true! Junior Finch was completely sterile as a result of the radiation leak that almost killed him when he was eighteen. He didn't produce a single gamete from then on. The histology report on the genitourinary system in the autopsy reconfirmed this, and I paid an ungodly sum to have that part wiped."

Jo's finger tightened on the blaster trigger. "But you said he isn't dead! How can you have an autopsy report on a man who isn't dead?"

Old Pete held up his hands. He was tired, defeated, and more than a little frightened by what he saw in Jo's eyes.

"Just let me continue. When your grandfather found out Junior was sterile, he was crushed. It meant there'd be no Finch beyond Junior to carry IBA into the future. That was important to him. He set great store by family—didn't start one till late in life, but once he had one, it became the prime focus of his life. Junior was one child, IBA another. He wanted them both to go on forever. Me, I couldn't care less."

"Get to the point."

"I am: your grandfather—a most persuasive man—talked Junior and his wife into cloning a child from Junior. I helped them arrange it." He paused. Then, regretfully: "You are that child."

"But I'm female. Junior Finch was male." The blaster did not waver. "A clone is an exact genetic duplicate."

"Surely you know that a female can be cloned from a male. All that needs to be done is to discard the Y chromosome and duplicate the already existing X. That's basic genetics. They decided on a female clone to head off any possible future suspicions. A male would grow up to look exactly like its donor, and if anyone ever raised the question, it would take only a simple chromosome test to put Junior in jail and you in a molecular dissociation chamber. There are laws against clones, remember? A female was safer."

Jo lowered the blaster. She believed him. The same instinct that had told her he was lying before, now told her that Old Pete was telling the truth. And it fit. It explained a number of things, especially the awe she seemed to inspire in the Vanek—they had recognized her for what she was.

Jo was inspiring a little awe in herself right now. She should be reeling, numb, crushed, shattered. But she wasn't. She felt strangely aloof from the revelation, as if Old Pete were talking about someone else.

"I've kept this from you all along," he was saying. "I never wanted you to know. When I went, I was going to take it with me since Junior's death left me the only one alive who knew. Even the technicians who did the cloning never knew whose cells they were working with."

"Why would you keep that from me?"

"Because I didn't see any purpose being served by telling you that you're not a real person under the law. I didn't know how you'd react to being a clone…that knowledge could destroy someone. Don't you see? Junior Finch isn't dead. He's you—and you're Junior Finch."

Jo answered without hesitation, her voice tranquil and full of confidence. "No. I'm Josephine Finch. I always have been and always will be. Junior Finch lies buried out there. Josephine Finch will go on living as she always has—as Josephine Finch."

It was a declaration of identity that brought Old Pete to his feet and made his face light with relief. Jo knew who she was and intended to remain who she was, no matter what her origins. He stepped toward her, falteringly, until he stood before her.

Placing his arms on her shoulders, he said, "I'm proud of you…Josephine."

She dropped the blaster and hugged him. She wanted to speak, wanted to tell him how glad she was that his only crime was trying to protect her, but her larynx was frozen. She could only squeeze his thin old body very hard.

Old Pete understood and held her until his arms ached. Then he pushed her to arm's length.

"Can we be friends now?"

Jo nodded, smiled, then began to laugh. Old Pete joined her and only the return of Larry and his bed prevented them from breaking into tears.

"What's so funny?" he asked. His voice sounded stronger than before. "And what are you doing here, Pete?"

Jo waited until the bed had moved back into its old position, then sat on it next to Larry.

"He came to see if we needed any help," she said with a smile.

'Well, we do. We've got to put some distance between Proska and us—"

"No," she said. "He's dead. The Vanek killed him." She then went on to tell Larry and Old Pete about Proska's blackmail scheme against deBloise.

"What a totally vile, amoral character!" Old Pete said when she was finished.

"Almost as bad as deBloise," Jo replied coldly. "He sent Proska to Danzer, then used my dead father's name to further his filthy career."

She realized she still thought of Junior Finch as her father, and no doubt always would. And someday, she would explain it all to Larry. But now was certainly not the time.

"But, Jo," Larry said. "A Vanek committed the actual murder."

"He did the right thing." Her voice was soft now. "I'd want the same for myself…you don't know what it was like. The Vanek did the right thing for Proska, too. But the deBloise account stays open."

"He's not even on Jebinose," Old Pete said. "Left for Fed Central yesterday. I heard it on the vid while I was getting dressed earlier."

"DeBloise is finished already," Larry said. "At least he is if what Proska told you about the recording is true."

"It's true. There was no reason for him to lie to me. He said the original would go to the Federation ethics committee if 'anything suspicious' happened to him. When the news of his death is released, I'm sure the person to whom he entrusted the recording will find the circumstances sufficiently suspicious to warrant its forwarding to the committee." Her smile was grim. "It should arrive within the next standard day. And that should put an end to deBloise's career."

"Well, that's fine," Old Pete observed testily, "and it's well deserved, and it's about time. But it doesn't do anything for the purpose for which we all became involved in this mess. What's there to keep the rest of the Restructurists from carrying through with the Haas plan, whatever it is?"

"That may not be a problem any more," Jo said, her smile brightening. "I'll know for sure after I make a single call."

She went to the vidphone by the bed and asked to be connected with the Jebinose brokerage house, galactic stocks division.

"At this hour of the morning?" Larry asked.

Old Pete explained: "The Galactic Board never closes, Larry; and on a sparsely populated planet like Jebinose, there's usually only one office dealing with galactic stocks. So, to take orders from all over the planet, they have to stay open 'round the clock. The younger brokers usually get stuck with the night watch."

"But what's all this got to do with deBloise and Haas?"

"I haven't the faintest idea," Old Pete said with a shrug.

"You will," Jo said as she waited for a connection. "I'll explain it all just as soon as I get a few quotes."

A youngish male face appeared on the screen. "Galactic stocks division," he muttered wearily.

"Good morning," Jo said with as much pleasantness as she could muster. "I've decided to buy stock in a couple of companies and would like to know the current selling price."

"Surely. Which ones are you interested in?"

"Fairleigh and Opsal."

The broker's hand had been reaching for the computer terminal built into his desktop with the intention of punching in the company names. Jo's words arrested the motion. He smiled wanly. "You and everybody else."

"What do you mean?"

"I mean that it seems like half of Occupied Space wants to buy shares in those two companies. I've been trying to beam in a bid all night and I can't even get through!"

"Why the sudden interest?"

"It started as an unsubstantiated report by one of the news services that Fairleigh had tapped a lode of natural Leason crystals and that Opsal would soon be coming out with the most revolutionary antibiotic since penicillin. When the companies confirmed, the Galactic Board began to go crazy. Everybody wants to get in on the ground floor. Let's face it, Fairleigh will be able to cut its production costs by a half—it's going to have the peristellar drive field pretty much to itself for a while. And Opsal's new product is going to make hundreds of other antibiotics obsolete."

"May I leave a buy order with you?"

"Yes," he sighed, "but I don't think I'll be able to do anything for you until the stocks split—which I expect to happen any minute."

"How about Teblinko?"

"Down. Way down."

"And Stardrive?"

"Same story. A lot of people are trying to dump their Stardrive and Teblinko for Fairleigh and Opsal. As a matter of fact, the whole Star Ways family is being hurt by this. Now, how many shares did you want to—"

"Thank you," Jo interjected with a pleased smile. "You've been most helpful." She abruptly broke the connection and the broker's startled visage faded from the screen.

"What was that all about?" Larry asked.

Old Pete shook his head in admiration. "My boy, you've just seen the largest conglomerate in Occupied Space knocked on its ear! And your lady friend here is the one responsible for the whole thing!"

"I had a lot of help from Andy...couldn't have done it without him, in fact."

Larry struggled to a sitting position. "Now wait a minute! Why does everybody seem to know what's going on here except me? And how did Andy get involved?"

Jo slipped into the chair next to the vidphone. "I said I'd explain, so let's start with the Restructurists. The main thrust of all their activities and all their rhetoric is to get the Federation into the free market and start exercising some controls on the interstellar economy—that's where real power lies. But the LaNague Charter prevents the Federation from doing anything of the sort. So, the Restructurists must find a way to nullify the charter, and the only way to do that is to activate the emergency clause."

"If you remember your Federation history, Larry," Old Pete added, "that's the clause that temporarily voids the entire charter and thus all the limits on the Federation as a government. LaNague disowned it, even though it was designed to be activated only in times of threat to the Fed and its member planets; he wanted no emergency powers at all and fought tooth and nail against the clause. But he was ignored and it was tacked on against his protests."

"I vaguely remember learning something about that once," Larry said, "but it's not exactly recent history."

"Maybe not," Jo replied, "but it's very important history to the

Restructurists. They've had their eyes on the emergency clause for a long time—it's the one weak spot in the charter. And this time they figured they'd found the way to get to it. The Haas warp gate was going to be the trigger to activate the emergency clause."

She leaned forward and alternated her gaze between Larry and Old Pete. "Now comes the tricky part. DeBloise and his circle were pouring enormous amounts of money into the warp gate and pushing Haas to market it prematurely—before the final improvements which would have made it a truly revolutionary product. No intelligent investor would do such a thing; it was financial suicide. And since deBloise is anything but a fool, I could interpret the situation only one way: the Restructurists wanted the gate to be a tremendous commercial failure.

"Why would they want to do that? It baffled me until two things clicked: Haas's statement about military contracts and Old Pete's joking reference to the Tarks. That's when I knew what deBloise was up to."

"I think I'm beginning to see," said Old Pete with a slow smile.

"I'm not!" Larry snapped. "What have Tarks and warp gates got to do with the Federation charter?"

"The Tarks are on their way to becoming a big problem," Jo explained. "There are numerous areas of conflict between Terran and Tarkan interests, and the list lengthens each year. Keeping that in mind, and considering the potential military uses of the gate in a wartime situation, you can see what a perfect lever it could be against the emergency clause.

"Let me give you the scenario as I believe it was planned. DeBloise and the other Restructurists involved were going to push the gate onto the market prematurely and wait for the inevitable: Star Ways would drop the price on its warp unit and suck off most of Haas's potential customers. When the Haas company collapsed, SW would make a nice offer to lease production rights to the gate—an offer that would make Haas richer than he'd ever dreamed. But Denver Haas, like a spoiled child, would take his ball and go home.

"That's when the deBloise circle would leap into action. They'd rush before the various defense committees and claim that continued sale and development of the warp gate was an essential preparation against the inevitable day when the Federation clashes violently with the Tarkan Empire. They'd claim that unregulated competition was depriving the Federation of the gate and would demand invocation of the emergency clause in order to intervene against SW and save the gate.

"It would be difficult to oppose them if they managed to generate enough fear. Not only would they be screaming 'security,' but they'd be painting the emotional picture of a huge conglomerate destroying a tiny company and the entire Federation suffering as a result of it. I'm sure they'd have got some sort of economic control out of it."

"And that would have been the beginning of the end," Old Pete said.

"Right. So I took aim at the one variable they figured to be a constant— Star Ways. Conglomerates are less susceptible to changes in the market, but they're by no means immune. With Andy Tella's help, I was able to put a few dents in two of SW's major subsidiaries. There's no way it can wage a successful price war against Haas now."

"That's all fine and good," Larry mused, "but without you the gate would have been lost. That doesn't say much for the free market."

"It says that the market deplores stupidity!" Old Pete replied in a loud voice. "It would be damn stupid for anyone to push the gate onto the market before the final refinements were perfected. Anyone with the idea of profiting from an investment would have waited. You forget—deBloise wanted the gate to flop; his profit was to be political, not financial.

"But enough of this talk. It's all worked out for the best. The Federation charter is safe, the warp gate will be on the market when we need it, and a certain murderer has received a long-delayed sentence. I think we should celebrate!"

"Not yet," Jo said, her facial muscles tightening and her eyes going crystalline. "Not until I've personally seen Elson deBloise thrown out of the Federation."

"You're not going without me!" Old Pete said.

# EPILOGUE

They arrived at Fed Central just in time. The ethnics committee had not delayed a moment after receiving Proska's package of damning proof. Its members confronted deBloise with the evidence that he was directly responsible for the murder of another man in order to further his own political career.

DeBloise, of course, denied everything, calling it a plot instigated by the various anti-Restructurist factions within the Federation. The ethics committee was unmoved and decided that the evidence would be presented to the entire General Council at its next session. DeBloise asked, and was granted, permission to address the Council before the charges and evidence were presented.

Jo and Old Pete arrived in time to catch the tail end of his speech:

"...that this is not government! We have tried to demonstrate this fact to you, but all in vain. We have tried for years, for centuries, to open your eyes, but you refuse to see. You refuse to see the chaos of the non-system of non-government in which you dwell. We have tried to bring order to this near-anarchy but you have repeatedly refused it.

"And now..."

He let those two words hang in the air. He was using his considerable oratory talents to the fullest, knowing his performance was being recorded, knowing it would be played and replayed on vid news all over Occupied Space.

"And now you have stooped to smearing my reputation! Do you really believe that the other progressive members of this body would accept the trumped-up charges against me as true? They are not fools! They recognize a cynical plot when they see one! We have caucused for days, we of the Restructurist movement, and after much soul searching and heated debate, after innumerable subspace messages to the planets we represent, a decision has been reached."

Again, he paused for full effect, then:

"The worlds that stand shoulder-to-shoulder in the Restructurist movement have decided that they can no longer be a party to this insane chaos you call a Federation!

"Be it known," he said into the rising tumult from the floor, "that we are seceding from the Federation—seceding from anarchy into order. Travel in the trade lanes through our sectors is here now restricted to ships of those companies that seek and receive prior approval from the new Restructurist Union. Unauthorized craft infringing upon our territories will be seized. We shall fire on sight at any craft bearing the emblem of the LaNague Federation. From this day on, we govern our own!"

With a dramatic swirl of his cape, Elson deBloise descended from the podium and strode down the central aisle of the General Council assembly hall. As he moved, other Restructurists, Philo Barth and Doyl Catera among them, rose and followed him. The rest of the Council watched in stunned silence.

Jo and Old Pete were standing by the main door to the assembly hall as deBloise passed. He glanced at Jo as he strode by but paid her no more attention than he did any other spectator. With the collapse of Teblinko and Star Drive on the stock exchange, his scheme to use the Haas gate against the Federation charter was voided; and with the delivery of Proska's blackmail package to the ethics committee, his personal freedom, as well as his public career, were about to suffer a similar fate. A Restructurist-Federation split was the only way to salvage anything.

And so he passed within a half-meter of Josephine Finch, never realizing that this tame-looking female had blasted all his plans, all his lifetime dreams of power to ruins. She was just another tourist and his glance flicked away as he went by.

A vid reporter was scrambling around the antechamber to the assembly hall looking for reactions to this startling, historic announcement. He spied Jo and Old Pete and approached at a trot.

"Pardon me," he said breathlessly, "but I'd like to know what you think about the Restructurist secession." He pointed the vid recorder plate at Old Pete. "Do you think there's a chance of war?"

"Hardly," Old Pete replied slowly. "It's a bold move, all right—certainly a surprising one—but to talk of 'war' is a little melodramatic. Oh, I'm sure there'll be skirmishes over resource planets. But these will no doubt be referred to as 'battles.' I foresee nothing on a large scale."

"Yes. Well, uh...thank you, sir," the reporter said, obviously displeased. Calm, rational answers were of no value to a good vid newscast—they slowed up the pace. He turned to Jo in the hope of finding a little feminine hysteria.

"How about you, miss? Do you think there was really a plot to assassinate Elson deBloise's character?"

Jo's mouth twisted mischievously. "Wheels within wheels, *bendreth*," she said in a solemn tone.

Then she linked her arm with Old Pete's and together they walked toward the exit, laughing.

It is given that the Tarkan Empire would never have initiated the Terran-Tarkan War if it had not been tempted by the inflamed rhetoric and spectacle of a civil war between the Federation and the Restructurist Union.

It is also given that the Restructurist secession from the Federation was precipitated when serious criminal charges were brought against Elson deBloise, the movement's most prominent member at that time. Restructurist apologists today say that the charges were false and never proven; other students of the period think otherwise. Both camps, however, agree on this: after the secession, the packet of evidence against deBloise was forwarded to Jebinose but mysteriously disappeared on the way.

One thing is certain: the contents of that packet significantly altered the course of human history.

from STARS FOR SALE:
AN ECONOMIC HISTORY OF OCCUPIED SPACE
by Emmerz Pent

THE END

# HIGHER CENTERS

He didn't know how long he had been sitting there, looking out through the dirty window without seeing anything, when a movement caught his eye. A small dog, a mongrel with a limp, rounded a corner and loped down the near-deserted street. Something about the dog made him lean forward in his chair and stare intently. And while his eyes were riveted on the animal, his mind reviewed the events of the past few weeks in a effort to make a connection between the dog and the catastrophe that threatened Morgan City and the rest of the planet.

DECKER EISELT GNAWED AT A STUBBORN CUTICLE as he gazed from the flitter window. He was short, very dark and had an intelligent, fine-featured face. He was presently engaged in marveling at Morgan City which lay spread out below him. This was hardly the first time he had seen it from the air but the perfect harmony of its layout never failed to stir him. This was a city as cities should be—a planned city, a city that knew where it was going, a city with a purpose.

Discounting a few large islands, Kamedon had only one continent and Morgan City occupied its center, a fitting capital for a world that had become one of the centers of Restructurist ideology and the pride of the Restructurist movement.

Yes, Morgan City was beautiful as cities go, but Decker Eiselt preferred the coast. The university was there and the years spent near the sea in study and research had instilled a narcoticlike dependency in his system…without the continual dull roar of the surf and a certain, subtle tang in the air, he could not feel quite at ease, could never relax and feel at home.

And then there were the fishermen. During his stay in Morgan City he would miss rising early with the sun glaring on the water and watching the fishermen head out the harbor as he and Sally ate breakfast. Most of the men on those slow, ponderous boats were salaried by the government fisheries but a few diehards still insisted on free-lancing and trying to earn more by catching more. Eiselt detested their stubbornness but their spirit struck a resonance somewhere within him and he was forced to admit a grudging admiration for them—until they got out of hand, of course.

He idly wondered if there could possibly be any connection between the disorder at the local fishery the other day and his being called to Morgan City, but promptly dismissed the thought. He was a research physician and had nothing to do with fisheries. And besides, the incident had been minor by any standard, just some pushing and shoving at the pay window. Some of the local fishermen—the free lancers especially—had become angry when the pay authorizations were delayed. Nothing to get excited about, really; this was the first time such a delay had ever occurred and would no doubt be the last. The Department of Sea Industries was far too efficient to allow such an oversight to happen a second time.

They were coming in for a landing, now. The roof of the Department of Medicine and Research's administration building grew large beneath them as Eiselt's darting brown eyes strained to recognize the figure waiting below. It was Dr. Caelen, no doubt. Eiselt hadn't liked being called away from his work for some mysterious reason that would not be explained until he arrived in Morgan City, but an unmistakable note of urgency had filtered through the message.

And so Decker Eiselt chewed a cuticle as he did whenever he was puzzled. What was the urgent need for a research physician? And why the mystery? He smiled grimly. No use in getting worked up about it; he'd know soon enough. He didn't have much choice in the matter, anyway: when Dr. Alton Caelen summons you to the capital, you go to the capital. Immediately.

* * *

THE FLITTER TOUCHED DOWN WITH A JOLT and Eiselt, the only passenger, hopped out as soon as the engines were cut. A lean, graying man in his fifties stepped forward to meet him.

"Decker!" he said, shaking his hand. "Good to see you!"

Eiselt couldn't reply. Was it…

Yes, it was Dr. Caelen and he looked terrible! Bright eyes gleamed from sockets deep-sunk in a lined and haggard face.

"Dr. Caelen!" he stammered. "I…"

"I know," the older man said quickly. "You're about to say I look like death warmed over and you're right. But we'll talk about it downstairs."

Caelen led him to the elevator and kept up an incessant flow of trivia on the way down, punctuating each phrase with quick, nervous gestures.

"How's the wife? Very pregnant and very happy, I suppose. Lovely girl, Sally. Dr. Bain's taking care of her, I suppose. Good, good. How about that little disturbance out your way? Unfortunate, very unfortunate. But things may get worse before they get better. Yes, they may well get worse."

Stimulants? Eiselt asked himself. Dr. Caelen was definitely hyper. He had never seen the man so worked up. After reaching. his office, however, he visibly sagged and Eiselt could no longer contain himself.

"My God, Doctor! What's happened to you?"

"I'm not sleeping very well," he replied simply and calmly.

Under normal circumstances, Eiselt would have waited for an invitation before sitting down but these weren't normal circumstances. He grabbed the nearest chair and, without taking his eyes off Caelen, slowly sank into it.

"There must be more to it than that. A sedative will cure insomnia."

Caelen followed Eiselt's lead and fell into the chair behind his desk before answering. "There's not much more to tell, really," he said, putting his hands over his temples and resting his elbows on the desk top. "I just can't seem to get enough air at night. When I doze off, I wake up a few minutes later, gasping frantically. And it's getting worse."

Eiselt repressed an audible sigh. Pulmonary diseases had been his field of research for the past ten years and he felt as if he were on firm ground again. His muscles relaxed somewhat and he settled more comfortably into the chair.

"Was the onset of symptoms slow, or abrupt?"

"Slow. So slow that I didn't become concerned until recently. But I can trace it pretty clearly in retrospect. The symptoms started showing up during my daily exercises—"

"You mean you have respiratory troubles during periods of exertion, too?"

"Yes…sorry if I gave you the impression that I'm only bothered when I'm trying to sleep. The problem isn't that simple. You see, about nine months ago I started noticing little irregularities in my breathing rhythm as I exercised. I didn't pay too much attention to it at the time but it's got to the point where short, simple exercises, that I formerly performed with ease, leave me gasping for air. Two or three months ago I started having sleeping problems. Nothing much at first: restlessness, insomnia, inability to sleep for more than an hour at a time. Things have progressed to the present stage where I can hardly sleep at all. And, unless I concentrate fully on my breathing, I can't exert myself in the slightest."

"Are you having any difficulty right now, just sitting and talking?"

"Only a little, but I find myself out of breath at the oddest times."

Eiselt mused a moment. "The syndrome, as you've related it, doesn't ring a bell. I'd like to make some tests, if I may."

"I figured you would," Caelen said and managed a smile. "The lab downstairs will be at your disposal."

"Good. But one question: Why me? There are plenty of others in Morgan City who could handle this, many of them right in this building. Of course I'm honored that you thought of me but I am, after all, a research physician."

"I wanted you here for a number of reasons," Caelen stated. "Central among them was the fact that there isn't much you don't know about respiratory pathology. The others I'll explain to you after you've made your tests."

Eiselt nodded. "Okay, but one other question, if you don't mind: What psychological symptoms? If you're losing REM sleep…"

"I'm as irritable as hell, if that's what you mean. It's only with the greatest exercise of will that I keep myself from biting off the head of anyone I meet, including you. So stop quizzing me and get on with your tests!"

"Well, then," Eiselt said, rising and smiling, "let's go."

He didn't know what was plaguing Caelen but was confident he could come up with an answer in a short while. No doubt it was a variation on another familiar syndrome.

* * *

LATER IN THE DAY he wasn't so sure. All his tests for pathology had come up negative. Strange, a man with Caelen's symptoms should certainly show some pathology. Feeling not a little embarrassed, Eiselt took the grav chute to the upper levels. Dr. Caelen had taught at the university before the Department of Medicine and Research decided to move him into Administration. He now headed that department and Eiselt, one of his former students, had wanted to look good for the old man.

Dr. Caelen awaited him in his office. "Well, Decker, what have you found?"

"Frankly, I'm a little at a loss," he admitted. "Your lungs are in great shape. You shouldn't have the symptoms you do."

He paused, but Caelen waited for him to go on.

Obviously crestfallen, he concluded: "I'm afraid I'll need some more data before I can even guess which way to go."

"Don't feel too badly about it," Caelen told him. "Nobody else knows what's going on around here, either—and we've had the best working on it. I knew you'd want to make those tests yourself and draw your own conclusions so I let you."

"Thanks. That makes me feel a little better. But now I'd like to know those 'other reasons' for sending for me."

Caelen nodded. "Okay. Tell me: have you noticed anything unusual about our personnel?"

"To tell the truth, the building seems almost deserted."

"True, that's part of the problem. But what about those you have seen?"

"They all look pretty beat," he replied after a pause, "almost like…Doctor, is there an epidemic of this syndrome?"

"Yes, I'm afraid so," Caelen said.

"Why haven't I heard anything about it?"

Caelen sighed. "Because we've been doing our best to keep the lid on it until we find out just what it is we're dealing with."

"Does it seem to be spreading?"

"Most suburban hospitals are packed with cases, but they're not as bad off as the city proper. It seems as if the entire population of the capital has come down with this…this syndrome. And we've also had reports of isolated cases from coast to coast. Figure that one out!"

Eiselt's teeth found a cuticle and went to work on it. "I have an instinctive feeling that this isn't the work of any pathogenic organism, known or unknown. Yet, an epidemic usually means contagion…" His voice drifted off into thought.

"Speaking of contagion," Caelen said, "I must apologize for exposing you to whatever it is that's plaguing us but we needed someone who was uninfected to work on it. The rest of us are so exhausted that we can't think straight about any subject other than sleep. We don't trust our own judgment. I hope I haven't endangered you, but you must understand that we're getting desperate. None of the departments can get anything done because no one can concentrate anymore. That's why the Department of Sea Industries made that error with the pay authorizations. And there have been a number of other, similar cases. The Department of Public Information has been keeping it quiet but little things have a way of piling up. We may have a very frightened planet on our hands if we don't come up with something soon. I tried to handle it myself but my stamina has been completely sapped."

"Could it possibly be a Federation plot?"

Caelen repressed a smile. Decker Eiselt hadn't changed much. He had been an adamant Restructurist during his college years and had evidently remained so.

"Ridiculous, Decker! The very reason we want to 'restructure' the Federation is because it limits itself exclusively to interplanetary affairs. A plot against Kamedon would be strictly out of character."

"But you have to admit that the Federation would hardly be dismayed if the people lost faith in the government and the planet ground to a halt."

"You've got a point there, but you must realize that the Restructurist movement will go on, with or without Kamedon. And you can't go around looking for a Federation plot every time something goes wrong."

"I suppose you're right," Eiselt reluctantly agreed.

"Of course I'm right! So let's not worry about the Federation or Restructurism. Let's worry about Morgan City. I don't want to have to call in the IMC."

Eiselt blanched. "The Interstellar Medical Corps is pro-Federation! Asking them for help is like going to the Federation itself!"

"Well, then," Caelen said pointedly, "I hope you've got some sort of a plan on how to tackle this."

"I've got the start of a plan. Those isolated cases might provide us with a clue. I'd like to have every one of them flown to the capital as soon as possible."

"Good idea," Caelen agreed, swallowing another stimulant.

After two weeks of testing and interviewing patients from the outlying districts, Eiselt was able to hand Dr. Caelen a piece of paper with a date scrawled on it. "Remember that day?" he said.

Caelen hesitated. "No, can't say I do." Daily he and all the other victims had grown more haggard and exhausted. Remembering was an effort. "Almost a year ago…wait! Wasn't this the day of the accident in Dr. Sebitow's lab?"

"Correct. And how does this strike you: every case I've interviewed was in Morgan City when the accident occurred!"

Caelen slumped in his seat. "Sebitow's ray," he muttered.

"What's that supposed to mean?"

"I don't know. No one really knew except Sebitow—and he's dead."

Eiselt's tone showed his exasperation. "But the department gave him the money! You must know what he was working on!"

"What do you know about administration, Decker?" the older man flared. "How do you handle a man who is one of the greatest medical minds in the galaxy but who has no concept of politics, who has no loyalty to anything but his work? To Nathan Sebitow the Federation and the Restructurist movement were just words! The only way to keep a man like that working for you is to give him full rein. A number of other planets had offered him unlimited funds and unlimited freedom so we had to match them. He said he was onto something big and wanted the money immediately, so we gave it to him."

"But don't you have any idea what he was doing?"

Caelen paused. "All we know is that he was working on high-penetration radiation with neuronal effects. When he worked out a few bugs he was going to give us a full report. Decker, you don't think the Respiratory Center could have been affected, do you?"

"Not a chance," Eiselt replied with a slow shake of his head. Your Respiratory Center is intact and functional. Were any of Sebitow's records recovered?"

"None."

"But wasn't he still alive when they found him? I remember a report about Sebitow being taken to a hospital...did he say anything?"

"He said a few words," Caelen replied, "but they didn't make too much sense."

"Remember what they were? It might give us a lead."

"Not really. Something about an over-reaction, I think."

"Please try to remember!" Eiselt urged.

Caelen shrugged. "We had a recorder going when he came around. If you think it's important, go down to Hearn's office and he'll play it for you."


Dr. Hearn, too, was gaunt and haggard and really didn't want to be bothered with retrieving a recording of Dr. Sebitow's last words. His last stimulant was wearing off.

"I'll tell you what he said, Dr. Eiselt: 'Over-reaction...danger...tell...ens...' That was all."

"Yes, but I'd like to hear it myself. I know what you're going through but I'm trying to find a key to this mess. Please get it."

Wearily, Hearn went to a file, pulled out a cartridge and fitted it into a viewer. For seemingly interminable minutes Eiselt watched the injured Dr. Sebitow toss his bandaged head and mumble incoherently. Suddenly, the man opened his eyes and shouted, "Over-reaction!...Danger! Tell...ens..." and then relapsed into mumbles. Hearn switched it off.

"What did he mean by 'ens'?" Eiselt asked.

Hearn shrugged. "That puzzled us for a while until we remembered that his chief assistant's name was Endicott. He must have wanted someone to tell Endicott something but never finished the sentence."

"Endicott? Where is Endicott?"

"Dead, too."

Eiselt rose wordlessly and started for the door.

"We've got to get to the bottom of this soon, Doctor," he heard Hearn say behind him. Stimulant supplies are diminishing. The Department of Production is so understaffed that it hasn't been able to issue the latest production quota and so factories and mills all over the continent have had to shut down. We've had food riots in some areas because the Department of Distribution has fouled up its scheduling. There's even talk of a march on Morgan City to demand more competence and efficiency in the handling of public affairs!"

"I'm doing the best I can!" Eiselt gritted.

"I know you are, and you're doing it almost single-handedly. It's just that I dread the thought of having to call in the IMC. But I fear it must come to that if we don't get a breakthrough soon."

"Never! If we can't lick this thing. They certainly can't do any better'" he declared, approaching Hearn's desk.

"Come now, Doctor," Hearn replied. "I know you're a dedicated Restructurist, as are we all, but lets be realistic. The IMC has the brains, talents and resources of a thousand worlds at its disposal. You can't hope to compare our facilities with theirs."

Eiselt slammed his fist on the desk top. "We'll solve this and we'll do it without the help of the IMC!"

"I hope you're right," Hearn said softly as he watched Eiselt storm from the office. "And I hope it's soon."

EISELT MANAGED TO COOL HIS TEMPER by the time he made his daily call to Sally. As her face came into focus on the viewscreen, he noticed that she looked distraught.

"Something wrong, honey?" he asked.

"Oh, Decker!" she cried. "They've gone!"

"Who?"

"Almost everyone! Students, faculty, administrators, fishermen, shopkeepers, everyone! They chartered groundcars and flitters and started out for Morgan City this morning!"

Eiselt remembered the march Hearn had mentioned. "What about Doctor Bain?"

"Oh, he's still here. His wife wants me to stay with them until you get back. Maybe I'd better take her up on it."

The exodus from town had made her somewhat anxious and Eiselt wished he could be with her.

"Good idea," he said. Bain would look after her. After all, she was his patient and in her eighth month and if her husband couldn't be there, someone should keep an eye on her. "Get over there as soon as possible and tell them I'll be eternally grateful!"

She ran a hand nervously through her brown hair. "Okay. Any luck so far?"

"No. Every time I think I'm onto something, I wind up in a dead end."

The frustration was evident in her husband's voice and Sally figured that the best thing she could do for him was allow him to get back to his work.

"I'd better get packed now," she told him. "Call me tomorrow."

"I will," he promised and broke the connection.

Depression was unusual for Decker Eiselt. In the past his nervous energy had always carried him through the troughs as well as over the peaks. But he felt drained now. He took the elevator down to street level and dropped into a chair by the window. That was when he spotted the dog.

It was the dog's gait that held his attention; the uneven, limping stride reminded him of another dog…years ago…at the university.

Suddenly he was on his feet and racing for the elevator. He shot to the upper levels and burst into Caelen's office just as the man was about to take another stimulant capsule.

"Don't take that! I've got one more test to make and I want you to try and sleep while I'm doing it."

Caelen hesitated. "I'm afraid, Decker. I'm afraid I may not wake up one of these times."

"I'll be right there," he assured him. "I want to monitor your cortex while you sleep."

"Are you on to something, Decker?"

Eiselt pulled him to his feet. "I'll explain as I wire you up. Let's just say that I hope I'm wrong."


Supine on a table, a very groggy Dr. Caelen tried valiantly to focus his eyes on the oscilloscope screen and concentrate on what his younger colleague was saying.

"See that?" Eiselt remarked, pointing to a series of spikes. "There's an unusually high amount of cortical activity synchronized with respiration. Put that together with the symptoms of this epidemic, the nature of Sebitow's research and his last words and the result is pretty frightening. You see, I fear Sebitow's last words were a warning."

"A warning against what?"

"*Telencephalization!*"

There was no sign of recognition in Caelen's eyes.

"It's a neurophysiologist's term," Eiselt explained. "If a lame dog out on the street hadn't reminded me of it, the concept never would have occurred to me."

"Forgive me, Decker, but I'm not following you."

Eiselt paused. "Maybe this will help you remember: the most common and effective means of illustrating telencephalization is to take an experimental animal and sever the spinal cord at midthorax, or at the neck. If that happened to a man, he'd lose the use of his legs in the first instance and also the use of his arms in the latter. But an animal with a severed spinal cord—a dog or possum, for instance—can still walk! His gait is often irregular but the point is *he can still get around while a man is rendered helpless.* Why? Because man has telencephalized his walking ability! As part of his evolution, the higher centers of man's nervous system have taken over many motor functions formerly performed by the lower, local centers.

"I have a theory that Sebitow might have developed a way to cause telencephalization, possibly for use as a rehabilitation technique…to let higher centers take over where damaged local centers are no longer effective. But I fear the city got a blast of the radiation he was using to induce this takeover and the symptoms we've seen led me to the conclusion that somehow the respiratory center has been telencephalized. The encephalogram seems to confirm this."

"But you said nothing was wrong with the respiratory center," Caelen rasped in a weak whisper.

"There's no pathology, but it seems that the voluntary areas of the forebrain are in command and are overriding the local peripheral sensors. Thus the diffuse respiratory malaise and broken breathing rhythm when you exercised. The voluntary areas of the cortex were starting to take over. They are nowhere near as efficient nor a sensitive as the local centers such as the pressoreceptors in the lungs and the chemoreceptors in the aorta and carotid arteries which work directly through the respiratory center without going near the cortex. But because of telencephalization, the respiratory center is no longer responsive to the local centers. And there lies the problem.

"It boils down to this: You and all the other victims are breathing on the border of consciousness! This means you stop breathing when unconscious! Without oxygen the acidity of your blood goes up and the local chemoreceptors start screaming. But the respiratory center no longer responds and so impulses are finally relayed to the cortex; the cortex is roused and you wake up gasping for air. That's the theory. I want to monitor the voluntary areas to confirm or deny it; if activity there falls off as respiration falls off, then we'll know I'm right."

"What'll we do if you're right?" Caelen asked.

Rather than tell him that he didn't have the faintest idea, Eiselt pulled a blanket over him. "Try to sleep." The exhausted administrator closed his eyes. Eiselt watched him a minute, then went over to the drug cabinet and filled a syringe with a stimulant. Just in case.

AS HE SAT AND WATCHED THE OSCILLOSCOPE, a dull roar filtered up from the street. Going to the window, he saw a shouting, gesticulating crowd marching below. They were frightened, and they were angry, and they wanted to know what was wrong. Kamedon had been running so smoothly... now, chaos. Some areas were receiving no food while others received more than they could use; some factories were shut down while others received double quotas; and no one could be sure when he would next be paid. What was happening? The famous efficiency of Kamedon was breaking down and the people wanted to know why.

Someone broke a window. Somebody else followed suit. Fascinated, Eiselt watched the march turn into a mob scene in a matter of minutes.

He glanced over at Dr. Caelen and realized with a start that the man had stopped breathing. He cursed as he noted the reduced cortical activity on the 'scope. Telencephalization of the respiratory center—no doubt about it now. He put a hand on Caelen's shoulder and shook him. No response. Looking closer, he noticed a blue tinge to the man's lips. With frantic haste he found a vein and injected the stimulant, then hooked up a respirator.

Slowly, as normal breathing returned, Dr. Caelen's eyelids opened to reveal two dull orbs. Cortical activity had increased on the oscilloscope.

Decker Eiselt's shoulders slumped with relief—and defeat. He was beaten. Telencephalization was an evolutionary process—although in this case the evolution was suicidal—and he had no way of combating it, no way of returning command to the local centers. The only hope for Dr. Caelen— and Kamedon—was the IMC. And Eiselt knew he would have to be the one to call them in.

They would be gracious rescuers, of course, and would do their work skillfully and competently. The IMC would find a solution, rectify the situation and then leave, no doubt refusing to accept payment, explaining that they were only too glad to have such an opportunity to expand the perimeters of neurophysiology.

But it would soon be known throughout the settled galaxy that Kamedon, the pride of the Restructurist movement, had found it necessary to call in the IMC. And pro-Federation propagandists were sure to waste no time in drawing an ironic comparison between Restructurist philosophy and the syndrome which had afflicted Morgan City.

He could see it now: "Centralists suffering from overcentralization!"

To put it mildly, the near future was going to be a most difficult period.

Outside, the roar of the mob redoubled.

# THE MAN WITH THE ANTEATER

*No discussion of galactic business, of course, would be complete without mention of Interstellar Business Advisers. Armed with the tried-and-true maxims of a free-market economy and a number of new and daring precepts for the conduct of business on an interstellar scale, IBA played an important part in shaping the course of trade in the galaxy.*

*The company was founded by one Joseph Finch, a man whose figure has taken on an almost mythical air in the annals of galactic trade. The most farfetched stories concern the period before the founding of IBA, when Finch was still a resident of Earth.—*

Excerpt from GALACTIC BUSINESS: A HISTORY
by Emmerz Fent

On a steamy summer morning, Joe and Andy the anteater stepped out into their backyard and surveyed their domain. Thirty-eight, slight of frame and a bit on the homely side, Joe Finch didn't exactly cut a heroic figure. But he was looked up to as a hero by many nonetheless. And there were, of course, many who thought of him as a stupid, eccentric, thick-headed, bull-headed reactionary. But they seemed to be in the minority.

You see, in a world that functions with the smoothness of a well-oiled machine, the man who insists on deciding when to shift his own gears becomes a hero of sorts. A man with few friends, who had yet to meet his wife, whose sister and brother-in-law, unable to cope with Earth any longer, were living as splinter colonists on a planet called Dasein II somewhere out in nowhere,

Finch was a loner. And in a highly collectivized, planned and patented society, loners, if they can avoid being swallowed whole and digested, become heroes.

Finch was mentally running through his plan to manipulate Arthur Gordon, Chief Administrator of Earth. Gordon was either a social idealist or a power-monger—the two not always distinguishable—and Finch knew from certain sources that Gordon was planning to manipulate *him*. The thing to do was to make Gordon show his hand before he was completely ready, and the strike going on at the Finch House plant right now could be the perfect lever.

"Stay here, Andy," he told his pet. "And if you get hungry, help yourself." Andy scanned the dry, virtually grassless yard and trotted off in the direction of a promising mound with his huge, furry tail held straight out behind him and his agile tongue seemingly licking his snout in anticipation.

"Don't overdo it or you'll have to go back on synthe-meat and formic acid," Finch warned. Andy glanced over his shoulder and stuck out his tongue.

Finch went out front, started up an old transporter with the words *Finch House* printed on the sides and back, and drove off toward Pete Farnham's machine shop.


As the last of the new equipment was being loaded, Farnham turned to Finch. "You sure you want to go through with this, Joe?"

"Look, Pete," Finch said, wiping his forehead on his sleeve, "you designed this stuff so I'd be able to increase my output by about another half without increasing my overhead or labor costs."

Farnham looked annoyed. "I'm not talking about that. I'm talking about the union…it's on strike, remember? They're very unhappy about losing their overtime."

"If the union had its way," Finch growled, "I'd still be using Gutenberg presses."

"But it's against the law to cross a picket line! Why don't you just wait it out as usual or maybe bribe the union president? All hell's going to break loose if you go through with this."

Finch locked the back of the transporter with a solid click. "That might be just what I'm after. Besides, this is as good a time as any to challenge a rotten law. Gordon's been pushing things a bit too…" His voice trailed off as he saw Farnham climbing into the cab. "Where do you think you're going?"

"With you, of course," Farnham replied and hefted a length of pipe. "I spent a lot of time designing that equipment and the only way it'll ever get to prove itself is if you get to use it. Now let's get moving."

*...the pickets/a truck in their midst/hey! /stop 'em! /get them! /Hold 'em/ don't let 'em through! stop 'em!! Stomp 'em!/but chain and bricks and barricades and bodies give way/a face looms/flail at it. /Someone fires a shot/miss! /The police arrive/made it!/ The pickets are being held outside and the police will deal with you later...*

Joe Finch watched the roiling crowds from atop the Earth Building. "You just can't figure people, Andy," he told the pet he had insisted on bringing with him. "They clamor for a law to be passed and then celebrate a man who breaks it."

"I believe you're oversimplifying the situation, Joe," said a voice behind him.

Finch turned to see Arthur Gordon: big, graying, about sixty, the man on whose "invitation" he had come to the Earth Building. It was their first meeting and the Chief Administrator of Earth got things off on the wrong foot by calling him "Joe;" Finch believed first names were for personal friends only.

"Oh, how's that, *Arthur?*" he replied, noting the CA's wince.

"Well, I mean...it seems you've become a symbol to them—"

(*My, what a phony smile you have, Arthur Gordon.*)

"...a symbol of Individuality—"

(*I'll bet he uses a capital "I" when he spells that word.*)

"And Individuality is something each of them feels he has lost."

(*Whose fault is that?*)

"I imagine that some of them, deep in their hearts, actually hate you for maintaining a quality they've lost."

(*I can think of a few union roughnecks who won't have to go that deep.*)

"As a matter of fact—"

"Get to the point!" Finch finally interrupted. "Why did you 'invite' me here rather than have me arrested for breaking the picket law?"

Gordon's fixed smile was replaced by one of a more genuine nature. "Okay, Mr. Finch, I *will* be more to the point, although what I've been saying isn't far from it. Let's go into my office."

It was not until Finch was seated across the desk from him in the Chief Administrator's spacious main office that Gordon began to speak.

"Mr. Finch, the reason I did not have you arrested is very simple: you are the only man on this planet who can be described as a hero."

"I think you've got the wrong definition of a hero, Mr. CA. I'm not a hero. I've never done a heroic thing in my life. I may stand out in a crowd, but otherwise I think you're overestimating me."

Gordon frowned. "I don't think I overestimate you at all. The public is hungry for an idol and you, unwilling as you may be, are the prime candidate. In fact your unwillingness to cooperate with the idol-seekers only increases your popularity. To them you're the last of a rare species. Just look at you! You wander around with an antbear at your heels, you're making a pile of money in an industry that should have been extinct shortly after the development of telestories, you had a shyster lawyer wheedle a private home for you so you could raise ants for that ridiculous pet of yours and now you've taken to busting picket lines!"

"Nobody keeps me out of my own business!" Finch stated flatly and finally.

"I wonder about that," Gordon mused. "This is hardly the first strike at your plant…You've bargained with the union before, why did you choose to defy it this time? Planning to challenge the Picket Law?"

"Would it do me any good to try?" Finch replied in a noncommittal tone.

"Maybe. I never liked the law. Didn't like it when it was passed and I like it even less at the moment."

Finch cracked his knuckles. "The Picket Law is a natural consequence of legalizing the picket line. You see, a picket line makes it possible to kidney-punch anyone trying to enter the building currently under siege and sooner or later you don't cross a picket line if you know what's good for you. Then, with typical political logic, crossing a picket line was declared illegal 'in order to prevent violence during strikes.'"

Gordon snorted. "I've heard all this before, Mr. Finch. And I didn't ask you here to reprimand your extralegal activities nor to discuss the Picket Law with you. Instead of having you arrested, I'd rather make a deal."

"I had a feeling you'd find some use for me."

The CA ignored the remark. "Look, Finch, here's the situation: we've become an incredibly complex society here on Earth; the average man feels like a cog, feels a loss of worth. Oh, I know it sounds very trite but unfortunately it's very true. We've been warned about this for centuries but it's something that's almost impossible to prevent, even when you can see it coming.

"You, however, have somehow overcome it all. You've bucked convention, legal restrictions…even technology! You've become a symbol of the Individuality people instinctively feel they've lost and want desperately to regain. And I've found a way to give it to them!"

Finch smirked. "How? Pills?"

Gordon was not in a light mood. "No, the plan's a little more complicated than that. It's a daring plan and will frighten people at first; they'll want the end but they'll balk at the means. Unless—"

"Unless what?"

"Unless someone they admire not only endorses it but actively promotes it."

Finch shook his head as if to clear it. "Wait a minute. Let's just go back a bit. You're building up to the means and I don't even know what the end really is supposed to be."

Gordon strode to a bookshelf and pulled out a huge volume.

"Ever hear of Gregor Black?" he asked as he laid the book on the desk.

"Some sort of technosociologist, wasn't he?" Finch replied. "But I believe his disciples are calling him 'Noah' Black now."

"Right. His theory was that both the individual and society are best served when the individual is doing the job for which he is best suited: the old 'right man for the right job' maxim. He figured that not only would you achieve maximum productivity but you'd also allow the individual the personal satisfaction and sense of fulfillment that comes from doing what he can do best."

"Where is he now?" Finch asked.

Gordon had opened the volume and was flipping through the pages. "Oh, somewhere in the Ninth Quadrant, I believe."

Finch snapped his fingers. "That's right! His group was outlawed so they decided to apply for a splinter colony.'

Ninety years ago they took up the government's offer to any large enough group that wanted to settle an Earthclass planet and got free, one-way transportation to the prospective utopia of their choice. Since they were registered as a splinter colony, the planet was then declared off limits to all government traffic and Black and company could do whatever they wanted with it.

"I'd love to know who dreamed up the splinter colony idea," Finch said with a smile and a shake of the head. "It's probably one of the few deals in history in which everybody gets what he wants: the government not only colonizes world after world, but it gets rid of all the local dissidents to boot. And the dissidents get their own world on which to live the way they wish."

Gordon was not listening, however. Pointing to the book on his desk, be said, "Here's the reason Black's group was outlawed: the Assessor."

"I remember the name," Finch remarked. "Gregor Black's miracle machine."

"Don't be too light with the Assessor… nor with old Gregor. He designed quite a machine. With the Assessor screening a population you wouldn't have, say, a potential physicist or chemist doing menial labor because his talents and abilities were never discovered and never developed. Nor would you have incompetents in important positions because of 'connections.' It's too bad the Assessor jumbled the minds of a few of his followers during testing—that's why its use was outlawed."

"Jumbled, hell!" Finch snorted. "It turned a few of his faithful followers into vegetables!"

"Well, you've got to remember that 'electrohypnosis'—which was the term for mind-probing in those days—was still in the experimental stages. Its use was integral to the Assessor but its control had not yet been perfected. Thus, the tragic accidents."

Finch yawned. "Just as well. Never would have worked anyway."

Gordon smiled and leaned over his desk. "Oh, but it has!"

"You mean you've heard from Black's splinter colony? I wouldn't put too much faith in…"

"No, no," the CA. interrupted, "it has worked right here on Earth!"

"Where?"

"The Rigrod Peninsula."

"So that's what all the secrecy's been about."

Gordon was enthused now: "We started a colony out there twenty-six years ago using a thousand deserted children, each about a year old. Each was 'assessed' once a year for the first twenty years and education was modified and directed for each in accordance with the Assessor's findings; we were thus able to give them twenty years of education in roughly fifteen. Six years ago they were all given the option of either going into their assigned fields or returning to the mainland."

He paused dramatically. "All stayed."

Finch affected a surprised expression. He had a few contacts in the government and knew all about the Rigrod experiment.

"And the advances in technology, the arts, the life sciences, business and hundreds of other fields in these past six years have been incredible!"

"I can see how it would work," Finch said, "but why tell me about it?"

"Because it's going to take a massive selling job to get the public to accept it and my advisers think that endorsements by popular personalities would be the best technique. You, Joe Finch, are going to help convince the public that the Assessor is the greatest thing ever to come along."

"Oh, really? Not without a little more than a spiel from you, I'm afraid."

Gordon sobered. "What do you mean?"

"I mean I want to see Rigrod and see exactly what it's like. If this Assessor can do all you say it can, then I'll back you on it. But I want to see for myself."

"I'm afraid not," the CA frowned. "We've allowed free access of outside information into Rigrod but all outsiders have been barred. We can make no exceptions."

"Better make one this time."

"Need I remind you, Mr. Finch, that your situation in regard to the law at the moment is quite precarious?"

"I endorse nothing sight unseen," Finch stated. He was gambling now, gambling that the Finch endorsement was important enough to the CA to make him back down. "And besides, you've said nothing about my legal situation after I endorse the Assessor…how will I stand then?"

If you're going to bluff, don't do it halfheartedly.

Gordon studied Finch with narrowed eyes and nodded slowly. "All right. All right, dammit! I'll publicly denounce the Picket Law and have the charges dropped after we go to Rigrod."

"Well, Andy," Finch said, scratching his pet's snout, "looks like we're going on a trip soon…and at government expense, no less."

✳  ✳  ✳

The Rigrod Peninsula had been turned into a minor city, a tiny nation of a thousand. Order and symmetry ruled its design and new structures of unique conceptualization were on the rise. The inhabitants came out in force to meet Joe Finch. They were only physically isolated here and the figure of the crusty individualist with his ever-present antbear companion was immediately recognized.

He wandered through the crowd of residents commenting on this and that, answering questions and shaking proffered hands. He was impressed. These people were friendly, articulate and every one a specialist in his or her field. But there was a subtle undercurrent here, an undercurrent he had been sure he would find.

After the tour, Gordon and Finch retired to the CA's Rigrod offices. Finch was skimming through a manuscript he had found on the desk. It was called "Interstellar Business: A Theory," by Peter J. Paxton.

"This Paxton is good," he told the beaming Gordon. "His logistical concepts will revolutionize interstellar trade. Does he need a publisher?"

"Sorry, Joe," Gordon laughed," but Rigrod is setting up its own publishing house—and it will be a telestories format." He was needling Finch and enjoying it. Changing the subject, he asked, "Well, now that you've seen our little project, what do you think of it?"

Now the touchy part: to stall for time. "I don't know. There's something about this setup that bother me."

"What could bother you? It's the perfect society! Utopia!"

"The whole idea of utopia makes me more than a little nervous," Finch replied. "Can you give me a week or two to think on it?"

"I'll give you a week, Finch. That should give you plenty of time to assimilate what you've seen here today. But remember, those charges still stand."

"Yes, I'm aware of that. But don't you think the endorsement would hold more weight if it wasn't so obvious that we had made a deal?"

"You have a point," the CA admitted and paused, thinking. "Why don't we try this: I'll get the charges dropped if you give me a tentative affirmation."

"Okay, Mr. Gordon. It's a deal."

And the Chief Administrator of Earth made good his promise the very next day.

\* \* \*

When Gordon and two other men burst into the Finch backyard, they found that he was not alone. Andy was there and so was a young, fair-haired man in his mid-twenties. Gordon instantly recognized him.

"Paxton! It figures I'd find you here! Go inside. I've something to discuss with Mr. Finch!"

The young man was cowed by the wrathful CA. He looked to Finch and Finch nodded toward the door.

"Do as he says. He brought a couple of his bully-boys along so we'd better humor him."

When Paxton had disappeared into the house, Finch turned to Gordon. "Now what the hell is all this about?"

"You're under arrest, Finch!" Gordon roared.

"What for?" Andy raised his head and wondered who was making all this noise on such a pleasant afternoon.

"You know very well what for…for destroying a government project!"

"You mean the Rigrod experiment?"

"Yes! The Rigrod experiment! The whole structure of the Assessor-built society started to break down soon after your visit. You did something out there. I'm going to find out what it was. I don't care how popular you are, you're going to tell me."

"I'll tell you what I did," said Finch. "I visited the place. That's all. You were with me all the time."

"You pulled something—" Gordon began.

"Damn right I did," Finch interrupted with a snort. "I destroyed that project willfully and with malice aforethought. And I did you a favor by doing it. It was bound to happen sooner or later! You thought you were creating the perfect society by basing it on human individuality, by making the best use of individual abilities. You took care of *individuality*…fine! But you forgot all about *individualism*!

"It never occurred to you that many people wouldn't be happy doing 'what they can do best.' As a matter of fact, many people don't give a damn about what they can do best. They're more interested in doing what they *like* to do, what they *want* to do. There might be a musician playing at the music center tonight who could be a brilliant physicist if he wanted to be, but he likes music instead. In an Assessor-built society, however, he'd be working with mathematical formulae instead of chord progressions. He'd sit around envying musicians for just so long and then he'd either rebel or go mad. When are people like you going to learn that utopia is a fool's game?"

Gordon was in a cold rage. The project, which was to be a monument to his name, was being torn to shreds by this man in front of him. He spoke through clenched teeth: "But why didn't they rebel before you showed up? The project was working perfectly until then."

"You've had no trouble on the peninsula until now," Finch explained, "because you've been working with a biased sample. Those kids have been told all their lives that they are pioneers, that they'll be the ones to prove that man can have utopia. And so all the square pegs in the round holes—the equivalents of our hypothetical musician-physicist—keep mum on the hope that their discontent will pass…they don't want to destroy 'man's chance at utopia' by a hasty decision. And in keeping mum they never find out that there are others like themselves.

"Then Joe Finch comes along.

"And I'm not a hero, Gordon. I'm a crackpot, an eccentric, a nut. I've known about Rigrod for over a decade now and spent that time building up a reputation as a rugged individualist. Many times I felt foolish but the press and the vid played right into my hands. I've been a walking publicity stunt for the last ten years. That's why my pet is an antbear instead of a dog—although I wouldn't trade Andy for anything now. I've been hoping for a chance to get to Rigrod and you gave it to me. And that was all I needed.

"Allowing someone with a reputation as a crackpot individualist to wander through the Rigrod Peninsula is like introducing a seed crystal to a supersaturated solution: all the underlying threads of doubt and discontent start to crystallize. But don't blame me! Blame yourself and your inane theories and ambitions! You were a fool to be taken in by Black's theory, you were a fool to bring me to the project and you were a fool to think that I'd have anything at all to do with such a plan!"

Gordon finally exploded. "Arrest him!" he told the two guards who had been standing idly by.

The guards, of course, did not know anything about antbears. The antbear has been long used in the areas to which it is indigenous as a watchdog. Its forelimbs have monstrous claws which it uses for digging into termite hills but it can rear up on its hind legs and use these claws for defense. And the antbear has an uncanny ability to roar like a lion.

The two guards were quickly made aware of these facts. Andy startled them with a roar as they made their first move toward Finch. A few swipes with his claws and the guards were down and gashed and bleeding.

Andy stood beside Finch and huffed warily as his master scratched his snout. Finch turned to the livid Chief Administrator.

"Now get out of here and take your friends with you."

"All right, Finch. You've won for now. But let me warn you that your life here on Earth from now on will be hell! And don't get any ideas about getting off-planet…you're staying right here!"

BUT JOE FINCH had been far ahead of the CA. He had already sold his house, a printing firm had bought his machinery and all the properties of Finch House had been picked up by a telestories outfit. A handsome bribe had reserved two seats and one animal passage out from Earth on a moment's notice, and Joe Finch, Peter J. Paxton and Andy were well into primary warp toward Ragna before Arthur Gordon had any idea they had left Earth.

With Finch's money and organizational experience and Paxton's business theories, Interstellar Business Advisers was born and grew with the expanding Federation. And Joe, at long last able to put aside his role of superindividualist, found a woman who loved him—and anteaters, too—and it wasn't too long before Joe junior came along. But that's another story.